The Unending

A. Sands

First Edition

ISBN: 1910667536

ISBN-13: 978-1910667538

theunending@outlook.com

This novel is written in British English (mostly).

Chapter 1

Knowing meant nothing.

Meryn had known this would happen. She had known for nine months. She had especially known about the pain.

She cried and moaned, and there was blood and more, as she strained to push the baby out.

She hadn't known it would take place in a lonely hut, lost in the middle of a meadow. Nor how little warning she would get. Nor just how alone she would feel. The timing had been unexpected. Herendak, the father, had left her to run to a nearby farmhouse, for water and someone to act as a midwife, if he could find anyone.

And Rilenheim came across the mess. He stooped into the hut, and took her hand.

"Thank God," Meryn cried, "I can't do this alone. Wait, where's Heri? Who are you?"

He smiled at her. She could barely see it through the pain.

"I am a friend. Now concentrate. Breathe. Here, squeeze my hand."

"It hurts!"

"It will be over soon."

And it was. She knew it was over when she found herself laughing and crying at the same time. She heard screaming and saw her baby girl. Only then, in that instant, did she realise just how little knowing meant.

She watched as Rilenheim severed the cord with his thumb and forefinger. She had done it. She reached out.

Rilenheim wrapped up the baby in his cloak, ducked through the door, and ran.

Meryn stared, then screamed.

Herendak finally found her in an irrigation ditch at the end of the field, ankle sprained, crying and sobbing, and no longer laughing at all.

* * *

Rilenheim took the baby to the wreck of the City of Ilris, taking secret paths, marching day and night. Herendak would be close behind, and furious. There was so little time.

Yet Rilenheim was delayed in the Haylen Plains. He couldn't see the way to Ilris. The horizon was awash with deep, thorny forests; a long, glistening swamp; a blinding desert.

None of them were real.

Ilris had long been locked away from the curiosity of men and women by a maintenance of magic.

Rilenheim cursed and cast about for the edge of the illusion. It was a such a heavy failing of his people that this lock now affected one of their own. He was shut out of his own home. Fooled by an illusion he had helped create.

He turned his head, sharply, this way and that, attempting to startle a glimpse of the stitches that would show him the way.

"Not now! This isn't the time for this!" He hissed out a breath and ran his fingers into the shifting landscapes. "Not now!"

There had once been a time when he would have needed neither *eyes* nor *fingers* for this nonsense...

Yes.

Of course.

He was not thinking like a Geomancer.

He shut his eyes. After a moment, he thrust his arm up to the elbow into the no-longer-distant desert. It faded. Ilris drizzled into view.

Ilris was a vertical city, a mass of pillars, ledges and arches, arrayed in a valley between two momentous, snow-capped peaks. Built without walls or ceilings, interweaving struts and supports twisted into an intricate labyrinth. The whole rose monstrously into the sky as high as the mountains nestling around it, with dignified clouds hovering among the higher levels, their tops brilliant with soaked sunlight. Walkways below seemed cold and proud in comparison, sunlight unwelcome, an unnecessary extravagance. Proof against gravity and the weather of an age, the city stood immutable.

Rilenheim set off at close to a run, the baby under one arm. Brooding vegetation concealed the city's roots. He tore through it, sheltering the child to his chest. The valley was still, silent, devoid of the mixed animal noises that could normally be expected.

He reached the first of many stone ramps. They were pristine, as if they had just been built. The air was somehow the opposite. It tasted stale. Unbreathed for so very long.

Boots pounding on the ramps, Rilenheim left the trees below as he sprinted into the sky.

* * *

Herendak's face was raw and bleeding. Thorns and nettles tore at him as he took the most direct of paths. He could sense his baby. He knew where she was being taken. He knew who had taken her. Meryn had described a tall but hunched man, gaunt like a spectre – who had seemed so kindly until the moment he'd snatched her daughter.

Rilenheim! How had he known about the child? How long had he been watching, waiting? This was the child who could solve everything. This was the child who could put back everything that was now wrong. Taken!

Herendak skidded to a halt on the slick grass at Haylen Pass. He turned, slowly. In the distance there was a mountain range, flickering under silver lightning, and a winding river, and a damp, foggy wood, and...

He smirked.

He could still sense his daughter. She was... *there.*

He pushed through the fog; Ilris slinked into view like a panther.

There was a clattering, high above, and movement, which slowed. Rilenheim, silhouetted, looking down, hand leaning on a pillar; then off in a ferocious sprint, head bowed low, bundle of cloak and baby in both arms, bounding up ramp after ramp. The child didn't utter a single cry. Was she hurt? Was she even alive?

"Rilenheim!" Herendak screamed. His voice crashed back and forth between the mountains, cut up on every ledge. He tried to calculate the quickest route up; his eyes slipped uncomprehending off fused stonework.

If Rilenheim could get high enough, where the magic dwelt, he would be able to mask the scent which let Herendak know exactly where his daughter was. And how was he then ever to find her?

Herendak plunged headlong through the foliage to the entrance of Ilris. The final leg of the race was on.

* * *

He should have been suspicious when he lost sight of Rilenheim. Flashes of the crimson overcoat of his prey had shown him the way, going this way and that, dancing through crossroads and under arches, leaping across unimaginable drops, clattering, boots stomping. As he closed, there was the desperate, concentrated tearing of bursting lungs, panting and gasping into disapproving emptiness; they were unwelcome intruders here.

Then: nothing. Herendak slowed to a walk. Dragging sweat off his face with his sleeve, he thought out, sensed his daughter. Not far, just ahead. He flexed his fingers, readying himself. If a fight between Geomancers on their home turf was what Rilenheim wanted...

There she was, on a dais, on a sundial, in the centre of a circular crossroads. She was still smothered in Rilenheim's cloak. There was no sign of Rilenheim. Did the old fool really think he was that stupid?

Herendak backed away, took two steps followed by a leap onto a neighbouring ledge, arms arcing wide to keep from toppling. He edged forward, circling the platform holding his daughter. He stared intently between struts and girders as he went, seeking Rilenheim, making sure the baby stayed where he could see her. The support pillars were thick here; thick enough to conceal a man.

He stopped one level up, jumping distance to the child. There was still no sign of Rilenheim. He frowned, clutching a hand to the stitch at his side. His breathing was calmer now. He dropped to his knees, used a thick block of stone for cover, listened carefully. Nothing but the wind. The stone was freezing cold against his side. His sweaty shirt was clammy against it. For the first time he noticed the deep chill of the city at this height. Droplets of moisture were tangling his hair, seeping into his bones. Below, there were wisps of clouds.

Where *is* Rilenheim?

A thought hit him. His stomach clenched. With a flying leap, unhesitating, he hurtled to the platform below, smashing his knee with a crack. He hobbled to the dais, flung the empty cloak wide.

"No!" he screamed. He could still sense the magic of it, fused into the cloak by Rilenheim. He screamed again, shouted curses to the empty city. He spun, around and around, brain whirling from the intricacy of the architecture. Rilenheim was nowhere to be seen. Could be long gone by now. Herendak could search for days – *would* search for days – but the chances of finding them now...

He sprayed magical flame into the cloak, until the sense of it dulled. He cast his awareness wide, in all directions, searching... nothing. Rilenheim had found what he was looking for. The spark of his daughter was dulled, countered, gone. She was lost to him. After hundreds of years of planning. How could he now undo what he'd done, without the child?

Herendak took in the clouds below, mingled with the ancient, criss-crossing designs of Ilris – those long dormant portals that had once intersected the world – and he considered jumping. He flung the burning cloak out to flutter and hiss and drop.

Thousands of years, and just two Geomancers remained. He would find Rilenheim. Eventually, inevitably. And his daughter.

This would all end.

Chapter 2

Herendak thought of Meryn, back where he'd left her, crying in the dirt and beseeching him to bring back her baby. He thought of the thousand year wait for there to be anyone *suitable* to have his baby. He thought of the ever-growing army, still building on the other side of this very mountain range.

He took Ilris's back door: a vast steel portal, leading into Ailtris High, the west-most peak. He cracked it open by flinging flame from his fingertips and darting into the inferno. Shielding his face with an arm, he heaved at the door while the air writhed and died. A hissing wall of musky air almost toppled him as inside and out equalised and the door swung wide. He swallowed as his ears popped.

The corridor stretching away into the mountain was perfectly smooth, perfectly square, and ended in darkness. Herendak shook his hair out of his eyes, resettled his cloak around his shoulders, and stepped inside. He heaved the door closed behind him with both hands, until the rumbling of gears took over and it sealed with an echoing boom.

In pitch-blackness, he eased forward, one hand stroking the metal-cold wall for guidance, until he reached the second door. This one should have been as difficult to open as the first, but after many rotations of the entry wheel it creaked wide at the slightest touch of his fingertips. It was perfectly balanced on massive iron hinges as thick as his thighs.

The sudden stench was gagging. Grey slime dripped down the other side of the door and splashed onto his boots. The corridor was saturated in it, like the inside of a sick nostril. The walls were visibly ragged and scored where the slime wasn't, as if a slightly-too-large cannon ball had been forced through the corridor at speed.

This was the work of weroms, a particularly unpleasant form of Wrilsch. Herendak considered for a moment the extent of the world's decay. All his fault, every last disgusting creature of it. How ironic that the only way to undo the damage was to make use of them.

He sank the first of many footsteps into the slime.

Chapter 3

It was a cloudless night and the rings were visible from the towers of Draneth Keep. They arced across the sky like a scar, the same off-blue colour as the moons. There was a sheen to their length, like the sky had cracked open to somewhere much brighter and, to Queen Aldrua, happier.

She sat rigid, cross-legged on the bed, hair tangled from the ordeal, alone. She was glad she was alone, now that the horror had passed.

"Go," she'd told the midwives. "I will tell the king." They'd filed out silently, closing the door so very softly behind them, as if the draft of its closing alone might break her.

She was exhausted. Every muscle ached. But sleep was as far away as it had ever been. She might never sleep again. This was the other side of exhaustion, where the least painful path was wakeful oblivion.

She concentrated on breathing; deep breaths, chest rising and falling. She smelt salt water, brought miles to the Keep on the warm sea breeze. She felt tiny now that the baby had gone. She'd got used to the weight of it. She felt like a child again herself.

Gone, so quickly. Whisked away, smothered in swaddling, covered to spare her feelings. Soothing words; so many words, so many platitudes. Didn't they realise words couldn't fix what had happened? She'd lost it, and she knew it wasn't her fault, she really did. She knew it was just something that happened, sometimes. Gone, before he could even open his eyes.

She had no idea what to tell King Rayant. She didn't really care. The baby wasn't even his. He might even be pleased it was dead.

She froze on that thought. For a moment she kept statue-still, as if this on its own could make her stone. Then she eased her shoulders up and down, muscles stiff.

Rayant hated her for what she'd done. But what had he expected? He was always gone, always fighting to expand his kingdom. Hadn't his marriage to her also been for that very purpose? Their fate had been decided before they'd even met. She was introduced to him once and suddenly they were married, and just like that the size of his kingdom had doubled. Was it any wonder she had found another?

But Ielenia. Oh, whatever was she going to tell Ielenia? She'd been so excited. She'd been bouncing around for months at the thought of a little brother or sister to play with. Only yesterday she had carefully laid out dolls around the cradle in welcome. Her least favourite dolls – typical Ielenia. Oh, my poor little girl!

But – still no tears.

* * *

A silent figure slinked among the shadows towards the Keep. Guards patrolled the grounds, clanking through the chequerboard courtyards: pitch-black shadows interspersed with the soft glow of the rings and moons; light on and off according to the position of towers, out-houses and crenulations. The figure bypassed them like a breath of wind, blew through locks with barely a thought. A wraith unaffected by neither flesh nor stone and steel. It moved slowly through the Keep, inexorably inwards and upwards.

It flattened itself against a wall, blending invisibly, as a breathless man thundered past. The man's shirt was untucked, his hair bristling from nervous tugging, his neck glistening with sweat. Yet he was undeniably the King of Draldorn, and the shadow recognised him as such.

The king had clearly received Rilenheim's message.

Once the path was again clear, the shadow gained the West Tower, tirelessly ascended the spiral staircase and slipped along the hall which ended outside the queen's chambers.

The door was ajar for an instant, and then the shadow was inside, the door closing softly behind.

* * *

King Rayant met Rilenheim in a copse of trees an arrow's flight from the Keep's walls. He thought he could hear the guards bantering on the battlements, the creak of their armour. They had no idea he'd slipped out from underneath them. The Keep held many secrets.

There were several underground passages that opened out into the woods.

It took the king a moment to place Rilenheim. The old Geomancer stood so still, so tall and gaunt that he could almost be taken for one of the birches surrounding them.

"Your Majesty," the old Geomancer nodded.

"Well?" Rayant was breathless. He ran his hands through his hair, started to tuck in his shirt. He stepped closer to the Geomancer and raised his fists. "Did you find them?"

"I did Your Majesty. Meryn is safe."

Rayant let out his relief with a curt nod.

"Good." But Rilenheim was too still. He was giving the impression of being nothing but an old man, tired and stretched out by time. But it was an act, Rayant knew. Rilenheim was far from that. They'd met once before, and Rayant had been subject to both Rilenheim's temper and his kindly, benevolent gaze, eyes twinkling inside a circle of crow's feet. The kind of gaze that would be called kingly.

"Don't try my patience, Geomancer," Rayant growled. "Where is she? Where is Herendak?"

"I presume they are together."

"Then what are you doing here? You said you would find them. You said you would bring back Herendak's head!"

"Events have progressed too far for that. I have discovered the cause of Herendak's interest in Meryn. He believes she is the key to reversing the Rift."

Rayant squeezed his eyes shut. For a moment he listened to the crickets and the wind. A single wolf cry sounded in the distance. Didn't one always?

"And what would that mean?" he said.

"It would mean the return of my people, the return of the immortals. The Geomancers would return to our place. In such a world, Rayant, there was never a place for man."

"Is that not what you want as well, Rilenheim?" A bitterness was rising in Rayant's throat. He spat it out into a bush. Rilenheim was silent a long while.

"I have been among you a long time," the Geomancer answered finally, voice so low Rayant had to strain to hear. If he didn't know better, it almost seemed like a confession. The king shook his head. A confession from Rilenheim would be a lie, just a trick for him to get what he wanted.

"We are at a dangerous point, Rayant, King of Draldorn," Rilenheim went on. "You may be the last king. This may be the end of Draldorn. You must understand that Herendak has seen what I have seen. But whereas I am content to fade away, Herendak wants to return to that time, that place. He will not compromise in his goals. He seeks an ending, at any cost, even if that ending is for everything.

"Rayant, I come to you because you are Draldorn's king. I have disrupted Herendak's plan. I have taken a piece of it and even as we speak it is being safely hidden. But – Herendak is not a fool. He will be coming. He will eventually find what he seeks. I beseech you to act before he does."

"What plan, Rilenheim? What have you hidden? Where? Stop speaking vague suggestions and tell me what-"

"Hush," Rilenheim leant forward from under the shadows of trees, face growing large and craggy, shoulders wide, cloak massive and black as night. Rayant took a step back: the old man seemed suddenly a giant.

"Rayant," Rilenheim's face was stone, "Herendak is gathering an army, in the desert plains to the north, over the Yastran range. An army of what Wrilsch he can coerce. The more time he has, the more he will gather. He gains the support of those with power, and they in turn bring their own forces. Already, there are many thousand. So what I ask of you is this: I need you to march. Gather every man who can bear arms and face them now. Before the enemy grow too many."

Rayant's hands were balled into fists. He wanted to argue. He had visions of sending scouts, to confirm what Rilenheim was saying. But he knew, with a terrible certainty, that Rilenheim was telling him the truth. Not the full extent of what the old Geomancer knew, or suspected – but enough.

He did not want to be Draldorn's last king.

"You will come with us?" he asked. "If Herendak is there..."

Rilenheim gathered up Rayant's gaze and held it. "You realise you must reverse my banishment?" he said. "You must formally reinstate me to the Council. Give me, again, the power to command. I do not ask you to forgive me, Rayant, but just for this chance to put things right."

Rayant glowered. Rilenheim had played his own part in Meryn's disappearance. It was hard to believe that less than a year had passed since that day. But, if what Rilenheim said was true, he could see no way around.

"Very well." Rayant's voice was thick. "I will do as you say, though trusting you again makes my palms itch." He stared off into the pale night. The woods were alive with rodents rustling among the bushes, the calls of night creatures. "Rilenheim, tell me what we will face. Will Herendak fight alongside those monsters?"

"It will take him a long time to get to them. He will have to take the long path around the Yastran range, and when I saw him last he was ill equipped for the journey. But, Rayant, I will be there by your side."

"Then we will march. For my people. For Draldorn."

Rilenheim towered over him, blotting out the blue light of the night sky.

"No, Rayant," the Geomancer said. "Not for Draldorn. For all places. For all people. For the world."

* * *

Aldrua started when the door opened.

"Hello?" she called. There was no answer. The door closed with a click. An undulating form of mostly darkness flitted in front of it. For a moment Aldrua doubted her eyes, then terror gripped her.

The thing flittered across the room, sliding and colouring itself across the wardrobe, the chest, the dressing table.

The door was clear. Aldrua leapt from the bed. She lunged for the door, tangled her feet in the mat and went down with a thud. Thrashing for purchase she regained her feet, got a hand to the door handle... and paused.

The thing had stopped, motionless, having placed itself between the candelabra on the dressing table and the wall. Thin, dribbly candles were giving it form. There was the shape of a man, but thick, and amorphous, shifting vaguely in the light.

Her heart was pounding. The door handle rattled in her grip.

The shadow raised a limb. An arm, a hand, palm out, as if in greeting.

She pursed her lips for a question but -

It folded in on itself, gathered itself together like black twine until it had become a ball of darkness. Just as quickly, it withdrew, elongating out, as thick syrup from a bowl, until it was massive. Taking form again against the wall, it bowed, placing a long finger of darkness where its lips should have been. Then it was in front of the window, its chest riddled with starlight, then on the sill; and finally gone.

Aldrua hissed out a breath. She ran to the window, leaned out, turned her hair from her eyes. No sign of it. The distant crash of surf, the continuing smell of salt water. Gull noises. Draldorn stretched out in front of her, a jumbled mass of grey dwellings, pinpricked with light.

On the floor by her feet, something gurgled where the shadow had settled. With a gasp she dropped to her knees.

Her heart turned over. Finally, finally – tears. It was a baby. A baby girl. Tiny, smiling, gurgling. She ignored the hairs standing up on her neck, her arms. It was a miracle. A gift. She took it up in her arms, held it close, stared into its crystal clear eyes.

What had done this? She gave the window a single glance, before turning her full attention to the baby in her arms.

Shoulders shaking, she dissolved into tears.

Chapter 4

Meryn lay a long while in the grass on the lip of the ditch, but Herendak did not return. She could taste sick in her throat. She didn't think this was normal after giving birth. Just turning her head made the sky spin. The sun passed overhead in fits and starts.

How had this happened? She should have just held on tight. She should have said no to the stranger: no, I don't need help, go away, go away, go away! But she hadn't. She had been afraid and alone and Herendak should have been there. He had left her. He had made for the farmhouse, looking for help and water. She had known there would be a midwife there. She didn't know how she knew, she just *knew*, and Herendak hadn't argued with her. It was the strangest thing, looking now: there was no farmhouse. There was nothing but meadow. Tall trees provided edges and shade. Buttercups were strewn about, and, in the distance, that nightmare hut. But no farmhouse. She was getting confused. She had been through a lot. Her memories must be jumbled. This was not how she'd imagined spending her first day as a mother. This wasn't... Her thoughts drifted, as pain gripped her stomach and everything blurred... How it was supposed to go.

Night came in a chill of blue-grey shadows. Meryn jolted upright, shivering, holding herself in her arms. The trick was not to think or feel. The light-headedness was useful. The aches and pains were a welcome distraction. Despair would not help her or her child and she would absolutely not fall into that sweltering pit of blame and regret. She was who she was. A self-pitying fool would not have helped Herendak in the first place.

She had to do something. She couldn't stay there. There were wolves about, and worse. The further north Herendak had led her, the more Wrilsch they had seen. They were mostly tiny things; spiny, little bristly things. There was one that had seemed to be stitched together with patches of white and crimson fur. Meryn had thought her sister would have found it cute, despite their past history with Wrilsch. She had mentioned this to Herendak; he'd told her it would eat their fingers. But no matter, there were others which did not need a pleasing shape to entice their prey. These just latched on to the smell of blood and were relentless in their pursuit.

Meryn held her hands up to her face. They were stained with dried blood. She tried to rub it off onto the grass. It wouldn't budge. And her legs! Blotched with red. She pulled out handfuls of grass and rubbed at the blotches, harder and harder.

"This won't do," she mumbled to herself, "Won't do at all." Crimson flakes came off pinkening thighs, but it had dried fast and stubborn and didn't come away until skin did, no matter how much it hurt or how blurred everything was becoming. In the end she dug her fingers into the earth and let out a keening wail.

She allowed herself that moment, then shut up.

Stillness washed back over the meadow. The silence of birds. No. She would not be wounded prey. She would get her baby back, if Herendak couldn't. She raised her chin, set her jaw, and heaved herself to her feet. Her bad foot wouldn't take her weight. Her ankle was a swollen lump on the end of her leg. She managed a few limping hops before she was again on the grass. Yet she had seen the meadow's edge: wooden fence and scattered trees and, beyond, the Wide Road. It stretched from Kilsmouth to Orton, splitting and branching and criss-crossing the entire kingdom. There would be travellers, trade caravans. Someone to help.

She crawled along the ditch until her knees were ragged. Stones cut into her hands. She backed her way through the fence when she reached it, slipping through the beams, lifting each leg over one at a time. She had to pull her hurt ankle over with her hands; she could no longer move it otherwise. A torn blanket of moss came off the wood and she sneezed away grey spores.

Over tree roots and through bracken she crawled, disturbing insects as she went. Her cuts stung, until they were encrusted with mud. Then they throbbed. When she reached the road, a kind of peaceful exhaustion washed over her. It was soothing and welcome and promised so much.

She passed out by the roadside.

* * *

"What's this?" A weasely voice. A shoe of cracked leather prodded Meryn awake. "A beggar?"

"She looks sad," rumbled a second voice.

A tongue clicked in reproach. "She looks like a carcass, you simpleton."

Hands were on her, checking her pockets, turning them inside out. They unfolded her fingers, pulled off her ring.

"Wait. Let me see that." A third voice. This one clipped and certain.

With difficulty, Meryn fluttered open her eyes. Three figures in the dark. They rose up at an angle against the sky. The sky was askew; her neck was crooked. They were featureless shapes, of boots and trousers, belts, scabbards and quivers. There was no colour to be had from them. She tried to speak, but her throat wouldn't work. She could still taste spores and her stomach felt like a sack of sand. She didn't think this was the same night she'd passed out.

"Where did you get this?" the third voice was asking her, holding out her ring.

My sister.

"Where's the rest of your party?"

Gone, all gone.

"She don't have anything else." The man with the weasely voice was the smallest, Meryn could tell now. He was fidgeting and shifting his weight from foot to foot. She thought she could make out the outline of a whiskery beard. He went on, "I don't like this, Drael. She's ain't got nothing worth taking – means someone else got to her first."

"Maybe she got lost," came the slow, rumbly voice. It sounded like it started somewhere deep underground.

"No, Brogan," said Drael. "Did either of you even look at the ring? See the circles of silver? See the spire? This woman is someone of importance."

"All the more reason to slit her throat and get away," said Weasel. "She'll have guards. We don't want to be caught like this. Compromisin'."

Meryn heard metal screaming against metal, a dagger being freed from its sheath. A blade glinted dully in the darkness.

Not like this.

One of them – Drael? crouched beside her with the creaking of leather. She felt the cool back of his hand against her brow. He scraped her matted hair back from her cheeks, which felt puffy and hot. He leant closer and his breath caught in his throat. When he let it out, it hissed; drenching her with the smell of stale mead.

"What's wrong?" Weasel asked from over his shoulder.

More creaking as Drael rose back to feet, his movements blurry and dreamlike.

"Shut up and let me think for a second," he said.

Meryn watched him and wished he wouldn't waver in and out so. Consciousness was slipping. Everything was getting distant. She couldn't focus. She wished they'd kill her soon so she could get on with finding her baby. No, wait, that wasn't right...

Drael had his hands together on his chin, as if in prayer. Weasel was rasping his dagger against stubble. Brogan stood back from the others, immense and silent.

At last, Drael shook his head and proclaimed, "We're taking her with us. No arguments. Brogan, you got her?"

Brogan grunted a, "yes", and she was rising into the air, gentle hands on her waist. Everything spun. In a brief flurry of movement she was upside down, slung over his back. Too much pain. Her whole body clenched. She cried out, before a kind of white-hot numbness began to take what little awareness she had left.

"But who is she, Drael? Do you know who she is? Will you tell me?" This close, Brogan's voice was strangely soothing. There was a delay before Drael replied. His voice was smaller, like she was drifting away.

"She's the queen's little sister," he said. "This, Brogan my friend, is Princess Meryn."

* * *

Queen Aldrua stood in front of the full-length mirror in the changing room which adjoined her bedroom.

She looked, she decided, perfectly normal. Big eyes, little nose. Dull, straight, brown hair. Like she'd always looked.

And, when she spoke, her lips definitely moved. She could see them. The mirror didn't lie.

She put her fingers to them, and tried again. She said, "You're not crazy." She could hear that fine, even if her voice was a little quavery.

She said, "What is going on?" and heard that, too.

One of the servant girls called to her from the bedroom. More proof, as if it were needed, that she wasn't deaf.

"Are you al'right in there, Your Majesty?"

"I'm fine, Pena!"

But the words didn't ring true. Three days wasn't enough time. Maybe there could never be enough time.

Nevertheless, she had been saying those words a lot. She had been forced to play host to a parade of visitors since the... She hadn't a word, yet, for what had happened. The visitors were dignitaries and nobles, mostly. A parade of congratulations for her new baby.

"I'm fine," had become Aldrua's mantra. If said in just the right way, with just the right fragile smile, it forestalled further questions.

To not a single one of them was she able to tell the truth.

In truth, her baby was dead.

To the mirror, Aldrua tried to state this fact again. Again, there was no sound. A pounding headache cut her off. She leaned on the mirror for support, leaving behind a smudged handprint.

"This secret, then, I must keep," she whispered to her reflection. Rayant could not be told, nor anyone else; some silent bargain struck with a shadow. Only the three midwives knew what had happened, and she had no idea where they were.

There was a strange kind of relief in this realisation. The decision to tell was no longer hers, which meant there was nothing to be gained by fretting. She thought of Meryn. Her sister would find no relief at all in being muzzled. Would find it intolerable. Meryn had never been one for acceptance – of anything. Aldrua smiled fondly, but only for a moment; when the smile reached her eyes it turned sad. Meryn never was able to accept that some choices should not be made.

What Aldrua *really* wanted to say she wanted to say to Rayant. That a shadow had come to the tower, that night. When she was alone. When she would have made a pact with anyone or anything to change what had happened. And it had gifted her something that wasn't hers.

But the baby looked like her. It had the same eyes, the same cheeks. But how could this be so?

"Your Majesty?"

Pena was there, in the doorway, folded clothing in her arms.

"It's fine. I'm finished here," Aldrua said, attempting another smile. But her reflection didn't seem to be in agreement. This smile looked insincere, almost sickly. There was worry around her eyes. "I'm just a little tired," she said to it. "Just tired, is all."

But it was time to get back to the latest parade. She had left Rayant presiding over it. He was in the throne room, but not on the throne. This he had given up to the child, who was being fussed over by a dozen nannies so the king could keep his distance.

She wished so much to be able to speak to Rayant because of that other secret. The one shared by only him, her and one other. That not even the baby she had lost had been his. Would it make him less hurt if he knew this new one wasn't even hers? That she didn't know where it had come from?

But she couldn't tell.

She couldn't even tell the real father what had happened to his son.

Chapter 5

Herendak slipped through the tunnels of Ailtris High, lighting the way with a controlled flame in the palm of one hand. He found the mountain a mess. He cursed as each ancient passageway ended in mangled slabs of steel and stone. They were completely impassable, even for a Geomancer. The original complex was lost. Something had gone wrong here. Something was amiss with the maintenance magic, or else the weroms would not have been able to interfere. The mountain was honeycombed with decay and the city within the stone was dead.

For a moment Herendak considered going back the way he had came. He could skirt the base of the Yastran range, take the pass north across its snowy back. But on foot this would take weeks, and Rilenheim had forced his hand. Far quicker – far more dangerous – would be to turn his back on the tunnels of his ancestors and risk a more direct route.

He made his way to the entrance of one of the new tunnels. Fresh and shiny, just glistening tubes, these were twice his height, and entirely the work of weroms. The danger was that he couldn't predict how long they'd stand. Weroms would not last long if they riddled their habitat with so many holes that they collapsed; and so they travelled in mating pairs, one opening up a path, the other closing it behind. He would have to keep moving, and quickly.

There were precious few werom tunnels leading north. Herendak tried prospecting east, and then west, backtracking as required, sometimes forced south; but always seeking a northern path through the maze. The task was made more difficult by the shifting of the tunnels. There were indeed active weroms near. He would retrace his steps only to find the way sealed with debris.

He wondered what Meryn would do. He was doing that a lot recently. She was a human, the younger race – the *lesser* race – and her ideas were just as laced with insanity as those of the rest of her kind. Nevertheless, humans did tend to get things done. Meryn would be livid, he decided. She would be angry at the rock itself. She would blame it personally for her lack of progress. But despite this – because of this – she would not give up.

Herendak went on. His luck changed. He came across a handful of tiny twinkling crystals scattered on the slime. They were diamond fragments, indicating a werom couple, and they were only in that very specific section of tunnel. He tested the walls north and south, and was able to crumble stone away with just his fingers.

Nodding to himself, he crouched in the slime, settling slowly, as if into treacle. There he waited, eyes closed, resting as much as he could. He thought of Ilris as it had once been. His people in their thousands working and playing in the cast-iron sunlight of a much younger sky. They'd had an eternity ahead of them then, or so they'd thought. So *he'd* thought. The sky was very different now, especially at night.

He wasn't sure how much time had passed, kneeling in the slime, but at last he became aware of movement. An almost imperceptible shifting of the surrounding stone, accompanied by a noise felt in the belly rather than heard. It grew and grew, that noise, building with the nausea in his stomach. His teeth began to chatter. It soon became a bone-grinding crescendo of sound which showered loosened stone around him. The mountain was shaking itself apart.

He got his first glimpse of a werom. It mostly resembled a chitinous worm, made up of ringed segments. It burst into the tunnel from the side, at right angles but too high. Rock fragments spun and tore and disappeared into the maw behind innumerable glinting mandibles. It sloped down into the tunnel when the hole was wide enough, and glided its obscene bulk across Herendak's path, oblivious to his presence. With a smack it ploughed without slowing into the opposing rock-face.

Heading north.

Rock dust swept over Herendak, getting into his eyes, his hair, down his shirt. He hacked cough after cough into his sleeve. Long stretches of white-grey bark-textured hide slid past, the creature's length immense, before a sudden snap of tumbling rocks.

Just like that it was gone. The slug-like trail of ooze settled. Flakes of chalk-white dust floated, twinkling, onto the glistening rubble. Herendak rose and kicked through the detritus with a boot. There it was: fresh diamond dust. This, it seemed, was a common route, and the creature blazing his trail was a female. The male would be close behind, sealing everything up behind him.

Herendak frowned into the newly revealed darkness. If he took this path, he would be trapped between them. He didn't know how often they would rest, or sleep; or even if they needed to. All types of Wrilsch were different and he hadn't made a special study of those which dwelt underground. How long could he keep up before *he* needed to rest or sleep? Would the female even keep going in the right direction? Maybe he could direct it somehow. Maybe enough fire scorched to one side would be enough to turn it the other way, to keep it straight enough until it rejoined the more permanent Geomancer tunnels on the other side of the mountain.

The worst outcome would be a clash with the creatures. They wouldn't win, of course. He would, however, become trapped. Becoming buried alive in the most ostentatious tomb in the world would not kill him, not in the mortal sense of the word. But he could feel pain, and frustration, and a lengthy wait for erosion to do its thing did not appeal. For a moment he envisioned the male catching up with him, the female doubling back. A brief skirmish, followed by centuries of him hacking through the mountain with a liberated mandible.

He was going to risk it, he realised. There was a time when he would have turned back. But going back and around would take too long. So strange for haste to rank above safety. He had fallen a long, long way from the ways of his people.

Once again he thought of Meryn. Risking everything was such a Meryn thing to do, even when the choices seemed trivial, even absurd. She'd once told him she'd rather die than roll over like her sister had. Rather be nothing than submit to the demands of custom and become Queen of Draldorn. It didn't seem much of a problem, to Herendak. Was oblivion really preferable? So strange to fight against demands that, if free of them, she would probably seek out anyway. He mulled over the strangeness, probing his tongue over his teeth, tasting rock dust.

He had been paying more attention to Meryn's comments recently. The topic of death came up all the time, casually, like she wasn't even aware of it. She'd say, "I'd rather die," or, "I almost died laughing." For the longest time death was something that could not happen to a Geomancer. Now, after the changes he'd made, there were only two of them left. He wasn't ageing – he didn't think he was ageing – but what other ways might it be possible for him to be ended? It was beginning to weigh on his mind.

He turned into the new path, following the trail of diamonds. Meryn had a saying about diamonds as well, about diamonds and women and friendship. It didn't really make much sense to Herendak. It didn't necessarily have to.

Meryn would not last long in her current form.

He hurried down the trail of sparkling stones, the only person ever to lay eyes on this new vein of the mountain, and likely the last. He continued until the feel of the air changed, became sharply muted like he'd dipped his head under water. That was it, then: the other werom was behind. There was no turning back.

He put on more pace, intending to catch up with the lead, all the while thinking of Meryn and diamonds and death.

Chapter 6

There were arguments coming from the Council chamber. Aldrua paced back and forth, shoes clinking on the giant slabs of the mosaic. A guard appeared on the balcony above, a circled spire emblazoned on his surcoat.

"They are ready for you, Your Majesty."

She clutched the bulky length of her dress out of the way and hurried up the stairs. From the balcony she could see what the mosaic depicted: a giant scaled Wrilsch, flattened and exploded into fragments, claws alone requiring several tiles each. This is what the Council was discussing, what they were to ride out and face. How could they hope to defeat such things?

Servants opened wide the ornate doors of the Council chamber and Aldrua faltered on the threshold. The chamber was an airy hall awash with ghostly light. The high ceiling was a false sky, made entirely of plate glass, depicting sun and stars and moons, as if day and night had merged. Muted hues of orange and blue cast conflicting shadows over the assembled Council. There were no blue planetary rings here, Aldrua noted. This was a *very* old mural, made before the sky had changed, or by those with memories as old.

She had never got to know the councillors. She knew them only as imposing men layered in robes and cloaks, faces concealed behind thick beards; which they would slowly stroke at moments of deep contemplation. They were doing this now. They hulked in overwrought oak seats and murmured words of deep import to each other. When they noticed her in the doorway, the chamber fell silent.

Aldrua was no good at this. She and Meryn had been born out of order. Meryn was the confident one. She was the one who should have been queen, not Aldrua. But it was for Meryn that she was here. As they had grown up together, Meryn had always fought for her: thumping bullies, arguing with tutors on her behalf, making unsavoury suitors think twice – and so now it was time to fight for Meryn.

Nevertheless, Aldrua stood uncertain in the doorway, until one of the guards felt the need to pointedly clear his throat. A deep, eloquent voice finally broke through her indecision.

"Come in, Your Majesty." Rilenheim stepped into view, tall, gaunt, his cloak bathed in fake starlight.

She shuffled inside and the doors were closed behind her.

"You summoned me?" she said, aware of the absurdity of her words – no one had the right to summon a queen. Nevertheless, she swallowed against the dryness of her throat. "Please – do you have news of my sister?"

"Sit, Your Majesty. There is much to discuss."

She nodded. She looked around for an empty chair, yet could make out none in the gloom. This was a horrible room, she thought. The light was so uneven. It was mostly dark. As Rilenheim paced, he faded in and out, shifting between night and day. Such a stupid place to hold council. If she had her way, discussions would be held outside in the light, not where secrets could be so easily kept. Maybe, she considered, that was the whole point. The idea made her weary.

The councillors stared at her, gazes stern under thick eyebrows, all shadowed under high foreheads, daring her to make a fool of herself. Rilenheim was pacing because he was waiting for her to sit. They were *all* waiting for her to sit. Her cheeks flushed. She already felt out of place, and utterly, utterly useless.

With enormous relief she spied Rayant among the men, his younger face in stark contrast to theirs. Yet he didn't acknowledge her, didn't say anything to put her at ease. She had fought with him about this. He had told her to leave it alone, this thing with Meryn. To let her sister go, as if she could ever do that. But it was Rilenheim who had called her here, not Rayant. The two of them must have discussed the situation in private. What had been said that had allowed Rilenheim to convene the Council for the first time since she'd been crowned?

Maybe it was out of mere pity, but at last Rayant stood and came forward, beckoning for her to come. She rushed over to him, stumbling over her own feet; how unworthy and ungainly she was among such people! After a moment of not knowing where to put his hand, he led her by her elbow to where he was seated. From there, other great oak chairs were visible against the wall of draped curtains. Aldrua sunk into one next to Rayant, grateful she could hide in its bulk, wishing it were big enough to sink into completely.

Rilenheim called the Council to session. He did not waste time. His voice filled the room, becoming a presence all to itself; a creature immediately at home under the intimidating mural sky. Maybe this was indeed the right chamber to hold such councils.

The Geomancer began a history lesson, about Wrilsch and what they had once been, about what Herendak had done to make them what they were now. He spoke of how they had been captured and controlled after the extent of Herendak's folly had become clear. How they had been hunted and crushed. None of it was clear to Aldrua. Rilenheim was speaking in riddles, in circles. She wondered if he was making sense to the others. They were nodding and stroking their beards, but, in this chamber of secrets, that meant nothing.

Herendak had meant to give vitality and hope to his people. Instead they had, one by one, become mortal. The world had changed. The sky had changed. Their new mortality had spread and, once their powers had fled them, they had fallen away into nothingness. A new creature had risen in their stead: Wrilsch. Creatures of despair and death.

Herendak had long sought a way to undo what he had done. He had now, this very year – after thousands of years of trying – found a way. He might succeed.

But, Rilenheim! But! Aldrua wanted to question him. She wanted to understand. The others interjected their own questions, seemed satisfied enough with the answers, but there was nothing straightforward about Rilenheim's responses. He was a master orator. Much of what he said she believed; so much of it, in fact, that it was difficult to determine which were the half-truths. Aldrua leaned on the mighty armrest of her seat and bit her nails. Which, then, were true: was Herendak to undo the Wrilsch? Undo the dying of the Geomancers? Return the magic from the sky? Which of these things were bad? Rilenheim did not seem to think Geomancers could live with humanity. He was not making it clear why.

Aldrua leant over to Rayant.

"Do you understand all this?"

His face was haggard, poor man. She went to touch his hand, but he jerked it away. Would he never forgive her for her infidelity, for Kendan, who he'd thought was his friend? Did he see the child that wasn't his every time he looked at her? Or maybe he saw only the mocking face of her lover? She again wanted to tell him there was nothing wrong. It didn't matter that he wasn't the father. Kendan wasn't either. She didn't know who was. She wasn't even the mother. But she still couldn't tell. That secret still protected itself with pain. The choice to tell had been taken from her.

Rayant didn't answer her question, just gave a curt shake of his head, indicating she should shut up and pay attention.

"Why am I even here, Rayant?" she persisted. "I wanted to get help for Meryn – but this is just history-"

She shut up. Rayant was shaking his head in warning. Rilenheim was standing right there, in front of her, arms crossed.

"Very well, impatient queen," he said. "Let us discuss your traitorous sister."

"She's not-"

"I know you think not. I know of your opinions, of your suspicions, your sentiments, your schemes. You think Meryn is still your sister and your friend? She is not. She abandoned you the very moment she abandoned Draldorn. The moment she gave herself to Herendak she aligned herself to his, and only his, schemes and devices. You are no longer anything to her, young queen.

"No, do not speak. You should know that I have discussed your concerns at some length with the king, and I believe now it is time to discuss our immediate situation. This affair with Meryn is one that you must come to understand and accept."

Aldrua pressed her fingers to her eyes. Rilenheim said nothing more until she finally looked up at him, until he had her full attention. False orange sunlight dazzled in his hair and beard. The fake sun had moved in line with the real one.

"You would do well to listen close, young Aldrua. I do not tell you these things to be cruel. Your sister has had a brush with immortality. She has given birth to the child of the enemy."

"A child? Meryn? But... I-"

"I took the child from her, to keep it safe. I am sure you, of all people, comprehend the situation. And, you must understand, the child of a Geomancer is a dangerous thing. The child of Herendak and a Princess of the House of Draneth is the most dangerous thing of all. Your line were installed here for a reason, Aldrua, or did you think your family a natural right to rule? You are not here because of past campaigns, past victories or because of the brutal seizing of power which has traditionally been the way of your kind. No, your past is not the accepted past of royalty. Your purpose was always Herendak's, set into motion so very long ago. Alas, that I did not realise until too late. And while I do not – yet – fully perceive the totality of the detail – for example it is unclear to me why he has deigned to wait a thousand years – I am of no doubt that we are approaching the final culmination of events.

"So now listen, and listen close. Meryn is no longer your kin. She is no longer, even, entirely human, and the more time that passes the more dangerous she becomes, for she will seek out the part of her that she is missing. It is vital that neither of them find it. It is vital that events progress with order. In order to remove this threat we must destroy all of its elements. Then, and only then, will the danger be nullified.

"Here, too, I have already set events in motion. Where that I could have understood what was required for Meryn when I saw her last-"

"When did you see-"

"But there was little time and to have brought her with me would have slowed me unacceptably. I was, however, able to put her upon a path, to wind her up like geared machinery so as to slow her transformation. Herendak, it would seem, does not realise her importance. He has still not figured all the pieces from his previous failure.

"And so, Aldrua, you must be patient. You must not seek out your sister, as I know you yearn to. She may attempt to seek *you* out, despite my efforts at preventing this, for as far as Meryn is concerned to the very end she will cling to what she once was. It may resolve, at the last, that the bond you and she once did share may well be all she remembers, the last remnant of her faded self; and so she may indeed seek you out above all others. I have tried to prevent it. I have a measure of influence over what she is to become. But her motivation to do so may be strong and, alas, I cannot be everywhere.

"So listen close, listen well. Stay safe. Stay in the Keep, stay guarded – I command it! Though the guards may not be enough against what she becomes. But, Aldrua, if she does manage to get inside, and get to what she seeks-"

Did he mean her, or the child? Did he mean the child *every* time he referred to *her*? Some of the time? Aldrua felt like he was talking to her alone now, that the room contained nobody but him and her and he was taking up most of it, squeezing her out, and that she was being told something that not even Rayant knew.

"-Aldrua, the two of you are made of such similar material you must keep her away from you and you must keep her away from your children. You must not, under any circumstances whatsoever, so much as touch a hair on Meryn's head. A single touch, from you or your children, would be disastrous. Until it is time."

Aldrua could barely look away. She couldn't believe what she was hearing. She felt sick. Was her sister lost?

"I don't understand," she whispered. "I really don't."

"You were not listening! I have explained this. You remove immortality from a Geomancer, and nothing but a shell remains!" Rilenheim's hand shot up, went over his eyes. When he removed it there was a moment – so brief – where his eyes looked sad, and she could have sworn he looked both kind and wise. It gave her a headache.

"But-" she begun. He raised his hand to cut her off. He was strangely still. But his eyes were moving and distant. Aha! He had not meant to say what he had just said! He had revealed something he had not intended!

"You remove immortality from a Geomancer, nothing but a shell remains!"

Was that it? Was that what he had intended hidden? What did it mean? She repeated it to herself, desperate not to forget.

"Enough, Aldrua," he continued, in a quieter voice – a more controlled voice. "I have said my piece. You must obey. Make no mistake, Meryn is not the person you once knew. She might seem it, but do not be deceived. You may not be able to tell the difference until it is too late."

"But what should I do, if she comes?" Aldrua asked. "I cannot turn my back on my own sister!" Her voice was tiny. A part of her wished that the chair would choose this moment to swallow her up completely. Another part – the Meryn part – was working furiously:

"You remove immortality from a Geomancer, nothing but a shell remains..."

"What should I do if she comes, Rilenheim?" she repeated.

He was watching her face, carefully. There was the tiny seed of a first doubt somewhere deep in his dark eyes.

"You must flee; and you must send for me if you can," he said at last. "I will come immediately, or send the swiftest aid. I will make sure you are safe."

How he would do so remained unsaid, but she could guess, and her guess was not favourable to Meryn.

Aldrua hadn't noticed Rayant climb to his feet. He stepped up, toe to toe with Rilenheim. His hands were fists. They often were, these days.

"Is this really necessary, Rilenheim?" He spread his arms, courtly robes billowing. "I understand if you say Meryn is key to Herendak's plans. I understand that we need be wary. I understand that she is dangerous now. But-" he jutted a finger under Rilenheim's nose. "Why must we behave like animals to those we love? Is that your idea of a new world?"

Rilenheim's voice, when it came, was low and thick and molten with slow burning anger. Aldrua felt it as scratches up and down her spine.

"Rayant, *Your Majesty*, when you have lived for many thousands of years, when you have seen loved ones become animals, and animals take over the world, then, and only then, can you begin to judge me."

The chamber went silent. The councillors sat still, hunched in thoughtful poses; kingly statues on their thrones.

Rilenheim looked from Rayant to Aldrua, back again, as if appraising them, taking measure of their worth.

"I have explained myself," he said finally. "You know what you have to do. If you cooperate with Meryn you will be destroyed. This council is over."

And he was gone. Long strides to the doors, twin thumps as they burst open and shuddered against the walls.

With his exit, Aldrua found it so much easier to breathe. The room seemed almost empty. She looked up at Rayant. She couldn't read his face. Why did she have to be so weak? Why did she cry so? Oh, to be more like Meryn: to be defiant and strong.

Of all the things Rilenheim was keeping back, which were about her sister? Would Meryn's lightest touch really hurt Aldrua and her child? *Meryn's* child, as it turned out! Hidden in plain sight, because she and Meryn looked so similar.

Why couldn't Rilenheim have simply told her this in private?

Because he needed everyone to believe it.

This seemed suddenly so clear it dropped her mouth open. Rilenheim was playing a deep game here. What he said was just as much for the benefit of the councillors as herself, and she realised how little of what he said she actually believed. And, also, just how alone that made her. The others were again murmuring to each other, accepting Rilenheim's words as truth and marshalling their plans from there. Rilenheim wanted an army to get at Herendak, and it seemed he would get it.

The only certain thing: Meryn was in grave danger. Rilenheim would kill her if he had the chance. The only reason he hadn't killed her already was because he'd not known, when he'd seen her last, that he needed to. But what could he have learned since then? She thought he'd come straight to the Keep as fast as he could to talk to Rayant. What could he have possibly discovered here to change his plans for Meryn?

And what of her sister's child? Was she to be killed also? And if so, why had Rilenheim not done so already? "*Events had to proceed to order,*" the Geomancer had said. So what would make him ready? Did he need Herendak too? Was that why he needed their help against Herendak, to tip the balance in his favour so as to capture him?

What did all this mean?

Again, she looked up at her husband; this time he was looking down at her. He touched his hand to her cheek, for the briefest of moments, his fingertips warm and so very gentle.

Before she could think of something – anything – meaningful to say, he pulled away, barked, "Dismissed!" to the councillors, and was gone after Rilenheim.

* * *

Herendak discovered, deep within the mountain, something that had remained concealed for many generations of men. He could age it precisely because he had been its cause. It had been hidden since the new world had begun, and he came across it now only by remarkable good fortune.

He had stumbled after the werom, his boots heavy with caked slime, his breathing harsh and rasping. The air had become very thin. For hours he had followed the creature, always in a northerly direction; thankful for that, at least.

Then all at once, without warning, the werom was gone. There was instead a blinding light and a warm wind on his face. He breathed lungfuls of a thicker air, which tasted stale, like the air itself had rusted. It parched his throat like it was from a time before water.

He extinguished the flame in his hand, shaded his eyes against the light and put on a final burst of speed. But something seemed wrong. That great sense of distance beyond the light did not seem entirely normal. Neither did its colour. There was a pale blue tinge to it, which he couldn't blame on his saturated eyes.

He stopped dead, giving his vision time to adjust. His footfalls absent, he could now hear distant stirrings. Scratchings and scrapings, from many sources. There were echoes to them, entwining them all together; a big bowl of ripping and tearing lay ahead.

This was not, he concluded, the way out.

Cautious steps took him to the edge of a precipice. The sense of great distance was not the outer world – but it was a world nevertheless.

The mountain opened out into a subterranean city. From such a height Herendak could see so much that it was impossible to take in all at once. There were buildings, or at least their remains, in every possible state of disrepair. Some were just starting to crumble, others had long since caved in on themselves; still others were more or less intact. Werom tunnels lanced through many of them. Great arches which had once joined the buildings had shattered, or toppled to lean on each other for support. Many were only recognisable by the thickset buttresses that remained to hint at their original forms. All were coloured the same obsidian black, dusted and scratched with grey.

There was movement, as well, down there in the ruins. Weroms skidded, slid and tore over and around and through the buildings. They had found this place and had made it their home. This made a great deal of sense – because of what was above.

The light high over his head was not from the sun. The city's roof – or, more aptly, its heaven – was a swirl of blue mist under crimson stone. This mist had risen up into each fissure, each crack, striving ever upward; seeking to join the rest of his people's remains. It – they – would have been doing so for hundreds upon hundreds of years, ever since he had caused...

Rilenheim had always called it the Rift.

The tunnel Herendak stood in was far from the only exit or entrance to the city. There were many others, at different heights and angles, dotted all around, some even jutting directly out of the city's floor, close to vertical. This was a werom crossroads, a meeting place; they had come from all directions. Some skulked in tunnels high to the roof, close to the mist. It was as if they understood what it was, but had no clue what they were supposed to do with it. They milled about, waving their mandibles, excited. Trying to get back what they had lost.

Herendak scowled. They didn't even realise this was what they were doing. Animals now, just animals.

The crimson stone was what was keeping the mist in. It was not a normal stone. Was it Rilenheim's doing? It must have been. No one else had realised Herendak's mistake until it was too late. But all the crazy fool had done was leave him a weapon, a means of control: something which would lure the more mindless Wrilsch.

Faint tremors, again, in the stone, nearby. Herendak looked back the way he had come. The second of his two travelling companions was almost upon him. Its mate lay far, far below, at the end of an oozing path, half of its bulk concealed in a smashed audience dome.

Enough rumination. Herendak turned and quested a boot sideways and downward. Found a ledge, which took his weight. He stepped out, stepped down. Began his descent to the writhing anthill of weroms below.

Chapter 7

As Drael approached the camp, Brogan stepped out onto the trail in front of him. The big man had been taking the safety of their special guest very seriously.

"You brought the princess her medicine?" Brogan asked.

"I did. Have you seen Whilpan?"

"He's making sausages."

"Good," Drael said. He paused. "Has he been here all day?"

Brogan nodded. "Why?"

"Just something Kippen told me in town. The price on the princess's head is quite a bit higher than ours and... well. Kippen's been wrong before, so we shouldn't worry."

When he got to camp, Whilpan was sitting in front of the fire at the cave's entrance, browning sausages on the edge of his knife. The open pig from which he'd pulled both the meat and its casings sat in a bloodied heap by his side.

"Here to dote on your new lover?" Whilpan said, scratching at his stubble, as always, with the very same knife.

Drael didn't reply. He scooped out a chipped mug full of warm water from the kettle by the fire, and ducked into the cave. The princess was at the back. She had come away from the bedroll again. He pulled and tucked it back into position, averting his eyes as necessary, and finally put a hand on her brow. The fever was still strong. But perhaps it wasn't as bad now as when they'd found her. It was difficult to tell. He unwrapped his parcel of medicines, crumbled arlney extract into the mug and stirred until the whole went brown.

Meryn was moaning to herself again. He couldn't make out the words. He cupped the mug in both hands, blew on it until it was cool enough to drink, then proffered it to her lips. He had to cup her cheek with his hand to hold her head steady enough. His hand came away slick with sweat.

There was one thing about her that opened a little well of anxiety in his chest, which he didn't want to explore. She looked a little – he wasn't sure the word – but... plump, maybe. But only in specific places, which didn't fit her frame. The horrible thought was: had she been pregnant recently? What had happened?

He really didn't want to know.

Even stranger: her eyes were mostly closed, but at times her eyelids would twitch open enough for him to glimpse...

He wasn't sure. But her pupils seemed to fill her eyes and her eyes seemed to be reflective.

A deep shadow fell over him.

"Is she getting better?" Brogan asked.

"I think so. I hope so."

The big man nodded, slowly. Everything he did was slow. Brogan gave a long look over his shoulder, making sure no one was behind, then moved into the cave, hunching down to avoid hitting his head on the sharp rocks of the cave's roof. He settled onto the ground, fiddled at the stones under his boots.

"Drael," he said after a time. Drael looked up. "We ain't got no more money. You said we'd get enough to get long from here. But you've spent it all on," he pointed, "her."

"I know, Brogan. I'm sorry."

"What are we going to do with her Drael?"

"I don't know. I really don't. There's a ransom – eighty D-s worth – but they wouldn't give it to people like us."

Brogan was staring at him, in a way that wasn't entirely comfortable.

Both their eyes went to the knife he'd used to cut the princess's bandages. Drael picked it up. He idly felt its edge. Sharp, uneven and cruel. It was an old knife, used for everything around the camp. He looked over at the princess, and remembered what Whilpan had suggested by the roadside. Her neck was a splash of glistening paleness in the gloom. He held the hilt tightly in his fist and thought how quickly things could change. He could rid them of this problem right now, with one movement of his arm. He shouldn't have brought her here in the first place. They had enemies enough already without the kind who would hunt a princess.

He leaned over with the knife, to put it down next to his waterskin. He straightened them both out, as if a cave could be tidied – for no damn reason at all.

"Don't worry, Broge," he said in a small voice, after a while. "You know I wouldn't do that. Not... again. This isn't the same situation." He looked over at Meryn. "At least not yet."

He grabbed up the waterskin, which hadn't been filled with mere water for a long, long time, and drank enough of the searing liquid until his chest felt like a furnace.

"What?" he demanded of Brogan's placid, cow-like gaze. It was unrelenting. "Don't look at me like that. We've done worse things than end someone's pain. Well, I have. I had no choice. You-"

"No," Brogan's shaking head was like one of the moons moving on a fast night. "I would not do those things." Brogan stared out into the light outside the cave. His round face was strained. "And you would not either unless you had to. But Whilpan isn't like us, Drael."

Drael's mouth curled into a grimace.

"I know. But he saved our lives. We owe him for that. And we're safer together."

They could keep an eye on him as well, if he was with them; but he didn't tell Brogan that. Someone like Whilpan needed to be kept under careful scrutiny, which would undoubtedly leave other potential victims safer.

Meryn was kicking again, thrashing about under the blanket. Drael held her shoulders down – with some difficulty – until the fit subsided. She definitely seemed to be getting stronger.

Was he wrong to be doing this? Would she be better off if he took her into town one night, left her by a Salo kitchen? They would have a better chance of curing her ills than he. But what then? She was an exile, but surely it wouldn't be a death sentence, for a princess? He could just carry her out to the road, lay her down on the path to Karbel, and his part in this would be over.

But some instinct said no. Something told him that Meryn was in far more trouble than that. He had gone back to the place they'd found her and he had searched. He had found a trail, along a ditch, and footsteps, faint grassy impressions. They had led to a hut. There was blood there, it seemed, and other liquids dried out on the ground. Sun and wind made reading the signs difficult, but there had at most been three people there.

Why would Draldorn's princess be exiled? No one knew. It had been almost a year, and still the king had not explained to his people. If what she had done was forgiveable, surely he would say? What had happened to her that day in the meadow?

What was wrong with her eyes?

He had asked Brogan to sit in Karbel's tavern several days running, just to listen, find what rumours he could. Brogan was good at that. His patience was legendary, and his size and manner made him trustworthy enough for people to lower their guard. Drael didn't really know what he was expecting. Perhaps a boastful highwayman to stride up to Brogan with a story to tell. But no one interesting had come, until finally, soldiers had arrived, asking questions about Meryn. This had never happened before. They must have had word she was nearby, or perhaps the king had intensified the search and they were being sent everywhere. Maybe both.

They had to go, Drael realised. They couldn't stay here. There were some, like Kippen, who knew where he hid. With so many looking now, and with the duke still seeking him, it was becoming too dangerous to stay.

There was something big at play here. Something bigger than his past. Perhaps if he helped the princess now it would make up for...

"I'm going to try and get some rest now, Brogan," he said. "I think you should too. Tomorrow, we follow the Ralman south."

"What about Whilpan?"

"I think, all in all, it's probably best he stays behind."

Drael laid down his head. A long while passed before the nightmare came.

* * *

Drael dreamed. A bright morning sky, a shimmering rainbow. On the horizon thunder, lightning and grey clouds. But it was warm and dry where they were.

The boats tethered to the tiny pier of lake Orthal sloshed up and down, wood knocking against wood. The lake shimmered and ducks paddled among fallen red leaves. Eyhold Castle rose up behind a wall of trees. The flag depicting the Rulnet Eagle was unfurled high on the Moons Tower.

No one had yet said they should go back. They were young and storms were exciting.

Drael clambered onto the sailing skiff with Ethi. The duke's only daughter, she was used to getting her way, and so she took her favourite position under the boom.

Milt and Noran had to settle for the rowing boat. They gave Ethi dirty looks and waved the oars at her and Drael like overlong swords. They were her elder brothers. Young Drael made a point of holding his arms wide while pointedly shrugging his shoulders and grinning.

Then the first voice of warning. The countess came down from the castle. She stood on the narrow beach, her thick, fur gown trailing in the scraggly sand.

"Come in, all of you! The storm comes this way!" Milt hesitated, before putting down his oar. The countess turned and walked back up the beach. She looked back, once, calling: "Drael, bring them in!"

"Well. You heard her," said Milt. Noran tutted. They climbed back onto the pier.

"You'll do anything to avoid being beat, won't you Milt?" Drael said.

He watched the sun play off the waters and felt the wind in his hair. He could smell the freshness of the distant storm, though it was so very faint. He wanted to be out there.

"Just one race," he said.

"You heard Mother."

"She's not *my* mother, Milt."

"No, she's your employer – so you'd better do what she says. She already thinks you're trouble."

Drael looked to Ethi. She was still smiling. Sunlight shone in her hair. Drael grinned.

"Come on, Milt. Just once around the Lights." He pointed, but the mysterious glow, submerged beneath the lake at its centre, wasn't visible in the daylight from that distance. "And, if the weather does get worse, that'll just mean we can see the turning point more clearly. Just around once. There and back again. It won't take long to beat you. We'll be back before anyone even realises."

That moment, right there. Two paths and a moment of balance. Things could have turned out so very differently.

"Fine. Come on, Noran," said Milt, "we can row that smile off his face and still get back in time for dinner!"

A delighted laugh from Ethi as they bustled back into position. Knots were undone, ropes unbound. The two boats slipped out onto the lake.

Grey clouds rolled in.

The second voice of warning that day on Orthal Lake was Ethi's.

"Maybe we should go back." She sucked on her lower lip. It was late afternoon and the wind had gone out of their sails. The sky was now fully grey. Milt and Noran were ahead, but had stopped rowing. They bobbed up and down instead.

The wind came back in an instant. The mast creaked. The sail filled and emptied, filled and emptied. Ethi pushed hard against the boom, jamming a foot to the lip of the deck to brace herself.

"Help me!" she said, the first note of fright in her voice. He joined her, his hands next to hers. "Take it down!"

But the storm didn't hit, not then. The wind calmed and steadied.

"It's fine," Drael said at last. He took her hand. "See, it's fine. And we can still win with this wind. We'll go as far as the-"

"Drael-" But his smile was big enough to stop her. Her hand felt small and smooth in his. She was so beautiful. Despite having Milt and Noran nearby, he felt like he was alone with her. This was all it took to make him happy. "We can beat them yet," he said, still grinning. She looked up at the sky. Grey, but... still. Everything was so very still.

They straightened up the skiff and, tacking against the wind, aimed for the other boat ahead. It was gloomy under the clouds, the figures of Milt and Noran small and indistinct. By now the eerie glow from the under buoy was brighter than the sky. It made everything look upside down, like they were racing on the underside of a rain-pocked sky. It had always been there, for as long as anyone could remember. Just some bizarre, glowing sculpture built right out of the lakebed.

Abruptly, Milt and Noran both stopped rowing. Milt begun feverishly to turn the craft about. Noran was on his feet, shouting something at them.

A single gust of hissing wind was the final warning. Ethi's hair blew back into Drael's face. As she turned to say something to him, the storm hit in earnest.

Water tipped down from the sky. The force of it took Drael's breath. Thunder roared overhead. The skiff toppled, the masthead scraped the water, threw him off his feet. The little craft spun onto a new course. For a moment it righted, teetering on the edge of the direction of the wind, sail at odds with it, the boat jerking this way and that as it caught and released.

Ethi was tangled in the sail ropes. She was spitting out water.

"Help me Drael!"

He tried to go to her, tripped. His jaw cracked on the deck. A bloodied tooth was taken by a wave washing over the boat.

Everything spun. He went under. Strangely calm underneath the chaos. But – he could still see Ethi, struggling with the ropes, bubbles everywhere.

He hadn't fallen overboard.

The skiff was upside down.

The water was streaked with rippling white light. Not far was the source of the ever-present glow: two rings of diamond-encrusted stone, partially submerged into the lakebed, joined by a thick length of metal. He kicked himself towards Ethi, climbing the decking hand over hand. He heaved at the sail ropes, tried to untie the ends of them, in the end biting them. But they were knotted and tough – and he couldn't breathe. Ethi's free hand pulled at his shirt. He saw her face, close up, the look in her eyes. But he had no breath, none left; just panic.

He struggled free from her grip. He kicked for the surface. Back into the crazy chaos of the storm, choking spray and hissing wind. He gasped at the air and coughed out water. He clung tight to the hull of the skiff, even as it tried to buck him off, all the while aware of what was going on under it. He couldn't see the rowing boat. Lightning crackled in the air. He held on for as long as he could, but his fingers went numb and his grip didn't last.

* * *

Drael woke, sweat dripping down his face. But it was Brogan who had woken him, not the familiar nightmare. In fact, Brogan was still shaking him – with some force.

"Stop that, what are you doing? All right, all right, I'm awake!" Drael sat up, dishevelled and cold. "What's wrong with you, man?"

"Drael, there's something big out there in the woods!"

Something about the sight of such an enormous fellow so worked up was almost comical. Also, at the same time, and for exactly the same reason, extremely worrying.

"What do you mean 'something big'?" was the question which died on his lips. He didn't need to ask it.

"Wrilsch," Brogan growled.

Drael shot to his feet. He fumbled around for his trousers, fell on his face trying to pull them on. His shirts were still drying on the line outside. He could see them dangling between the cave and the tree closest to the campfire.

"Where's Whilpan?" he asked.

"I don't know. I don't see him. He's not in his tent."

"Right." Drael grabbed his sword belt. He rang the sword out of the scabbard and dropped the rest. He slinked barefoot, as quietly as he could manage, to the right side of the entrance of the cave. Brogan followed, completely soundlessly, slipping over to the left.

Drael peered out into the night. The campsite was draped with shadows. He could almost believe Brogan had made a mistake, except for the absolute silence. He couldn't even hear crickets. His eyes asked Brogan for directions. The big man stared out, a perplexed expression on his baby face.

"Stay. Here," Drael mouthed across to him.

Crouching low, Drael stepped out.

"Whilpan!" he whispered. "Where are you?" He crept to Whilpan's tent. The canvas entrance hung lose. The tent was indeed empty.

"Up here!"

Drael looked up. Whilpan had climbed a tree. He stood in the nook where the trunk split into two thick branches.

"Get down from there!" Drael whispered. "We can defend ourselves from the cave!"

But Whilpan just shook his head, and Drael noticed how he slumped. One arm hung loose, the sleeve bloody and torn. Whilpan had his bow with him but it hung by its drawstring from strengthless fingers.

"Where'd it go?" Drael asked, arms wide.

It came out of the darkness, talons first. Drael leapt backward, brought his sword up, caught a mottled limb. The thing was massive, undefined, blocking out starlight. It lunged at him again. A face of sharp edges etched out of the darkness. Drael's sword bit, tore, wrenched free from his hands. It spun away across the campsite. He fell back over a guy-rope, sprawled in the dirt. A whistling hiss. An arrow dug into the Wrilsch's neck and it bellowed. Another glimpse of its face as it came, a face of scars and sagging yellow flesh.

Drael scrambled backwards in the dirt and leaves. The thing loomed over him.

Then Brogan was there. He had his mace. He swung it with both hands. The sick thump of metal on flesh. A second swing, lower this time; a savage crack. But the mace head snapped clean off. The Wrilsch cried out in rage and slashed a claw across Brogan's chest. The big man staggered back, arm over the wound, blood flowing around it.

Drael bounded across the camp, scattering embers and kindling. He snatched up his sword.

He turned and froze. Their attacker was nowhere to be seen. A pool of something glistening lay where it had been.

"Where'd it go?" he asked Brogan.

Brogan just shook his head.

"There!"

It crashed into Whilpan's tree. A crack, and the tearing of branches. Whilpan leapt away and rolled as the tree came down around him.

The Wrilsch faced them, clear in the starlight for the first time. Its face was angular, rotten, sagging. Its physique was that of a bear twice normal size, musculature bulging behind mottled grey skin.

The leg Brogan had hit slumped with splintered bone. Something glinted around its neck. It was wearing a collar? A necklace?

Its eyes were disconcertingly human.

Drael darted forward, ducked a talon, pulled back and with a cry slid his sword straight into the creature's mouth.

It bellowed a scream of pure rage, its breath searing around him. Its teeth chomped down. Drael staggered back with only half a sword in his hand. The Wrilsch spat out the rest in his direction.

"Brogan..." Drael said, not looking away from the creature's eyes. "Go get Meryn."

Whilpan was at his side.

"We run?"

"Unless you have any objections..."

"No. Good plan. *Good* plan."

Chapter 8

The chase went on too long. Hours passed. They were getting tired, but didn't dare slow. Brogan was clearly hurting. He stumbled on ahead, setting a crazy pace, not looking back. He carried Meryn with one hand under her knees, one under her neck.

Drael called a halt to take another look at Brogan's wound. Brogan laid the princess down on the grass and Drael pulled his tunic away from the tear. It started on the big man's shoulder and ended at his navel. It was ragged and deep. His chest was beginning to look like a side of ham.

"I'll take Meryn," Drael said.

Brogan grunted.

"I'm fine," he said. His expression gave no hint of pain, or anything else. It just glistened.

They settled for carrying Meryn between them. Her feet dragged on the ground. That black ankle of hers was still swollen and Drael winced when it caught on roots. His own shoeless feet weren't faring much better.

"Higher, Brogan."

Brogan didn't reply. He was just staring ahead down the narrow trail, unseeing.

Whilpan brought up the rear. His arm appeared to be broken. The bowshot earlier had been drawn partially with his teeth, which meant it had lacked the power to do much, if any, damage. Drael was surprised he'd helped at all. He noticed Whilpan's distracted fascination with the undergrowth on either side of the trail, but didn't blame him. If Whilpan made a run for it, away from them and the Wrilsch that followed, he would not hold a grudge.

And it *was* following. They could hear it when they stopped to listen. But why? Why them? Why not seek weaker prey? Brogan had hurt it, that much was clear. It wasn't able to run. But, thanks to the princess, neither were they. They were outdistancing it, but for how long? They should leave her. *She* was the weaker prey. If it was after food, they only had to outrun *her*.

But the thoughts which he couldn't outrun were that this Wrilsch was far too far south, so much further than its kin had previously dared venture; and that it had found its way to their hidden cave, which was backed to a cliff and difficult to get to by accident. And that it was following a woman with eyes as reflective as its own.

Leave her, damn you. Save Brogan. Save yourself!

He thought of Ethi; saw her face, creased into a smile.

He gritted his teeth and pressed on.

He almost despaired when he heard wracking, wet coughs. But it wasn't Brogan. Meryn was trying to bend forward over her stomach. They came to a halt.

After coughing up something that looked vaguely like frogspawn, Meryn uttered her first words to them:

"Darkness," she said. "Pools in the light."

"What? Princess, you have a bad fever."

Her eyelids opened to a milky-white blankness, before her eyes rolled down and she focussed.

"Water," she croaked.

They lowered her to the ground, where she slumped.

"Don't have any," Drael said. "Princess, I have a lot of questions-"

"Water, water, water!"

"Calm down!" She was frantic. He thought for a moment. "We're near the Ralman. We'll come across tributaries soon enough."

"I'm *so* thirsty," she said, and it was such a terrible plea, like a dying soldier calling for his mummy.

"Come on," Drael said, reaching for her, "we'll get to a stream and -"

Branches shook as Brogan crashed to the ground. He knelt for a moment, unmoving, then fell backwards like a felled tree.

"We rest here," Drael declared. "Maybe," he said, catching Whilpan's pale expression as he peered back down the trail. "Just maybe, that thing has given up."

"It hasn't," Meryn said, voice cracked. "Dark pool in the light."

Drael cupped her head in a hand and gently pushed her onto her back. "Get some rest. We'll stay here for..." he looked at Brogan, staring up at shivering branches. "Until Brogan is done. We'll find you some water soon, princess."

"We go that way," she said, pointing very clearly and deliberately, though her finger shook. "We must go that way." She was shivering all over, in fact. She was in no position to issue orders. Again the thought: all they had to do was leave her and run. He could still save three of them.

Assuming he and Whilpan could drag Brogan away.

But damn it all, not again. Not this time. They had to try.

He turned to Whilpan.

"Can you take a first watch?"

Hesitation. Don't abandon me now, Whilp...

"First of two?" Whilpan said at last.

"It'll have to be. Let me know as soon as you see or hear anything, no matter how distant, even if it might be something else. Thank you. Thank you, Whilpan."

"Don'tmentionit," Whilpan mumbled. He stepped off back down the trail, unslinging his bow with his one good hand, easing straight his injured arm, testing its strength. He turned back. "What're *you* gonna do?"

Drael looked at Brogan.

"Get us moving again," he said.

With Whilpan gone, Drael felt suddenly alone. The night closed in around him. It was warm and smelt of wet soil. What the hell was he doing? Where could they go? The only one of them to have hurt that thing was struggling to stay conscious.

He took a close look at Brogan's wound. It was a deep pink-green in colour and clearly poisoned. He should have guessed Wrilsch wouldn't be content to just slice and tear. He tried to clean it as best he could with water from the stream. Brogan didn't respond in any way.

Drael rested his back against a gnarled tree and grimaced his eyes shut.

The problem was, he knew where they should go – it was in exactly the direction that Meryn had pointed – he just didn't want to acknowledge it. Eyhold Castle was near, across the river. The duke kept soldiers there. They could defend against the Wrilsch. They could protect the princess. And they could take her back to be judged at Draneth, if that was to be her fate.

The only certainty, Drael thought, was that *he* couldn't help her. She'd just end up like Ethi. At that thought, his hand clenched around an imaginary waterskin. He'd left it behind, in his haste. Why did he forget the things he wanted to remember, and could not forget the things he yearned to leave behind?

No. He was decided. They would take her as close as they dared to his old home. The rest of them would hide. They would wait to ensure she was safely escorted inside. And then they would flee.

He was sure the Wrilsch would not follow them once they were shot of the princess.

Meryn startled his eyes open. She had crawled to his side. Her hand was cold and damp on his bare chest. The night was deeper, the sky obscured by branches and clouds.

"We go now," she said. "It comes."

He stared into those bright brown glittering eyes and nodded.

"What happened to you?" he whispered, but she just shook her head.

* * *

They reached a stream at midnight, when the moons eclipsed into one. Clear water trickled over pebbly shale, carrying twigs and leaves along to the Ralman.

Drael was carrying Meryn by himself now, and so struggled to make any kind of pace. Brogan just walked blindly in whatever direction he was pointed. They had only managed to get him back on his feet by pulling him up by his hair. Drael tugged the back of Brogan's tunic to stop his march. He put Meryn down by the stream. He cupped some water in his hands and held it to her lips, but she pushed them aside and plunged her face straight into the water. She slurped like a horse. Whilpan stepped a little way downstream. The stream had carved an easier path through the foliage.

"Drael," rumbled Brogan. Drael turned. "Drael, I need to sleep."

"I don't think we have time, Broge."

"I'm going to go to sleep now." Brogan lay himself on the ground and curled up around his stomach.

Meryn pulled her face out of the stream, gasping, shaking water from tendrils of glistening hair.

"I..." A shadow passed from her face. "I appreciate your helping me," she said, suddenly lucid. She looked down at herself with clear disapproval, and her face tightened.

"Where are we?"

"Near the Ralman. South of Rulneth."

She nodded, slowly.

"I think I can help your friend," she said.

"He's poisoned."

"I know." She brushed her wet hair back behind each ear. "I see the poison."

He stared at her.

"Something... has happened to me," she said.

Drael noted the pause. She chose those words with deliberate care. She was afraid to say: *is* happening to me.

"I mean it. I can see the poison in your friend. So let me see," she breathed a sudden difficult breath, "see what I can do."

She made to move towards Brogan, but gasped instead.

"Can you walk?"

"I don't think so. I can't feel my legs, and my arms are tingling."

"You're very sick. You had a bad fever."

"Help me." He hoisted her up and they stumbled to Brogan. They uncurled him, with difficulty, his limbs stuff and unyielding, until he was flat on his back.

Meryn sat still for a moment, then touched her fingertips to Brogan's wound. Her hands were thin and mapped with blue veins. She ran them over the tear.

"It's the *absence* of..." she said. "Drael? I need you. Put your hands over mine."

"I-"

"Hurry now."

He did so. The poison came up, then. Drael could see it as well. Black and oily and smelling of sick. It seeped from the gash in Brogan's chest and...

It leapt straight for Drael.

But Meryn snatched out. She caught it before it reached him. She tensed and fell away backwards, a single piece of black-liquid night writhing impossibly in her grip. It shot out and down, stretching for her face. Holding it at arm's length she screamed, then managed to twist it sideways. A sudden snap. It folded. She wrestled it into a blob, put her hands together and squeezed *hard*.

When she let go, blackness trickled to the earth. Grass and dirt bubbled and hissed. Her chest heaved for air.

"How did you do that?" Drael gasped. She stared at him. She didn't know, he could see. She was just as lost as he was. She didn't know and it terrified her.

* * *

In the silence and darkness under the craggy trees of Homefire Wood, Meryn watched Drael replace the splint on Whilpan's arm, and finally, she *understood*.

"This is the end," she said to Drael, and Whilpan, and Brogan, who was now awake, his knees drawn up to his chest, his tree-trunk arms wrapped around them. She stared out, past Drael's face, pale in the moonlight, and out along the stream. She stared down the path they'd taken, and though she shouldn't have been able to, for many miles she *saw*.

The trail they had made was clear to her. It was warm and sticky, with a scent that was hers, and at the end of it, the shape of the Wrilsch. It was a hole rent in the darkness, a sucking, twisting, tearing bulk, reaching for her.

She scrunched her eyes closed and concentrated. When she opened them: nothing but regular blue night, cool shade and the faces of those who had helped her.

"Herendak sends it," she said. "The thing after us. It's his. I *know* this." Thoughts – shadowy, indistinct thoughts – were tumbling through her head.

"Meryn, Your Majesty-" Drael said, his voice soft with a kind of warning, though for which of them she wasn't sure.

"Hush," she said. "Let me say this." She closed her eyes tightly once more, trying to hold on to the thread. She couldn't let it fade. "He told me the child would be first of many, would bring things back. He said it was wrong that we have to live as we live, as things with endings."

"What is she talking about, Drael?" snarled Whilpan. But in a whisper, so as to not provoke her. "Herendak is a myth."

Drael nodded.

He asked her, "Herendak? Herendak... the founder? Who laid

the first stone of Draneth City?"

"Herendak," she said, "the father of my child."

He stared at her. She stared back, but could barely see him. Her condition was getting worse. Her vision was a blend of what was actually in front of her, and what was distant but relentless in its approach. Just a condition. That's all it was. She insisted on it. A condition implied a cure. She gritted her teeth until the moment passed, feeling so endlessly lost that the world itself would never be able to find her.

Let go.

It was her own thought. Right in her head, where they normally came from. Yet it seemed so unfamiliar.

"What?" she said. There wasn't an answer, of course. There wouldn't be, unless she did the answering.

Just let go.

So what if she did? What if she did lose herself to the world? What if she embraced this change? It would be freeing, to let go, in the way vertigo was freeing. Falling, falling, free from constraints, knowing that nothing you did could save you, that the only thing left was the falling...

She noticed, almost abstractly, Drael give Brogan a subtle look. This prompted the big man to his feet, to stand over her with a large, sharp rock at the ready. A rock! She was well past rocks. In the distance, the Wrilsch lurched along the trail, calling to her, mocking.

"Oh, I see you," she said. "Oh, I see you coming!" Then, she blinked, and there was Drael again, closer, his mop of hair tangled with sweat, a look of sweet concern on his face – or maybe not concern. Some other kind of sentiment that set his face sternly to hers. That was abstract, as well. She wasn't sure what it meant. A face, features, concern, sweet. It all *meant* something. She desperately tried to concentrate. She tried to feel some kind of response. Just a blank, terrifying void.

There was no way across.

"It's mercy," she said, scrabbling to get back to them. Into the emptiness was coming a new understanding, a different, seeping kind of knowledge. She skirted its edges, sensed the weight of it, its pull, was afraid it only went one way. "Mercy is what has had Herendak take action. He has seen his people end, he knows what will happen. He was to do it himself, if he could. That was his original intent. He said he loved me, you know, Drael, do you believe that? But maybe it was all just mercy."

"I'm not sure I'm following," he said gently, clearly not sure what to say, and just as clearly unwilling to break her train of thought; afraid, no doubt, of what she might do next.

"Do you know why my sister is queen?" she went on. "Do you know why I am 'royal'? Do you know how Herendak, the founder, chose who were to reside in the Keep and rule? It is no accident we are where we are, and neither did we choose ourselves, like the Houses of other kingdoms.

"No. We are whole people. We are not Geomancers, we are not Wrilsch. All others from us, when free of them. We are the first of the new people. Do you see? He never could make them whole.

"But now – now, he has made another! He has taken from me and made one more, but one who is different. She is a creature of this new world, my child, a daughter of time. Do you not see what it is for a creature which is ageless to make a new one of itself?

"*She* is the key. He spoke to me of this, but I did not understand. He said he would make the world great again, but would need a mortal child. Do you know how I know this? I can *feel* the others. I am slipping. I must not let go.

"He said he loved me.

"He said he would take care of me.

"But this is all about endings. I see that now."

* * *

She fell silent.

Drael took the sleeve he'd cut off Whilpan's broken arm and recycled it as a bandage for her ankle. Black lines criss-crossed her foot, like it was cracked and waiting to fall apart. His eyes met hers. They were startlingly dark. He looked away quickly. Brogan was slumped nearby, staring at the patch of earth bubbled by poison.

"If you had a crutch, could you move?" Drael asked her. "We're running out of people who can carry you."

"I think so," she said, from a long way away. "Maybe."

"Brogan?" After making no move for a long while, the big man raised his head abruptly. He heaved himself to his feet and started foraging for a suitable branch with a grim determination. His movements were slow and deliberate. Drael figured it best he be kept busy and distracted.

"We need to go as soon as possible," Meryn said. "It'll keep coming. It's a wonder it hasn't already caught up with us."

"Yeah, well," Whilpan said, his shadow dropping over them. He had been lurking at a vantage point with a view of the way they had came, but close enough to keep an eye on her. "What I want to know is, how do you even know what 'it' is? You were sick. We carried you. You were out of it. Unconscious. Or were you just pretending?"

"This isn't the time, Whilp," said Drael.

"Oh, yeah, you would side with her. That was always your way, wasn't it, Dray? You always had a thing for your 'betters'. Wasn't that why you were at Eyhold?"

"That's enough!"

"Look. One minute she's unconscious. The next she's awake and knows something's coming. And *then* she's *folding* poison with her bare hands! Only darkness can handle darkness! We can't trust her!"

"I said that's enough!"

"No," Meryn put up a placating hand. "Let him speak! The way out of this mess isn't to stop asking questions."

And for the first time Drael realised who he was dealing with exactly. Her words, if not her voice, were clear. Her gaze was angry and unflinching. Beneath the pain and fear was something stone.

Even Whilpan seemed taken aback. He crossed his arms over his chest and pouted.

"Good. Well, then. First you tell us what everyone else in Draldorn wants to know: just how is it the king wants you back so bad? First he exiles you, then he's offerin' a huge reward for your return. What did you do?"

For a moment, she gazed up at him with the kind of irrefutable expression that could only come from a lifetime of being obeyed. Then, she sighed, and just looked ragged and spent.

"I've already told you about Herendak. I'll tell you everything, but let's get somewhere safe first. I don't think our pursuer needs to rest, as we do."

"Brogan mangled one of its legs," Drael said. "I expect that's why it's yet to catch up with us."

"Really?" The princess looked up at Brogan, who had now taken to standing in the shadows behind Drael, leaning on a newly smoothed branch that was ready to be pressed into service as a crutch. Or possibly a cudgel, depending on her behaviour. "So maybe we *can* outrun it," she mused.

"How is it tracking us?" Whilpan asked.

"I can only guess."

"Then guess."

"I... for *me*, it's kind of a hole in the darkness. Like a whirlpool dragging the darkness in. It's... enticing. Maybe it can see us – me – in a similar way." She shook her head slowly. "I'm not sure."

"Then we can't hide," Drael nodded. "Wherever we go, it will follow. So we run. What will the king do with you if we turn ourselves in for protection?"

"Kill me."

"Bah!" Whilpan kicked a drift of muddy leaves at her. "You're a princess! They wouldn't dare!"

"You don't get it. You just don't understand. This is bigger than you know."

"Then explain it to us, Meryn," said Drael.

"That may take more time than we have, and I do not know all of it. But," she rolled her eyes, "you are not going to trust me until I tell you, are you? Oh, very well. I've mentioned Herendak. Rilenheim is also involved. What do you know of Geomancers? Answer quickly. We cannot delay long."

"They're the people who used to live here, before Draldorn," Drael said.

"There are two of them left. Those two are still alive."

"Meryn, they wiped themselves out. They exist only in stories now, as told by the superstitious, to scare children. They exist only in the sky." Drael spoke slowly, deliberately calmly. Meryn looked so frail, and after what she'd been through he didn't know if he'd trust what she had to say.

"Rilenheim," said Brogan. They all looked at him. "They were talking about him in town. They say he's called the Council. They say he is telling the king what to do. I suppose he gets to do that. He was the one who named the kingdom, all that time ago."

"Your friend is right," Meryn murmured. "He was here at the beginning – in fact, before the beginning. He is the reason we had to flee Draneth. Herendak and me, I mean."

"And Herendak," Brogan continued. "He started building it. I hear many stories about the Geomancers."

"Yes." Meryn's eyes sparkled. "The people of Draneth speak of the works of those two constantly. Why not believe that these are the same men of old? No, listen. You've – all of you – risked your lives for me. So let me tell you this. For, however strange it may sound, the fact is that Herendak is the father of my child, and Rilenheim stole her from me. Rayant was warned, I think, by Rilenheim, that I would betray him. That I would help Herendak, help him by bearing..."

She fell silent. This time, Drael was certain he knew the reason for it, which was far more mundane, and did not require this sudden weight of history.

"It sounds to me," Drael said, "like you made a mistake."

"Maybe I did. Though is it really a mistake, if what he promised turns out to be true, even if it costs me myself? Mercy. Yet, I cannot help thinking that, if he has kept this transformation from me, what else has he kept back?" She sighed. "But it's more complicated even than that. Let me explain. The fact is – the simple fact of it is..."

"Go on, Meryn."

"Herendak went to my sister first."

Chapter 9

She had found that out the very same day they had fled from Draneth. It was a bright day, cloudless and warm; the sun overpowering the rings. It was the kind of day where chirping birds distracted even from the melancholy of leaving everyone behind.

The knowledge that they were being chased also helped with that, of course. And, if she'd have known this was just the first chase of many, maybe she'd have turned back.

"We should have told her!" Meryn told Herendak, shouting so as to be heard. She wanted to take him and shake him. But she needed both hands for the reins. Their coach crashed wildly up and down. It was meant for the paved roads of Draneth, not these unkempt tracks into the wilderness. Rows of trees jolted past, and occasionally lost branches. Terrified robins chirped sweetly as they fled for their lives.

"And what would we have said?" Herendak screamed back. They were moving fast. Around one bend, they were suddenly on two wheels.

"You could have told her the truth!"

He shook his head, insomuch as that was possible to tell at this speed. "She's not like you, Meryn!"

"If you just gave her the chance-"

"No!"

"No? Just no? I still don't know why you had to involve her at all."

She cocked a glance at him. He was looking at her funny. *Intently.*

"What? Why *did* you insist on meeting her? It's something to do with all this, isn't it? There's something about both of us?"

He was shaking his head again. He looked bemused, perhaps even a little confused. She loved that about him. Despite his vast, century's worth of knowledge, and the confidence that came with it, she could still cast him adrift with a few well-aimed questions.

"Am I right?" He didn't answer. "I'm right. I'm always right!"

The road straightened and the ride became smoother. She took the opportunity to again check his expression. Yes, he was holding something back. Sometimes she didn't think she entirely trusted him. But how *could* she truly trust someone she could never understand, someone who had such immense experience that they had so little common ground? She couldn't, not entirely. But it made a big difference that she understood that. She was no fool.

And besides, other things made up for it. Like the stories he told, to her and her alone, in secret moments, when they were by themselves. They made her shiver. And he wouldn't tell them to anyone else. *He* didn't trust anyone else. Just her. Not even Aldrua.

"She's my sister, Heri. We should have told her."

"Told her what? Everything? That you had agreed to bring back my people? She would not have kept *that* secret."

"I'd have made her understand!"

"It's not a matter of understanding, Meryn. We are going to change things. It will not be the same for your kind after this. It will be better, with us back – though some might argue otherwise. But better is still different. Do you really think others of your kind would not resist?"

"Aldrua would understand. We can't leave your people in so much pain."

"Not everyone has your compassion."

They went on in silence for a while, barring the crunch of the wheels, and the creak of the coach's tortured frame, and the occasional crash as yet more gilded lettering was torn from it; all framed within a furious wind which sucked at their breath.

Herendak had insisted on the king's highly impractical, ceremonial coach, as they wouldn't be questioned on their way out of Draneth. He had been right to insist. They'd got out unchallenged, with him driving and her hidden inside. She wondered how much time that had bought them, before someone noticed she was gone. She wondered who'd be the first to notice, and whether they already had. Once they were free of the city, she hadn't wasted any time in taking the reins and whip from Herendak to make sure they didn't lose whatever time they'd gained.

"We're still not going fast enough," she said. "Throw out the seats."

"We're sitting on-"

"The ones *inside*, you idiot. For someone thousands of years old, you're not too bright."

"I can't get to them unless you stop-"

"Take the reins back for a second."

"No! It's too dangerous to climb over at this speed."

She fixed him with a cold stare. Or tried to. It was made difficult by the jarring bouncing.

"You think I'm such a fragile thing, don't you?"

"No."

"Yes you do."

His eyes were hot. "No. You have to take greater care. I need you, Meryn."

"What we need is to go faster. *He* is coming."

"You can't know that."

"I do."

"You've never even met him."

"I still know him."

"But you're-"

"Only human. I know. But some things I can tell."

He grinned, which she judged this time to be rueful.

She decided something.

"You changed the subject, earlier," she said, "or you just shut up, I can't remember which. What did you need from my sister? Is she getting Rayant on your side?"

"Keep your concentration on the road. It's narrowing!"

It was, and was also veering sharply to the left, and then quickly to the right, following the contours of the landscape. The wheels spun and threw dirt up into their faces. Meryn laughed, even through their coughing.

"Slow down, you fool!"

He looked so perturbed she reached out to lean her hand on his knee. And she slowed.

"Fine. In fact, I'll stop. We can get rid of the excess bulk of those seats. And you can answer my questions."

He didn't look pleased.

"We should keep moving."

They slowed to a stop.

She turned to him.

"Tell me."

She could hear his breathing. It was fast. She leaned in closer. He had been afraid of her driving. For her? Or for him? She knew he didn't like it when she took risks.

Spontaneously, she kissed him lightly on the nose.

"Tell me. Or we sit here until Rilenheim comes."

"Meryn-"

She pulled herself over and straddled him, so they were facing, his warm breath on her face.

"I said: tell me."

Awkwardly, he pushed her off him and got down from the coach. He opened the door to the passenger area. He pushed and pulled ineffectually at the seats.

"Heri. Look at me." She waited until he did so. "Whatever it is, you know I'd prefer to know."

He closed his eyes. "I know. But I don't want to tell you. I hate the way you look at me when I tell you things like that."

"It's bad, isn't it?"

"You have to remember what is at stake."

"Your people. Thousands of them. More. Not something I'm likely to forget."

"Come down from there."

She did so. The grass was springy underfoot, and smelt moist where the wheels had torn it up. They stood there face to face – almost. He wasn't a tall man. She looked down at him, and tried to quell a rising dread.

"I- Meryn, you could not bear a child with me on your own."

"What? What do you mean? Isn't that the whole point of this? What else are we running away to do?"

He looked at his feet. His lip was trembling. She waited, knowing she had no choice. She had to know. Always had to know.

"Tell me."

"Meryn. I took the life from Aldrua's child. We need it for our own. Hers will never be born, and she does not even know it."

Chapter 10

It was like in a fairy tale: it happened three times. These things so often happened in threes; otherwise sevens. Aldrua mused on this later, once she truly understood just how dark things were going to get.

She would later look back at this very moment as the last time she was truly carefree. Which was strange, when she thought about it, given everything that had already happened up to this point.

She walked down the perfect lawn over to the Old Palace on her own, not wanting to bother Pena or the other servants with the trip. She had left Ielenia and baby Elhrinna safe with them. It was chilly, but bracingly so, and short spells of cold were almost pleasant when she knew she would soon be snug and warm. Like Ielenia liked to do, she floated her fashionably baggy sleeves to trail in the wind and imagined she were sailing herself along. It was a game that had been her mother's, and which Ielenia now kept.

Movement. That was what she liked about that game right now, about what she was doing right now. Keep moving.

Because if she stopped, she would start to think and-

There, ahead, look at it. The Old Palace was where the Retts now lived, and Aldrua saw no harm in asking Yenna Rett about *that night.* She could even bear to think back on it now. Nothing she did was going to change what had happened and sometimes, after enough time had passed, and when there were enough things to do, everything more or less seemed-

No. Focus on the practical. She wanted to see if Yenna could talk to her about what had happened. To see if Rilenheim had stopped everyone who was there that night from discussing it. He probably had. He was nothing if not thorough. But possibly... there was a chance they could still talk to *each other.* The secret would still be kept in that case, and what did Rilenheim care for the opinions of Aldrua and her midwives if they were to be kept amongst themselves?

Besides, she wanted to thank Yenna and if she stayed holed up in the Keep much longer she would go mad. She hated watching Rayant trail around after Rilenheim like the Geomancer's very own lapdog.

She hastened up the long, spacious steps which rose to the Old Palace's entrance, and idly wondered why the doors were open and there was no doorman. Maybe a party was on its way out.

Figuring to wait for one, she stepped back down a few steps to admire the place. She had always liked it. It was giant and bright and very pillared and had always given her the impression it was carved out of a massive block of chalk. It was one of Draneth's biggest buildings, and it was where her family had used to live, a long, long time ago – long before she was born, in fact. Although of course nowadays it was entirely dwarfed by the shadow of their new home, the Keep.

She waited only a short while before deciding it was becoming the unpleasant kind of cold. She went inside. All the inside doors were closed and there were no servants. She hesitated. She never normally had to open doors. Maybe that was one of the things that had driven Meryn so angry: the fear that her sister would become hopelessly helpless and forget even how to open a door.

Aldrua grinned and went down the main hallway, which was all tapestries and rugs and warm wooden panels, until she arrived at the audience chamber.

She opened the door gingerly.

This was where all the servants were. They were arguing with each other and it took a while for them to notice her arrival.

"Your Majesty! I-we-what are you-please, Your Majesty, you should talk to him! I-we fear he will do something rash!"

"Who? What is it?"

"Lord Rett, Your Majesty!"

Rett was ranting in his study. His face was very red. Yenna was gone, it turned out. She had taken nothing with her, nor even said goodbye. Rett couldn't understand why she'd left. He couldn't understand what he possibly could have done to make her leave. He speculated she might be being blackmailed, or was hurt – or worse. He didn't know what to do.

His wife had been a little quieter than usual recently, he confessed to Aldrua, his eyes wild and sweat dripping down his forehead, but that didn't mean a thing. She had always told him everything, and that hadn't changed, would never change. She had always told him everything whether he wanted to hear it or not. So what if she had been a little ill, as well. That, also, had nothing to do with it – he insisted. Why would that make a difference? They were just headaches. Just headaches!

Aldrua felt sick to her stomach.

What had poor Yenna thought was happening? She must have thought this secret dangerous. A child swapped in secret for a royal baby who had died, like it had suddenly come back to life? And no way to tell of it, instead only a crippling pain to the head? What had Yenna done? Had Rilenheim spoken to her? Is that why she had run away? Did she think she had no one to turn to?

And that was what had happened to the first of the three midwives.

* * *

The second of the three was dead. No surviving relatives. All gone in the same house fire. The servant Aldrua sent to fetch her said there was nothing left but ash.

Coincidence?

When Rilenheim asked her what she was doing with her time lately, she threw up over his boots.

* * *

The third of the three was of no fixed abode, but Pena knew where to find her. They had used to be friends, though long since separated by differing vocations.

Aldrua didn't know what to believe or who to trust. She made Pena promise to talk to no one about where the midwife could be found. She knew she shouldn't be doing this. She should trust – or at least obey – Rilenheim. Someone who was cursed with an inability to talk about something might well panic and run away, and houses could so easily catch fire. So maybe these things were unfortunate but innocent. Aldrua could leave this thread all alone and go back to the Keep and not say a word more. Maybe everything would all work out if she just left it all alone. Maybe Pena's friend was perfectly safe.

Maybe she would find out the truth soon enough.

She had never before been to this part of the city, only through it; and it was an entirely different experience on foot. Previously she'd been seated comfortably inside a coach escorted by soldiers in dress uniforms. There had been trumpeters and flag-carriers and all the other paraphernalia of a royal procession, which, she could see now, also included the exclusion of anyone who didn't look the part.

These people didn't look like they'd fit into any politely clapping crowd. They scurried, or loitered, or stood staring with arms folded. The closest they would ever get to a coach would be to rob it. But she was being uncharitable.

On the ground *everything* was different. The smell, for one thing. It smelt of dead dog, which turned out to be because there was a dead dog. It was washed up against a drain, sodden, its hind legs tiding up and down over and over like it was trying to run – or maybe do something else.

She couldn't stop staring at it.

"Someone should do something about that," she muttered to Pena, hoping that "someone" would be understood as "you".

"You'll... get used to it, Your Majesty," the chambermaid replied. "I'm sorry."

"We're just going to leave it?"

Pena looked at her as if she'd gone mad.

"How far?" Aldrua couldn't keep still. She fidgeted with her cowl. They both wore one, along with wide mantles, and Aldrua had in addition a veil and burlet to be absolutely sure no one would recognise her. Aldrua didn't like the result; she couldn't easily turn her head to see behind her. And this was unnerving not just because this place was plain *horrible*, with every other person looking like they might try to rob them, but because at any moment she expected Rilenheim's giant, ancient hand to clamp down on her shoulder.

"Not far, Your Majesty. Just past the Alleys."

"*The* Alleys? I've heard about them..."

"They're safe during the day."

They didn't look safe. Aldrua held her nose and refused to budge when she saw the first of them.

"Do we have to go this way?" she asked.

"If you definitely don't want to be seen, Your Majesty."

Having previously heard the Alleys described didn't do justice to actually seeing them.

They used to be waterways, Aldrua knew, carved out of the hard clay upon which Draneth was built. They were the result of harnessing a river, splitting and directing it to supply the original town. The town had grown up into a cramped city, and so the water had been architected underground, where it ran still, honeycombing under their feet. Leaving this forsaken maze of refuge behind.

In practise, in front of her was a half-tunnel in the ground, which was wide and shallow enough for her to be able to run up the side and climb out the top. Interesting, she considered, that this was the first thing she thought of. It was filled ankle-deep with thick, brown, what-she-hoped-was-mainly-water, in which things floated, and from which bubbled strange smells that made her think of peaty marshes.

She had heard that when it rained hard the Alleys became waterways again, and she wished very hard that it would do so now.

"We really, really have to go this way?"

"Yes, Your Majesty, if you really, really want to see Sahine in secret."

"I do," Aldrua said. "I can't say why, Pena, I'm sorry. I'm *unable* to say. Come on then, let's get this over with."

She clenched her hands into fists to stop them from shaking. What if her worst suspicions were true? She could imagine the look on Rayant's face when she told him what had happened to everyone who was there that night. *Then* he would see who it was he should trust. He would be sorry. And it didn't matter what Rilenheim would say. She *knew* what he would say. He was smooth. He would claim that the secret of the baby's identity was so important that the fewer people that knew about it the better. But he would lose Rayant's trust.

Meryn would be safe.

They would together have her fetched back to them.

"Come on," she muttered to Pena, and eased into the filth.

They walked down half-tunnel streets which seemed lined with grey scarecrows; people unkempt, underfed. *Under* in general. Many of them tended frail-looking stalls filled with merchandise, all of which looked equally careworn. These stalls were temporary, whisked to safety when cleansing waves swept by or into hiding when questioning authorities passed, to be unveiled again only to those who weren't overly concerned with either the quality or the legality of the goods for sale. Aldrua stayed close to Pena. She couldn't help but stare, which was misinterpreted.

"Ladies? You want adjustments? I can make better fits-" A tailor frowned at their cloaks, which were all Pena's, but still had too few holes to blend in.

"Just had 'em done mate," Pena said, not slowing, not meeting his gaze.

They hurried on, Pena leading. The sodden tail of her cloak left a little wake of yellow surf as it was dragged through the muck. Aldrua's own begun to feel heavy. It was difficult to walk on the curved surface. Aldrua noted how the stalls and the occasional rickety chair to each side were kept in place by ropes tied to the tunnel's edge, and were cut shorter on one side to stay level. She wondered how the tunnels had been made. They didn't have the usual rough and uneven manner of a riverbed.

She was soon lost. The Alleys meandered maze-like through a third of the city and only those who were familiar with them could shortcut from place to place with ease, and as the only people who became familiar were those who tolerated the filth there was a high barrier to entry. Which didn't include, to Aldrua's mind, what she would consider decent people. She wondered how Pena knew how to navigate them.

Funny, but she felt like a little girl following her mother, losing and gaining distance to Pena amidst pauses to observe some unusual new sight. There were some very busy streets. Aldrua didn't know what many of the things being sold were for. Many of those she *did* actually recognise were in very poor condition. She couldn't understand why anyone would want to buy them at all.

When a handcart was wheeled past, piled high with clothes, Aldrua noted how heavy it looked and how the wheels screamed and creaked. There was something... the clothes were moving up and down... like they were *breathing*.

"Excuse me," she asked of the woman pushing it. "Is there someone-" The woman pushed past, acknowledging Aldrua only by turning her shoulder to her. "What is that? I- Pena, did you see that?"

"Hush, Your Majesty!"

But now she'd attracted attention.

"Meat? Fresh off the bone!" A butcher – a profession she recognised at least – waved meat on a stick. The meat was furry.

Aldrua recoiled but couldn't look away. Pena had to pull her away from the butcher's scowl.

"You have not to be starin', Your Majesty!" Pena said into her ear.

They hurried past an old woman who watched them from beneath a broad hat, her face concealed except for cracked teeth, the hat turning to watch them go.

"You're speaking differently," Aldrua said. "Is this how you normally talk?"

"Normally I'm in the Keep, Your Majesty."

"How far now?"

"Still not far. Pull your cowl down more."

"You didn't say 'Your Majesty'."

"I'm sorry, I didn't mean-"

"I don't mind, Pena. Thank you for doing this." And she was, she realized. Even though the girl had to do everything the queen asked of her without question. This felt different though. This was Aldrua's own business, and not entirely the kingdom's.

"Yes, Your Majesty."

"Where did you used to live?"

"It ain't – isn't – there any more. It was bought and torn down. Come on, we'll go this way, harder for anyone to follow."

"Follow? Rilenheim doesn't know we're here. He can't be

everywhere at once."

Pena nodded.

* * *

But he did. He knew. He knew a lot of things. He knew who Aldrua trusted. He knew where Pena's family lived. He knew how humans worked and how to get what he wanted.

They *were* being followed. They had been followed all the way from the Keep. Pena had no idea why Aldrua wanted to see Sahine, but apparently Rilenheim knew. Apparently he had been prepared for it.

Pena was glad of her cowl. She had been Aldrua's chambermaid for a long time and didn't want to see her die.

Pena had tried to shake off their pursuer. She had taken a difficult route, taking many turns and shortcuts, circling around adjacent cul-de-sacs in figures of eight, and then having them climb out of a half-tunnel and jog down into another nearby. But all to no avail. She hadn't even managed to get a good look at him. He was just a miscellaneous figure in grey. If she hadn't been given an idea as to what was to happen by Rilenheim she wouldn't have been looking out for anything suspicious and would never have known. She'd have put it all down to her imagination.

Aldrua clearly had no idea what was going on.

So now Pena had to do exactly what Rilenheim had told her to do, or else he would know.

She had to lead Aldrua into a trap.

* * *

They arrived at the tenement Rilenheim had designated. It was in a normal part of the city, and looked like any other along the long street. Pena's heart was pounding. The outer door wasn't locked, just as Rilenheim had told her it wouldn't be. She opened it to a dark, steep stairway which led straight upstairs. One of the steps was split. Slivers of wood jutted out where someone's foot had gone through. There were no signs of a repair.

"This is where Sahine lives?" Aldrua asked her, with a raised eyebrow. "It doesn't look like *anyone* lives here."

Pena swallowed before answering.

"Lots of places like this," she murmured. "Listen, you can hear neighbours." Barely audible voices gave the stairway an uneasy thrum. She stared up it. "This is definitely the place."

Aldrua nodded.

"I'll wait here," Pena said, exactly as Rilenheim had told her to.

"No," Aldrua said. "You don't want to be seen."

"It won't be a problem. I'll wait across the street." Rilenheim hadn't furnished her with a good excuse. He'd just told her to say she had fallen out with Sahine, which suddenly seemed like the kind of excuse only a Geomancer who *didn't* truly understand people would come up with. He'd warned her to be convincing or she – and others – would be very, very sorry.

"I can be a lookout. In case anyone comes." She was muttering, she noticed.

Aldrua nodded again. She bit her lip, before starting up the stairs. The stairs screamed as she carefully trod around the split step.

Pena found herself moving. Without thinking, she seized the queen's forearm.

"Wait! Don't go up!"

"Pena? What is it?" Aldrua looked up the stairway, following Pena's gaze, then back at her.

"We need to go!" Pena whispered. "Please! This isn't safe."

"What's... what's up there?"

"Please, Your Majesty!"

"You're hurting my arm!"

Pena dragged Aldrua back outside. The queen seemed too surprised to resist. Pena thought she saw something move behind the upper windows of the tenement, first at one side, then the other.

There were other people on the street. Whatever Rilenheim wanted to do here, Pena sincerely hoped he wanted it kept secret.

"You're scaring me, Pena!"

"We have to go!" she told the queen. "I'm so sorry! But we have to go!"

But Aldrua was being stubborn. They struggled for a moment in the street.

Then something hit Pena on the shoulder and she fell. She cried out. Someone *was* behind the window. But Pena wasn't hurt – just startled. She picked up fragments of what had hit her. A cup?

One of the windows creaked open.

"Get up here you idiots!" Sahine called.

* * *

The first floor living room was a mess of broken furniture, the larger parts of which had been swept haphazardly into a pile. It looked like a fight had broken out recently, and then the victor had lost interest in cleaning up.

There was also a woman gagged and bound to the only chair still intact. She looked suspiciously like Sahine did. Same narrow, pallid face, same curled brown hair. Her eyes were wide.

"Sahine?" Pena swallowed. "I... don't understand."

"Neither do I. What the hell are *you* doing here? It's been a long time since I've seen you."

"I-"

"And who is this?" she said, about Aldrua. Without waiting for an answer, she was at the edge of a window, peering out unseen. "Is it just the two of you?"

"Yes," Pena said, quietly.

"What are you doing? I was expecting..." But Sahine trailed off. Aldrua had removed her cowl.

The queen's face was white. "Are you sure?" Aldrua said to Pena. "This is Sahine?"

"Yes, I-" Pena stared at the floor.

"Then who is *she*?" Aldrua pointed at the woman in the chair.

"They look so alike."

"Your Majesty!" Sahine was kneeling. Aldrua waved her back up impatiently.

"Answer the question, one of you!"

"She was to be me, Your Majesty," Sahine said.

"You better explain, Sah," said Pena. Her face felt very red. She had no idea how Aldrua would respond to her own part in this.

"Your Majesty," Sahine said, rubbing her brow with a hand holding a small knife. She noticed it and put it down on a table. "I already got the truth out of her. She was to be me according to... She was to pretend everything was fine if anyone asked. But I never expected that someone to be you!"

"She looks so like you..."

"I don't think so. Maybe. Maybe Rilenheim has that kind of power. I don't know. And you and I only met that once, and it was dark."

"Rilenheim? You're talking about Rilenheim the Geomancer? How do you know all this?"

"You were to think she was me," Sahine said, "and she was to tell you that she was perfectly fine and you were to leave here knowing that he had done nothing to hurt anyone. He knows you've been poking around, and decided to put an end to it."

"You're sure?"

"Rilenheim came looking for me," Sahine explained. "But I've been an orphan all my life and on these streets no one's going to give me up for some creepy lurch. When we found this..." she kicked the chair, "traitor willing to play his game, we reckoned we could try and find out what he was about. But I never figured you'd come yourself, Your Majesty."

"I wanted to talk to you, Sahine."

"I know." Sahine wrinkled her face up into a pained expression. "But I can't talk about it."

"You can't?"

"She is our queen, Sah," Pena muttered. "You'd better-"

"How did you even know to come here?" Sahine interrupted.

"This isn't where you live?" Aldrua asked.

"No. People there would know *she* wasn't me."

"I came with... Pena, how did you hear about this place?"

Pena looked up from the floor just long enough for them to see what was in her eyes.

"He said he would hurt my family," she croaked, barely audibly. "I am so sorry."

The room was very still for a moment.

Sahine stepped toward her, but Aldrua put up a hand.

"No. Not now. She tried to warn me. I... Sahine, I do need to talk to you-"

"No, I'm sorry, Your Majesty. I just *can't*. He made sure-" and Sahine. She put one hand to her head and groaned. "I think, maybe, you might understand, Your Majesty."

"I don't-" Pena begun, but Sahine interrupted.

"But I can show you something. *Your* something. Something that may be important. We'll go out the back way."

"What about *her*?" Aldrua indicated the woman in the chair.

"Leave her to me and my friends. We'll make sure she cooperates. Best if Rilenheim thinks his plan has succeeded."

Aldrua nodded slowly. "Then I guess you need to show me. And Pena?" Aldrua said nothing more until Pena forced herself to look up at her. "I thought *you* were *my* friend."

* * *

They didn't have far to go.

The graveyard was little more than a converted back street. It had been fenced off and gated with black iron. Nettles entwined the fence, but had been cut away from the gate, which itself looked like it had come straight from someone's garden. Sahine opened it for them then latched it closed, after first ensuring there was nobody else around.

There were three rows of graves, with paving slabs leading rough paths through them. The graves themselves seemed to be made of smaller, broken paving slabs. Mossy dirt leaked out of every gap. The graves were very small; too small for adults – or even children. It was dark and Aldrua had difficultly reading the headstones as they passed. The buildings down each side were high and unbroken and cut out the light.

Sahine knelt where loose soil indicated a freshly laid grave. The headstone was blank. She started to pull apart the broken slabs. It took a moment for Aldrua to realise what was happening.

"What are you doing?" Aldrua started. "You *can't* do that-" She was stopped by Sahine's expression.

But there was no coffin. There was just a wooden box. Sahine put it down in front of Aldrua.

"I'm sorry," she whispered, "but you have to see."

"What's in there?"

The box was a large tinderbox. It still had the graven image of a flame on its lid.

"Remains," Sahine said.

"You are *sick*," Aldrua managed.

She looked to Pena for assistance, out of habit, but the servant girl was standing further back, in the exact centre of one path, one foot on top of the other, as if to get as far away as possible from everything around her.

"I don't know what I can say," Sahine went on, her voice barely audible. "I don't think it went according to his plan. I was told what to do with it. But I ran. I didn't know what else to do. And when he came looking, I did what I had to. I know people. I found out what he planned. I warned Yenna. Then I waited back there to see who would come. And I think you need to know this. This is not normal. You must take care, Your Majesty. Aldrua... please listen to me."

"Open it."

Sahine opened the box.

Aldrua's baby boy had become a thick, sickly, black liquid, like oil.

Chapter 11

Rilenheim stood under the trees by the Wide Road at the entrance to Draneth and watched the army grow. Soldiers arrived in all formations. King Rayant had sent the call to arms to all corners of Draldorn. Entire battalions marched in from outlying fiefdoms, led by minor nobles on tired steeds. Smaller columns marched back from exercises, war-dogs yapping and straining at the end of leashes. Ragged mercenary troops sloped in. Others turned up individually, old hands coming out of retirement or young men seeking their fortune.

The fields around Draneth had turned into a makeshift town. Grass had churned into mud. Tents had been pitched wherever they didn't sink, around which fires had sprung up, contained in cairns of stone. Men were everywhere.

Little pockets of commerce had come into being. The opportunistic roamed among the soldiers selling hot pies. Some stood on the back of wagons full of mismatched armour and weapons and offered them to the highest bidder. Brown-robed men offered prayer and blessings for those seeking comfort. A few women moved among the camps, offering a different path to enlightenment.

Rilenheim watched with a detailed eye. Humans doing what they did. His people had never had need of armies. The Geomancers of Ilris would have simply combined their magics and imposed their desired solution. They had been so much stronger as a group, before Herendak had decided they should be greater still.

Rilenheim scratched at his wrist. The child's powers were growing. Already they extended beyond the gates of Draneth. He could feel the strength Herendak had dumped into her. How long before Herendak realised where she was hidden? How long before Meryn? Even that fool Aldrua might eventually realise her own part in all this.

Meanwhile, the army grew far too slowly. Rilenheim had only so much time to expend.

He watched a figure smothered in coats come out from under the city's great arches, head bowed and concealed under a hood. The figure paused at the edge of the field, facing the chaos, watching two men fencing with wooden swords. Another runaway, Rilenheim decided, defying his parents' wishes to go fight and so make something of himself, even if that something was a mangled corpse.

Rilenheim shook his head. This should all have been done years ago. He should have destroyed the Wrilsch before Herendak had managed to organise them. But who could have predicted Herendak would have found a way – that it would even be possible? And destroying them would be painful. There would be those he still recognised.

But now was now, and he couldn't alter the path that had led here. Thinking back, these circumstances almost seemed inevitable, the road back to those days as implacable and straight-line as an arrow; back, back, back to Ilris and the shattered sky, that time of change, from here, now, where his old friend had struck – and Rilenheim had to counter where he could.

If Herendak sought conflict, Rilenheim would oblige by striking first.

Yet this was all wrong. Rilenheim had learnt to listen to his gut when it spoke to him, and it was speaking now, insistently. The key here, it whispered, did not lie in strength of arms. This fate would not be decided on the battlefield. This fate was greater than both of them.

But he could not just stand back and let Herendak diminish them.

Rilenheim watched as the bundled up figure took a first tentative step into thick mud. The Geomancer frowned, though wasn't sure why.

No matter. Herendak did not understand. His lack of understanding was what had caused the first Rift. So much had been learned since then. Rilenheim allowed himself the slightest of dour grins. He had his own plans now.

The figure hurried off into the camp.

Wait. His – no – *her* movements were strangely familiar...

* * *

Aldrua slipped through the camp. It was sweltering under her disguise, and the smell of smoky flames and half-cooked meat and unwashed soldiers was stifling. Mud got everywhere. She kept stopping to try and wipe it off, kicking clumps off her shoes. She would ask Pena to fill a tub as soon as she got back. Maybe she should go back now. This was dangerous, stupid and both Rayant and Rilenheim had forbidden it.

Some parts of the camp were calm and disciplined. Fires were well-tended and smokeless. Tents were arranged in lines. Everything was regimented and the men were cordial. Other areas were more disordered. Play fights ended in lost eyes. Drinks were quaffed rather than drunk. Rayant's drinking ban among the standing army did not extend this far. Men gambled for trinkets with dice, then took back lost pride with rusty blades. Even laughter here was boisterous and hard-edged.

Aldrua tried not to look too hard at anyone she passed. She turned her head from the sounds of flesh on flesh, as men punched and wrestled in the mud, others egging them on, cries and screams. There were other sounds of flesh on flesh as well, from tents, accompanied by other screams of an altogether different nature.

Aldrua hastened through it all, a single, slight figure, despite the coats. She felt calculating eyes on her. She tried to walk differently, step with her legs wider. She tried to puff out her chest. But she felt too obviously a woman and welcome in a way that she didn't find welcome. Her throat was too dry and her breathing too fast.

Rayant had forbidden her not just from leaving the city, but even from the Keep – at Rilenheim's request, she was sure – so if she were caught here... She swallowed. Maybe Rilenheim would hesitate to treat her like he'd treated her midwives, but she really didn't want to end up in any dungeon. Rayant would do with her whatever Rilenheim commanded, queen or no queen. In the same way, she was suddenly sure, Meryn's banishment was also Rilenheim's doing. It must have been. What exactly was this bargain her husband had struck with the Geomancer? How could Rayant possibly trust the old man? Rilenheim was needed, of course he was, to fight the Wrilsch. But his motives were so unclear, and the fact that Rayant listened to him, obeyed him, and needed him more than he needed her – well, that hurt.

Maybe a certain amount of it was just payback. A part of him must hate her. She had hurt him first, after all. When he'd found out about Kendan, when she'd had to go to him for help, when she'd told him she was pregnant and it wasn't his, the worse thing, the absolute worst thing, was his calmness. He had listened to her confession and decided exactly what they should do, and then they had done it. He hadn't screamed at her, or cried, or even raised his voice. She had become someone else to him that day, someone alien and untrusted.

Maybe he didn't even hate her, maybe she was just nothing to him, and that would be worst of all.

"You can't come this way, ma'am."

She hadn't been paying attention to where she was going. Tree trunks were laid out in rows in front of her, being hacked into sharp points by soldiers with axes. It didn't make sense until Aldrua stumbled over gears and other tiny pieces of metal being fitted together.

"What are you doing?" A soldier seized her arm.

With one twist of his hand, he pulled down her hood.

Her heart seized up. He took a long look at her face. She was doomed. He would make a fuss, the whole camp would find out the queen had come among them. Rilenheim would find out and how could she possibly explain what she was doing there? When she should have been holed up safe in the Keep, where she could be protected – and where she could in no way interfere with his scheming.

This was all the excuse he would need to keep her locked up somewhere even safer.

But – the soldier didn't recognise her! Relief made her giddy. Though it only took a moment for that relief to fade into panic, because, well... he really didn't recognise her.

He was grinning.

She pushed him back and hurried away. His barely audible goodbye comments made her neck flush; she wasted no time hiding again in her hood. Except this time she kept one hand to it, holding it up.

In a quiet corner of the camp she finally found what she was looking for.

The White Ravens had found themselves a prime spot shaded by a giant oak. Two vast tents hulked under its branches, twigs scraping at them in the faint breeze. Weather stains gave them an old tea-towel look.

Three men, all with the same close-cropped hair, sat around a map laid out on a timbered stump and held down with a dagger. They were arguing.

Lying with his back against the oak's trunk a more ragged man smoked a pipe, blowing grey rings in her direction. He took the pipe out of his mouth and nodded to her.

"You're doing it wrong," he said. When she didn't reply, he explained, "The cloak. Covering up."

The others looked up from their map.

"Wrong part of camp, Missy," she was told. "Be off with you."

The pipe-smoker shifted to a more upright position. "Ignore my companions," he said. "They can be unsociable. I am called Drak." He grinned a cracked grin. "If you really want to help us poor warriors out, you could go fetch me some more of *this*." His hand went to a length of papyrus folded around black powder.

"I need to speak to you," Aldrua babbled. Then she said it again, because her words were barely legible even to her. She looked around. No one was near, but she still couldn't risk anyone recognising her. "In the tent."

He grinned, but half-heartedly. "Not taking no for an answer, eh?"

She didn't say anything. Too busy swallowing. Instead, she ducked into the nearest tent. It was surprisingly well-furnished, for a tent. There was a bright gold-weaved rug, three bedrolls, and a number of saddlebags forming a little store topped with dark red apples. It was big enough to stand straight, but Aldrua still hunched.

When Drak ducked in after her, she pointed to the raven insignia on his tunic.

"You are the White Ravens?"

"Settling only for the best, eh?"

"I want to hire you."

He laughed. The hearty, easy laugh of a man who took his mirth where he could.

"You really, really don't understand how this works, girl!"

Aldrua rushed on, "You've worked for King Rayant, many times. In secret. You've kept your silence. You've been paid well to keep your silence."

"Yes. That's us." He cocked his head, while his hand went to the hilt of his sword. "But you can't know that, you see. Because, if you do, than we haven't done our job right." He jiggled the sword in its scabbard.

Taking a deep breath, Aldrua pulled down her hood. Drak's mouth clamped shut. He stared at her in a most discomforting way.

"Do you recognise me?" she said. This time, it was essential that he did. He raised his eyebrows. She went on, "I've seen *you* before. I saw you go into my husband's study one night."

"I'm going to get the others-"

"No!" She went to reach for his arm, but stopped. She didn't want to touch him. "No fuss. No one can know I'm here."

"Why *are* you here, your queenliness?"

"My sister is missing."

"Exiled, you mean. I know. You know I know."

"*Missing.* I'm here because the White Ravens are the best trackers Draldorn has. And you keep secrets."

He paced, in the limited fashion allowed by the tent. She noticed the ash in his fingernails as he spun his pipe around them.

"So, am I to understand that the king is to know nothing of this?" Aldrua nodded.

"How very interesting," he said. "You know our fee? Enough gold for at least a month's carousing is customary."

"I can pay."

"Yes. Yes, of course you can. So, assuming this is something we'd be interested in, where do you think we should start looking for this missing sister of yours?"

"I don't know."

"And when we find her?"

"Bring her to me."

"I see." Drak took an absent pull on his pipe, before realising it was unlit. "This is all most strange. I don't wish to offend, your Majesterialness, but you've always been considered, well, a bit of a wet flannel. Please don't be insulted. Tell me, what is it Rayant intends to do should his men find her first?"

"I... I don't know."

"You realise he has thousands searching for her? Yes, of course you do. And we, of course, would be in competition."

"Please. Will you help me?"

"Do you smoke?" He offered his pipe.

"No."

He rubbed his hands on his trousers. "Do queens shake on the conclusion of business? Or should I kiss your ring, or something?"

"You'll do it?"

He shrugged. "We've always been more the hunting and finding kind of group than the line up and rush the enemy sort. There's more living involved in the former. I can speak for the others. We'll do it."

Aldrua smiled at him before she could stop herself.

"There will be," he went on, eyeing her carefully and now chewing the pipe, "some additional expenses, however. We do what we're asked to. We get the job done. We have special talents no other group can lay claim to. Sometimes all this entails extra costs and additional rewards which we ask our employers to cover."

"Yes." Aldrua's hands fluttered. "That's fine."

"You haven't asked what extra rewards." Drak licked his lips and continued staring at her until she looked at her feet.

"I-"

"Do you want your sister back or not? If we succeed, you'll do what I ask. We deal harshly with people who go back on their word."

"I... I understand."

Drak pushed his shoulders back, stretched his arms.

"You're different," he suddenly declared. "From the other royals and nobles, I mean."

"I'm sorry to hear that."

He grinned around the pipe.

"No. I like you. You've got..." he searched for a suitable word. "Balls."

"Is that how you talk to the other royals?"

"Like I said, you're different."

"Please find Meryn? She could be in trouble."

"If she can be found, we'll find her."

"How will you let me know when you do?"

"Discreetly."

* * *

Aldrua almost broke into a run on her way back to the Keep. She'd done it. She'd gone against both Rayant's and Rilenheim's decrees and she hadn't folded.

If Rilenheim ever found out, he would probably kill her.

She felt eyes on the back of her neck as she stepped back under the arches. She peered around, but saw nothing amiss. She hurried away, wanting to get back to the two girls as soon as possible.

* * *

Aldrua slept restlessly. She woke in a tangle of sheets. She'd been running, in her nightmare, from something that stalked, something big and dark and mocking. But she couldn't get away from it, not ever, because it hulked in the back of her own mind.

She sat up. Blue moonlight infused the chamber with an otherworldly glow. Not yet morning.

"Mummy?" said Ielenia, lying on the other side of the bed, little hands clutching the tops of the sheets. "Can't you sleep, Mummy?" She'd come in during the night because *she* couldn't sleep.

"It's al'right, Ili, try and rest." Aldrua leaned over and smoothed her hand over Ielenia's brow. She offered her daughter a big smile.

"But you're all fighty," Ielenia said. She pulled the blankets up, crossly.

"Sorry."

Elhrinna, Aldrua noted, was still fast asleep in her cot alongside the bed, a beatific expression on her ever serene face. The steward had not yet replaced the nurses who'd normally be looking after both children. Aldrua wondered if Rilenheim was involved in that somehow. He might want to minimise the number of people who were in contact with Elhrinna.

He certainly hadn't hesitated as far as the midwives were concerned.

"I can't help feeling that..." Aldrua said, to no one in particular, "I may have put people in danger today."

Ielenia nodded, in a most adult-like fashion. Aldrua smiled, a smaller yet more genuine one than before. She kissed her daughter lightly on one cheek then lay back down, settling as best she could. She reached out and touched the cot, offered it a silent goodnight.

Inside, Elhrinna's eyes moved under her lids as she dreamed.

And, hidden in the dark cracks of the ceiling, Rilenheim's shadow watched the dream.

* * *

The White Ravens slipped away from the rest of the army that night.

They packed up with practised efficiency. They folded the tents and their furnishings into the saddlebags of obedient warhorses. Nine horses and nine riders picked their way through the town-sized camp, stepping over packs of provisions and between rows of soldiers sleeping in bedrolls. The horses snorted around piles of refuse, mounds of chicken and boar carcasses, scattering flies.

Drak led them on a wide detour of the large, hissing fires that burnt day and night. Around these music played, mostly drums, fuelling shadowy movements which flickered wild shadows across the night.

They hit the road one by one and broke into a canter. Drak took the lead, back straight, waist loose, deftly absorbing the impact of hooves on compacted mud. Two swords crossed in a baldric on his back. Another was contained in a scabbard at his belt. Clasped to the saddle by his side, an enormous crossbow faced the sky.

Although Drak took the lead, the Ravens had no real leader. They prided themselves on their independence, each man the full equivalent of any normal mercenary group in its entirety. Someone to command was unnecessary: they were the best, they knew it, and fully respected each other as equals – or, in truth, very slight inferiors.

Yet they picked up a tail almost immediately, and not one among them noticed. Riding in the woods parallel to the road, kicking through smaller bushes, leaping fallen branches, this tail quickly overtook them, passing twig-and-leaf flecked silhouettes of man and rider until it was clear to gallop ahead.

When the Ravens arrived at the first major crossroads from Draneth City, Drak called a surprised halt. A slight figure on a massive horse stood there in the road. It trotted slowly toward them, until a slant of moonlight revealed the rider.

"Aldrua?" Drak tapped his horse's sides, clopped closer, pulled the reins back hard as the horse suddenly snorted and fought him with a lurch of its head.

"Good evening," said the queen. She sat with a slight hunch, face tilted down, her horse utterly still. "I am sorry to startle. I know you did not expect me. I need to be clear about what it is I want you to do."

"Worried about the price?"

"No, no. I just need to understand that you understand..."

Pierton, one of the oldest members of the Ravens, dismounted and stepped up beside Drak, leading his horse forward with a hand on its neck.

"What's going on, Drak? Contract problems? It's very clear, Lady. We go fetch your sister, we bring her back. Clear as blood."

Drak watched Aldrua carefully. Her eyes flicked to his, held his gaze... for just a moment. Then she dropped them. Batted her eyelids demurely. Drak frowned.

"Good, we understood each other," she said. "But we don't under*stand* each other. I've spoken to Rayant and got it very wrong. My sister... my sister is no longer my sister." She put her hand over her eyes. And she started to sob.

"Your Majesteryness," Drak began, but she held up her hand to stop him.

"I'm sorry to be so emotional. Rayant told me to give you this." She held out her other hand, a piece of parchment folded in her grip.

Drak made to spur forward, but his horse resisted, clopping in a half-circle, before Drak reined him in with a firm, "Whoa!"

Pierton stepped up and snatched the parchment. He unfolded it and stroked his moustache.

"Attention White Ravens," he read. "I the king... blah, blah, blah, further orders, unfortunate yet necessary. Not wise to tell the – oh." Pierton passed the parchment up to Drak. "Take a look *here* and *here.*"

Drak read the relevant sections: "Find the princess and escort her to the plains of Haylen; there to await further instructions," and, "Do not tell the queen."

It was blunt. Drak was still frowning. He flashed another look at the queen.

"You remember our terms of payment?" he said. She nodded, her dark hair glistening in the moonlight.

He spurred forward, the firm kick and strong grip of his thighs forcing his mount alongside Aldrua.

"You recall what I said?" he said. "I know what you think I meant." He looked at her closely, then reached out a hand, hesitated. She remained still. He touched his fingers lightly to her left breast. Her eyes went down again. He squeezed. She closed her eyes.

But she did nothing else.

"Watch out!" he cried, and, in the same breath, drew the dagger from his boot sheath.

There was a flash of white and he was bucked over backwards. He crashed to the ground. His horse screamed and reared. The rest of the Ravens reacted instantly. Pierton's sword rung out. But a lance of red heat disintegrated his arm. A thunderous clap echoed after it.

Drak's horse bolted and where Aldrua had been, Drak saw Rilenheim, disguise dropped, a snarl scarring his lips. The Geomancer lanced another bolt among the Ravens. Drak leapt to his feet, had his sword out, and lunged. Another thunderous lance; Drak was on his back. He choked on the bacon smell of burning flesh, sick rising in his stomach. He was sizzling. There was a hole in his forearm.

Savage cries. Arrows notched and fired. Rilenheim fell sideways off his horse, but, like a dancer, rolled up to his feet in one smooth movement. Two more booms and a horse and rider fell. The horse bellowed and rolled, screeching like a dying child, and brought down another. Trees roared into sudden light, crackling with flames.

Felton, coming out of nowhere, was behind the Geomancer, long dagger sliding into Rilenheim's stomach from the side. A gasp from Rilenheim, then the Geomancer punched his hand into Felton's chest and ripped out a lung. It wheezed for an instant in his hand, before he discarded it to a bush.

Rilenheim raised both his arms.

"Retreat, flee, regroup!" Drak screamed. Stumbling over his feet, he half-leapt, half-fell, into the undergrowth. The others scattered. A final arrow shot towards Rilenheim, but he flicked a wrist at it and whooshed it into flame in mid-flight. It dribbled apart into ashes and smoke before it reached him.

Rilenheim swung himself back on to his still motionless horse, and leapt into the undergrowth in pursuit.

* * *

Aldrua woke a second time. A scrabbling noise. She turned over. Ielenia's little face by her side, scrunched up in that wonderful way she had, as if she was concentrating in her sleep. Elhrinna, in her cot, also still slept, though *her* expression remained one of beguiling serenity.

"Won't last, lucky girl," Aldrua whispered with the faintest of smiles. It was almost dawn. She could hear distant wagons crawling up the hill to market. She pulled her legs over the side of the massive, queen-sized bed – far too big, to Aldrua's mind, for any actual queen.

That scrabbling again. Mice? Or – Aldrua clutched her nightdress closer around her neck – rats. She got out of bed. The Keep was cold, always cold at night, even with the many well-tended hearths warming the stone. But she needed the garderobe.

Wait.

The scrabbling... from the door?

The lock! It clicked open and a bulky figure pushed inside. A hand shot out and grabbed her round the face, pressing into her mouth.

"Quiet!" a voice growled. "I've had to take out three guards to get here, don't force me to hurt any more!"

She screamed, but silently, around his hand. The girls, she had to protect the girls! She had to fight, but felt suddenly weightless. Her arms felt like they'd come loose. She tried to batter at the man, but he pushed and lifted her back across the room. A flash of early morning sunlight caught his face.

"Drak?" she tried to say, but it came out, "Krk!".

"I said quiet!" he said. "I haven't got long! Just keep quiet, all right?"

And he let go of her. She stumbled back against the wardrobe.

"Your Majesteri, ah, hell with it – Aldrua! You've been less than fair with me this night!"

He was hurt, she saw then. His arm was bandaged with the same tunic he was wearing. It was splattered with mud, and blood. His hair was missing along one side, all torn and wispy, like it had been burnt away. He face was red and blackened on the same side. His earlier casual manner was altogether absent; his eyes were hard and dark.

"There is so much more to your story," he went on. "Oh, there normally is, when the Ravens are called. And normally, hell, we don't care. But when a Geomancer is involved..."

"A... what happened?"

"Rilenheim happened."

"Ril- he... did that?"

"My people are scattered. Some," he bared his teeth, rang his tongue along their edge, "are dead. Or maimed. The White Ravens are not easily slain, but the Geomancer..."

"I'm sorry! I didn't know he'd... I didn't realise he was so serious as to..."

But she had, she realised then. There was only so long she could pretend everything was normal, that everything was going to turn out all right. They needed Rilenheim. No one else could stop Herendak. And, right now, he also needed them. But *his* need would, someday soon, end – and she trembled in advance of that day.

"Tell me why," Drak was saying. "Tell me why your sister is so very important." When Aldrua didn't answer quickly enough he lurched closer, his shadow smothering her. "Tell me why, or I will share with you my pain..."

"I... I think Meryn will become a Wrilsch! Or she will dissolve! I don't know if... Rilenheim thinks if the immortal is removed from... but she isn't so... I don't know but I think she's in very immediate danger! I think she's important! I think Rilenheim is up to something and somehow she can stop him!"

"No. He's looking for her. He wanted her taken to Haylen.

You're babbling."

"Please don't hurt me! I'll do anything. I can help you, your arm-"

"Shut up!" Drak was watching the door, hand on the hilt of his sword, scabbard tilting as he put weight on it.

Aldrua bit her tongue; felt blood dribble down her chin.

"Please, I'm so sorry!" she rushed in an urgent whisper. "I didn't mean for you to get hurt!"

"What is Rilenheim up to?" he growled, when he deemed the coast clear.

"He spoke about Herendak restoring his people. I think... I think we're talking about the end of... everything. Humans, I mean." They stared at each other.

When he spoke, his voice was slow and controlled. "How sure are you?"

Aldrua waved her arms. "I'm not, not sure. I'm never sure of anything!" This was the first time she'd told anyone what she thought. This was perhaps the first time she even *realised* what she thought. That was the problem of having no one she trusted to talk to. How could she know her opinions unless she could share them with others? Poor missing Meryn would have listened. "I think, I really think, that I'm right," she said, in a small, almost petulant voice.

He drew himself up over her.

"Please, I'm sorry! You don't need to hurt me!"

"Don't be a fool." Drak strode across the room and paused in the doorway; he was big enough to almost block it entirely. "I am Drak of the White Ravens. We have a contract. When I find Meryn, I will find you. We do not fail."

And he was gone, footsteps clattering on stone and the cries of guards as they caught sight of their prey.

But they could never catch a Raven.

* * *

"Rayant," Aldrua said, later that morning, tugging on his sleeve. "Rayant, I need to talk to you." He brushed her off. She trailed him through the banquet hall. Minor nobles around long benches watched them pass, chicken legs paused half-way to their lips. Aldrua collided with a servant and a basket of loaves upturned onto the floor.

"Sorry, Your Maj-" Her expression stopped him.

She followed Rayant out into the bright sunlight of the training yard, which was filled with soldiers and their trainers. Her heart was pounding. Well, let them all watch, let them all think their queen had lost her mind; she didn't care. Rayant was fussing with his shirt, once again loose, as he strode. There was once a time she would have told him to tuck them in; though never any use.

They stormed across the yard, where drills were being drilled, weapons swung and fired; soldiers preparing for the war to come. The place was musky with sweat and dulled by the smell of hay. Aldrua recoiled on passing horrid scarecrows with woody limbs and ghastly yellow faces of hay-packed sacking. These were having the hay smacked out of them by men with quarterstaffs, or were being peppered with arrows.

Rayant turned and strode straight across a firing range to where the doorway to the barracks beckoned.

"Rayant!" she shouted.

The king finally stopped, turned with a swirl of his velvet cape. An arrow snapped and pinged away, narrowly missing his raised arms. The courtyard fell silent. Bows creaked as their strings were slackened. Final sword clangs rung themselves out.

"Aldrua, no! Go and whine to the servants. I don't have time for your foolish worries. And who is minding Ielenia... and... and..."

"Elhrinna," Aldrua said in a low, dangerously sweet voice.

He grunted.

"I know her name."

"Rayant. We need to talk about Rilenheim and what he said." Rayant had to know Rilenheim wasn't to be trusted. She had to tell him what she thought, even though she didn't even trust Rayant, not properly, not like she should. "Rayant, I've been thinking-"

"Well... well you shouldn't!" Rayant raised his fists. He seemed to notice for the first time that he was standing on an archery range. A dozen bowmen stood, heads bowed and slick with sweat in the sun, not knowing how to react.

Rayant pulled her roughly aside by her arm.

"I have a war to win, Aldrua. You have absolutely no idea what's at stake, do you?"

She gritted her teeth.

"I know I can't trust the Geomancer. Can I trust you?"

"Trust isn't your concern. This isn't your business!"

"Rayant! I can't just hide in the Keep and do nothing! Meryn is out there! She was with *him*. And she's hurting!"

"All her choice, if you remember! I sometimes wonder why you didn't run off with him yourself. Oh, but yes, you had another to keep you entertained, didn't you? Good old Kendan. The man who offered to save you from your dreary life. To change your boring world for you-"

"That's not fair!" She lowered her voice. "That's nothing to do with this."

But it *was* fair. Of course it was fair. She'd had Kendan; Kendan, the father of her dead child. Kendan who *had* made promises to make things better. He'd asked her if she was happy with her lot. He'd held out his hand and with smiling eyes asked if she wanted to change her world. What woman in her position would have said no to that?

Aldrua looked at her feet, something she did far too often. She felt her fight slipping away. She tried to grab hold of it. Rayant always clenched his fists. She closed hers tight. Her nails cut into her palms and she whimpered. Maybe men got angry more because their nails were shorter.

She suddenly felt foolish. She looked up into Rayant's face, the sun right behind him, haloing through his hair. There were bags under his eyes, his cheeks were haggard. He still wasn't sleeping right.

"Meryn made her choice," he murmured, "and you made yours. You're still here, and we should be grateful for that; that you, at least, are safe."

"Rayant. What did Rilenheim say to you, when you were alone, about my sister?"

"Nothing."

"You're lying. I can always tell when you're lying. Your cheeks suck in and your eyes go hard."

"No they don't! They're not! That's not the point. I have to do what he says. We all do. He knows so much, he has so much power..."

"That's... that's not what I asked. What do you mean do what he says? What has he told you to do?"

"Keep your voice down! This isn't the place..."

He waved a hand to encompass the yard. Trainers were glaring the grins off their trainees. A young private leaned on his quarterstaff, smirking, until he received a knock to the back of his head. The whole yard was as thick and oppressive as a desert by day.

Aldrua felt something, just a tingle at first, grow from the pit of her stomach. A foreign feeling, one she barely recognised. It became powerful, washed over her like a wave.

She opened her mouth and let it out.

"No!" she cried. "No! I won't keep my voice down!" Her words travelled far in the still air. Her voice was shrill, but she didn't care, not this time. Soldiers shifted, looked at each other, sensed a shift in something intangible, that they somehow knew would greatly affect them, someday, somehow. "You tell me, Rayant! Right now! Rilenheim can have secrets, but I will absolutely," she poked his chest with her forefinger, punctuating each word, "not. Take. No. For an answer! From you! I mean it! I can be as stubborn as Meryn if I want to and I'm not moving from this spot until you tell me."

"I..." Rayant shook his head. Then he leaned in and spoke so that only she could hear him, "Your sister can't be saved. Rilenheim wants her captured and held at Haylen. I am sorry, but she is the only one who can stop Herendak now. And it... it will cost her everything. Rilenheim will do what needs to be done himself."

"I hate you! I HATE you!"

She punched him on the jaw. He stared at her, eyes wide. Possibly as wide as hers. No, hers felt about to burst. Rayant swallowed, over and over, somehow too surprised to even lose his temper.

Aldrua felt an apology immediately leap to her lips. She fought the urge to put her arms around him, to seek comfort, for both of them. Instead she clung to the anger, balled it up inside, feeling like it might consume her.

"I'm making a different choice now," she told him, leaning in yet closer, feeling her cheeks twitch, her eyes pulse. "I choose my sister. I will *not* help you hurt her."

"What are you going to do?" he said at last. "There's nothing you *can* do, not against Rilenheim..."

"We'll see. You'll see."

She turned and hesitated at all the eyes on her. She made sure to keep her chin up, made sure to gaze in a manner she hoped was haughty. She walked stiffly across the yard, back toward the banquet hall. The banqueters were clustered in the doorway. She ignored them. A path opened up for her and she marched through into the permanent coolness of the Keep. She kept walking until all of them were behind, until she clinked alone down an empty, marble-slabbed corridor. When she was certain she was completely out of sight, she ran, wildly and recklessly, until finally she fell against a door deep within the Keep.

* * *

She hadn't realised this was where she was going.

She had a key; she was one of very few who did. This was one door servants were not expected to open for her. She was not expected to have need to open it at all. Inside was windowless and dark. Not dusty though; this room was sealed tight, and its contents had been treated and polished and sharpened before they had been shut up.

She took up a candle from the stack by the door and lit it.

Reflections took up the light. She ran narrowed eyes along long rows of purposeful metal, laid out on shelves from floor to ceiling. Some were scabbarded, others lay raw and some were set in ornate display cases. Still more had been lumped into piles.

Many generations of her family's weapons.

Her fingers ran along them.

At the end of a shelf, laying alone, and not bringing attention to itself, she found a narrow dagger, sheathed in light leather, with a matching cord designed to be used as an inconspicuous belt. Its hilt was beginning to suffer from age, though the blade was sleek and clean and the leather had been well cared for. It smelt of tallow, when she held it up to her nose. She rubbed at the hilt with her thumb. Behind the grime, the brown-red of a gemstone.

She clutched it close. She had never been armed before. She belted it on, ensuring it was tucked away out of sight. Walking without giving away its presence was difficult at first. She considered that she was too conscious of it, as it didn't look like it should be particularly bulky, so she practised walking normally, pacing back and forth in front of the silent shelves like she was on some kind of marching practise. Until even she could almost forget she carried it.

And she vowed to herself that, when the time came, she and the blade would act.

Chapter 12

The thing Herendak sent to take Eyhold Castle came that night. There was little opposition. It had waited until the bulk of the humans had marched away, as Herendak had said they would.

And now it made its move, so slowly at first, moving like a long first breath after the deepest of sleeps, and deep down on the bed of Orthal Lake, there was no one there to notice.

What little light made it this far was scattered into the faintest of glows. Currents curled fronds over shelled creatures which clung to the muddy scree. Fish darted about them, swallowing at the invisible, occasionally scattering as something larger darted into them.

The scree skipped and danced for a second. Anything which could move, did so. Schools of glinting green aronons zigzagged away. Shells closed tightly in on themselves.

It came with only this brief warning, from where it had lain since before the castle had even existed. It was a special kind of Wrilsch, which was why Herendak had given it a special kind of task. The sediment of ages held it down, but it was still able to rise, lifting the lake's bed almost in its entirety above it, curled as it was around the ancient stonework hidden below, and as the sand and fronds and shells poured over its sides it could move ever faster. The very ruins it had been smothering jolted and twisted, pivoting up and out of the lake. The eastern bank flung up high and rained into the wood.

Then the Wrilsch was out, and rising over Eyhold, blotting out the moons. Just a giant, amorphous bulk, punctuated with a single bulbous eye.

Below, pulsing brightly in the now greatly reduced lake, the twin loops of the ancient portal hummed in anticipation.

This doorway would be ready when it was needed.

By the time the alarm was raised, it was too late.

* * *

Herendak finally cracked open the main gate at the northern edge of the Yastran range. Cool air washed around him. He stepped out into blinding sunlight. It was day? Which day? He shielded his eyes with his hand. He'd lost track of time in that deadly race between weroms, and lost more in taming them, but, while not wasted, it was nevertheless time he couldn't afford to lose: if he was to undo his mistake, he had to find the child before Rilenheim could interfere.

Meryn again, in his mind's eye. She wouldn't understand, Herendak decided. She was so young. But she would see he was right. She understood about taking risks. She had given up much to help him... if only he could talk to her, to explain. But she would never understand. She would never be immortal. Humans were just so temporary, and this clouded their vision so very dangerously.

Forget her. He had to forget her. He could only preserve so much.

He stepped out onto a ledge, dislodging snow. It rolled, beginning slowly, down the mountain's side, washing against the sharp peaks which jutted out of the white expanse at intervals. It dribbled to a halt. A kind of mist billowed on, peppering and pockmarking the smoothness of the snowfield.

Then – a gigantic section of white slid away. It built up speed, rolled itself into an unstoppable force and blasted out in a roar over the army miles below.

Distant faces – or at least what passed for faces – craned in his direction, some on necks, some on stalks, others built into other body parts. Snow rained around them.

The Wrilsch had gathered in their thousands. They milled and schemed and fought below, in one unceasing tableau of horror. A ripple ran through them as word – or at least awareness – of his presence spread.

He ran his eyes over them. So many different kinds, mashed together, all different shapes and sizes. There were as many different type of Wrilsch as there were monsters from the nightmares of children. There were many that were alike, but also plenty that were unique, with their own twisted forms and strange and unpredictable talents. Perhaps most dangerous of all were those who could almost pass for human. Those who could wear – haphazardly, awkwardly –

human armour, and carry scavenged human weapons. Those who could get close enough so that by the time they were recognised for what they were, it was too late.

Herendak looked upon them, all ruined and scarred and eager, and as they looked up at him a deafening roar rose up, collecting in mass just as the avalanche had, as more and more realised he was back. It was the kind of roar that enveloped. Herendak vibrated with it. The Wrilsch beat their hands – and other appendages – on their chests. They stamped their feet – or what passed for them – and they screamed and hollered.

Herendak raised his arms for silence. It was a long time before they quietened themselves, and stood or sat still, some of them with difficulty. They stared up at him with a focussed concentration that was terrifying, and Herendak told them in detail how this had all come to pass, and how it was to be.

* * *

It had taken a long time for the full effects to become known, all that time ago.

Herendak had, in the end, when his suspicions had solidified, gone to Rilenheim, because Rilenheim was the first of them to have seen what was happening. Rilenheim had always been the one with the most interest in the other creatures of the world, and could see changes where others could not.

Herendak was formless then – or vaguely formed, at best. Just like Rilenheim. Just like all of them. They knew, back then, of no other way to be. To see a Geomancer was to see out of the corner of an eye, to see mist or smoke, a disturbance in the air. Something not quite normal which broke up the graph of *here* and *there*. They were the thing inside the thing. They were the hosted, and anything and everything else were the hosts.

When Herendak went to see Rilenheim he was, firstly, in a nest. An enormous nest, which covered a hilltop. It was made of entwined trees, many of the branches and trunks curved almost to shattering point, still more already splintered and cracked. There were many eggs, cosily nestled amidst large piles of gleaming bones.

Rilenheim had always taken a particular interest in flighted creatures, though they seemed to have little interest in him. They moved most similarly to Geomancers, though it was not really similar at all. They needed wings and the currents of wind to move about, whereas, originally, Geomancers had needed nothing. Indeed, Geomancers might have looked like wind, to the flighted creatures. Visible winds. Inhabited winds.

Later, more sophisticated creatures than the flighted creatures had come and named everything, recklessly, thoroughly, as though by naming they could do anything other than reduce.

The flighted creatures became "birds". Geomancers had not yet become "Geomancers". They were named later; they were to be given many names, over the times to come. This was still too early, before the portals had been built, as a necessity against the encroaching changes, as a way of attempting to hold on to the way things were. One of their earlier names was an amalgamation, then an abbreviation. They became "g'hosts", and then the apostrophe was lost.

It was in that nest that Rilenheim had first explained to Herendak that time was creeping in, change was coming, and that to weather the change they needed forms, needed a mechanism to ride the currents which made things grow and decay and come together before falling apart. They could be hosted by the physical world, but they would not survive it unless they could be part of it.

Rilenheim had explained what he had learnt by studying the other living things which had come. He had seen them live and die – mostly die. That's just what happened. They died and died and died. But they were relentless in creating more of themselves. They were driven to be more. They grouped in pairs and they became so many more, so much more.

Rilenheim had shown him everything. They had left the nest, with its cracking eggs, its squawking and cawing, and they had gone to larger nests, nests made out of buildings, nests made out of streets. Nests which never stopped growing. New creatures everywhere. Bawling and gurgling, tiny and helpless – but only at first.

And so it was Rilenheim who had given Herendak the idea.

A child.

What if he – a Geomancer – could have a child? A vessel through time, a way to survive it.

For all of them.

Chapter 13

"Your Majesty, Rilenheim has called for you."

Aldrua put down her cup, nodded to the servants, and went with them without a word.

They led her in silence down the hallways of the Keep, two in front, two behind.

She had been expecting this.

"Since when," she asked them, "do servants wear swords?"

"He told us to carry them," one of them answered.

All the servants were doing what Rilenheim told them to now.

"Does it really take four of you to tell me where to go?" she said. "I'm perfectly capable of finding my own way."

No one said anything.

She ignored the stares of those they passed. They could see what was happening. They could see she was being shepherded around her own home. She wished they'd stop looking at her. But then she was in the older parts of the building, where no one went anymore, the original places built when the Keep was a rock behind which to hide from enemies, and she wished there *were* people there to stare.

Witnesses would make her feel safer. Rilenheim would not dare harm her in front of others.

Or would he?

"Well? You never answered!" she snapped. "Where are we going?"

"I'm sorry, Your Majesty. He told us not to talk to you."

"Just remember who's queen here," she shot, but in a low voice. Something about these long, cold corridors made it seem wrong to use a raised voice. It was dark and there were few windows. Those there were consisted only of narrow slits from which to fire arrows. They didn't even look to the outside, but to other rooms and corridors. Had the Keep been built outwards from here, or had there once been a need to kill the people within?

"This place would be far less creepy if one of you said something," she whispered, without meaning to whisper.

"I'm sorry, Your Majesty." She squinted at the speaker. She didn't recognise him. Perhaps he worked in the gardens, but she wasn't sure. His eyes were red. Something about the way he spoke slowly sunk in.

She stumbled to a halt.

"Sorry?" she said. "Why are you sorry?" She looked back at the two behind her. Two maids. They wouldn't, surely they wouldn't?

She considered just asking directly what they'd do if she refused to continue, but was afraid of the answer. Because who were they more scared of, her or Rilenheim?

She should run.

They would intersect another hallway ahead. She could see it head out in the direction of the harbour. She could climb down the ragged stones of the Old North Tower, which for a long time should really have been called the Old North Ruin, and get down to the ships. But what then?

"Please, Your Majesty," one of them said, his voice sounding just as small as Aldrua's. "I-I don't think he means to harm you."

"How do you know?"

But the man didn't answer.

They arrived finally at a staircase leading down. She could hear dripping, and smell water.

"He's in the *vaults*?" she said.

"He said to knock, Your Majesty. We'll... we'll wait here."

She tried to glare at them, but her eyes felt too moist. A kitten trying to scare off wolves. Well... puppies, possibly.

Besides, she couldn't blame *them* for any of this. She knew who to blame.

She walked down the steps into the darkness, alone.

* * *

But she didn't knock, because to hell with Rilenheim.

The vault was cramped. It was never meant to contain so much junk. When it was first built it was just for emergency supplies; grain and blankets and medicines and the like, in case of sieges or bad winters.

Now it was full of centuries' worth of discarded rubbish, forgotten as the Keep had grown up over it all, its foundations made up of the old and forsaken. In time other vaults had been built surrounding the original one, as need had dictated, and these had then been haphazardly connected. She could see them branching away by the light of flaming brands attached to wall brackets. The light flickered in a wind which seemed to circle, as if some perpetual sentinel of its lair. Rilenheim must have lit them. She was surprised he couldn't see in the dark.

He was at the other end of the chamber. He had his back to her and hadn't heard her opening the door. She picked her way over and between the piles of scrap.

He was looking at a scroll, unrolled on a battered side table and held open by goblets. He was too tall for her to see the scroll's contents over his shoulder.

He turned, and his face was shadowed in the light, craggy like a broken cliff face.

"You wanted to talk to me, queen," he said, without preamble.

"*You* called *me* here... Geomancer."

"You came because you wanted to." He seemed to hesitate. "Look at this." He stood aside and beckoned to the scroll. She had to move closer to him to peer at it, so close she could hear his breathing, which was slow and controlled, but hissy, like air from a pinholed pipe. He didn't sound well.

The scroll showed a landscape, of sorts, but of broken rivers and hills and trees, like they had been snapped and twisted and reformed in a way that somehow still had them functioning as rivers and hills and trees. The scene was one of chaos, but chaos made out of regular things. Aldrua looked at it for a long while.

"What is this?" she asked. "Where did it come from?" But Rilenheim's eyes were unreadable under his jutting brow, and he didn't answer. "What do you want with me, Rilenheim?"

"You act against me, queen," he said. She stepped back from him, keeping the entrance to one of the other vaults to her back. Ready to run. She looked for a weapon on the Geomancer, but of course he didn't need one. "Of all the humans here," he went on, "it is you who have your little rabbit teeth in me. You told me in the Council chamber that you understood. But perhaps you were not listening. Perhaps you were lying when you said you understood."

"I don't know what you're talking about."

Rilenheim picked up the scroll and, very deliberately and calmly, tore it into strips.

"This," he said, letting the strips fall about him, "is what Herendak has done to our world. And you dare stand there with your gaping eyes and your quivering lip and expect me to believe you are not in league with him? Why so frightened, queen?"

"I-" She wondered if the servants were still outside the door. What they would do if she were to scream.

"Nothing to say? But you will be talking soon. Come with me."

He seized her arm and, before she could utter a word, she was being yanked through the darkness. He was unheeding of anything which got in their way. She stumbled and was dragged, scattering small objects out of her path. She couldn't tell what they were. One tore at her and she felt trickling blood.

"Slow down! I can't see!"

He didn't slow, but they didn't have far to go.

He took a lantern and blasted it alight with a bolt of flame from his hand. The lantern's wind-guard shot across the room and clattered into a dark corner. She could hear it pinging as it cooled, keening like a wounded animal.

The lantern lit up a trapdoor in the middle of the room. It was open. One of its rusted hinges was misshapen and twisted, like it had melted and then cooled.

Rilenheim had come this way already.

"You will soon see just how Herendak has hurt you," he said, and dropped the lantern through the trapdoor.

The passageway below was narrower, the stonework cruder. An older passageway.

"We're going deeper," he said.

* * *

He made her go first. At times the corridors were so narrow she had to squeeze through sideways. When Rilenheim did so, stone came loose and she was blinded by dust. She pushed the lantern out ahead of them, but it didn't do much to counter the darkness.

The rooms of these original chambers were mostly empty. Some of the outlying ones they passed were half collapsed, just wedges of rock, ramps leading up to nowhere. The main structure looked to have been reinforced more recently. By which she thought maybe a hundred years or so ago. She guessed everything had been moved upward at the same time, and then these lower sections had been abandoned.

Though not everything had been moved. There were dusty bones still piled up in old cells. She stood staring at them with her hands to her mouth. Sinuous beetles the size of her fingers plodded about them. One waved its little antennas at her from the eye socket of a skull.

"Keep moving," Rilenheim said, his voice startling in the silence.

"Who would have left people down here?" she asked.

"Keep moving."

She wondered how many times she had unwittingly stepped over those bones, high up in the Keep above. They had been under her feet her whole life.

Unless, of course, they hadn't. Unless someone else had been down here more recently. This seemed a convenient place to dispose of people who were not wanted.

But who even knew of its existence?

"For the last time: keep moving! It isn't far now."

She almost fell apart right there, right then. But she thought of Meryn, who needed her, and even Rayant, who didn't, and most of all she thought of Ielenia and Elhrinna.

She was grateful for the darkness which hid her terror from the Geomancer.

"Let's get this over with," he said to her.

* * *

What Rilenheim wanted her to see was scattered around the floor of a long forgotten library. Bookshelves were sunk into its walls. The walls had been hollowed out so as to cram in ever more books.

What he specifically wanted her to see was the beginnings of a book. It was a book which had started a thousand years ago, and was still being written.

On the cover, which was unbound, to allow the book to continue to grow, was one word.

Roarst.

Her surname.

She recognised the book's latest volume. She had seen it not so long ago. She had stood in the steward's study and he had asked her for a name. She had mouthed it three times before she was able to croak it out, and he had carefully inked it down in the book. He had added two dates. A birth date and a death date. They were both the same.

But what Rilenheim had laid out on the floor down there were the earlier volumes. She ran the lantern along the rows of them. They illustrated a history of writing, although Rilenheim's ordering seemed haphazard. There were slate tablets, wax tablets, wooden carvings, papyrus scrolls, sheets of parchment, which became thinner until they ended up stitched into the later volumes of what were more recognisable as books.

"Look closer," Rilenheim said.

She crouched and looked.

"What am I looking for?"

He took her through the assorted records, one by one, until she'd got the point but was far too afraid to tell him to stop. They were a history of her family. Many events had been recorded. There were many names and many dates. The Geomancer shoved slate after slate, scroll after scroll, page after page in front of her face. He pointed out each name and each date, throwing the tablets and parchments and books aside when he was done. Some were so fragile they fell apart.

What he showed her were the names forgotten. Those of her ancestors that were never remembered because they had never done anything to remember. The names of those only a few had ever known, though they had burnt deep memories of pain into those few. The one thing they had in common was that they were all babies. Dead baby after dead baby. Over and over. Through every generation of her family. From every woman who had ever born her name.

"What is this, Rilenheim? What does this mean?"

"Now look to the others. Go through them all. Observe how their spouses lived or died."

She did so. Accidents, so many fatal accidents. Often after a first child had died.

"What does it all mean?" she asked him again.

"You have been helping Herendak in secret. I know you have. Now you see why this was a mistake."

"I have not! I don't understand!"

"I wondered how he did it. After all this time. How he managed to father a child with a mortal. Now I see how long he has been planning this."

"No...."

"He has treated you like cattle. He has fattened you up until you were ready."

"No!"

"Herendak has been killing the children of your family for a very long time. He has been killing those who would veer the line off his path."

"No! Sometimes babies die!"

"This often? And all those accidents?"

"How do you know it was him? It might not have been him."

What she wanted to say to him, but couldn't: "It could have been you, Rilenheim!"

"I know. So do you. Do you remember the day your father died?"

* * *

She did. Of course she did. Even though she had been a child at the time. Maybe because of it.

She had been fighting with Meryn when it had happened. They

were always fighting as children, at Meryn's insistence – apparently because Meryn understood that good children didn't.

That was why they were going up to their father's study. They were going to him for arbitration, as they always did. If they hadn't been fighting, they might not have been told the truth for a long time.

Aldrua remembered that walk all too clearly. She remembered how angry she had been and how much her cut cheek had hurt. She couldn't believe Meryn had punched her in the face. It was deeply confusing that she had.

She understood now, of course. Father had never hesitated to solve disputes in the most expedient way possible. Meryn was only trying to make him proud of her. He was always so much closer to Aldrua, and that wasn't something which Meryn could stand.

They hadn't paid any mind to the absence of the overly tall guards who normally stood on watch by the entrance to the Great Hall. Those guards never did anything anyway. They had always just stood there glistening in plated armour whilst holding their pikes unwaveringly straight, pointing to the sky, like they were somehow frozen in place.

Aldrua and Meryn had skittered across the hall in a haze of words snapped back and forth, tiny in a place they would be out of breath running across, and which rose so high they could forget had a ceiling.

At the door of the king's study there was a guard, but he was lying face down.

Aldrua remembered looking at Meryn, and Meryn looking back at her. The argument was instantly forgotten. This was new. They stood there lost for a moment. Neither of them had a pattern of what to do.

The door was ajar, but too slightly for them to be able to see inside.

Meryn unstuck herself first. She walked in a big circle around the dead man, stepping carefully over his outflung hand.

She put her head to the gap in the door.

After a time, she had gone inside.

"Meryn! Meryn!" Aldrua called after her sister, as loudly as she dared.

There was a loud thud. There was a clattering sound. A shadow over the door, as of something big moving fast.

Later, Aldrua could not understand how Meryn hadn't screamed. She knew *she* would have.

When Aldrua finally gathered the courage to follow, she saw her father lying over his desk, his head torn, his neck split open, shiny with fresh flowing blood. One of the side tables had been upended. A decanter dribbled its contents into a rug. The rug was rumpled and into it was ripped a rough claw-print. There was a hole smashed into the wall nearby and through it she could see a sunlit courtyard.

Meryn stood in the midst of all this with a look of wonder on her face. Her own neck also glistened, though not with blood.

"It nuzzled me," she said. "Like a cat."

They exchanged a long, wordless look again.

"There was a Wrilsch," Meryn explained. "It killed Daddy."

* * *

"I was the only one who believed her," Rilenheim said. "I spoke to her at length."

"I believed her," Aldrua claimed, knowing as she spoke that it was more complicated than that. "But she lied about the Wrilsch still being there. How could it possibly have been? It would have killed her."

"It was there. I did not think to link the events at the time, but it was then that Herendak started showing an interest in Meryn."

"What- you can't mean that. She was a little girl!"

"Would you seriously contend that someone who has lived for many thousands of years – indeed who has lived from before there was even such a thing as 'time' - could not be many things to those whose lives flash past meaninglessly?"

"But-"

"Once again I find myself having to explain the obvious. The Wrilsch knew what Meryn was, right there in that room. It knew Herendak's plan was finally on the verge of success and it took this message back to him. If he had found out another way, your father might still be alive. The point I am making is that there would have been no need to continue to direct your lineage down a different line. But that is exactly was he has done just lately. I sincerely doubt killing your child was mere force of habit. And so this is why you are down here, my queen. To explain to me your part in all this."

Aldrua found she was shaking her head, over and over.

"You are a cruel man, Rilenheim."

"You would do well not to mistake me for a man. You would do better to answer my question."

"He didn't kill..." But the words trailed off, crushed by the enormity of what she had seen in the chronicles of her family. So many deaths. Death in childbirth was common, but not this common, especially for those of her station. And what of the others; all those fatal accidents which had resulted in alternate lineages? It was almost too painful to believe.

And, of course, there was what she had seen with her own eyes, in that graveyard of lost babies, which had somehow managed to become more terrible still.

"I don't know why he did it," she whispered. "Perhaps he wasn't certain." She felt sick, talking about her son this way.

"Perhaps."

"Sometimes they just-"

"Do not be petulant. You know I'm right. Why would he do that to you unless you also were important?"

"I... I don't know. I don't feel important."

"You have a hand in this, my queen. And you will explain it to me."

"A part in this, Rilenheim? I don't-"

"After all I have demonstrated, you still will not cooperate? Here." He shoved the most recent volume at her. She clutched it to her chest. "You will want to think on the latest entry. Follow."

She did so. He moved fast. She had to jog to keep up, fearful he would outpace the weak light from her lantern.

He led her back, but not all the way.

"Get inside."

"What? Rilenheim? No. No!"

"A few quiet nights to understand what it means to defy me. Did you think I would leave you unpunished for hiring mercenaries behind my back?"

"No, Rilenheim! I promise. I promise!"

"I will be back to ask you once more about Herendak. You would do well to think upon how you will answer."

"No!"

She was frozen to the spot.

With surprising gentleness, he pushed her into the cell. Bones clattered underfoot. Disturbed beetles fled in all directions. She felt their tiny feet crawling around her calves.

Rilenheim took the lantern from her unresisting hands. He closed the door. He locked it with a rusty key.

He blew out the lantern.

"Good night, Aldrua."

Chapter 14

There were trails through the scraggly wood that hadn't been there the week before. They were of all different sizes. Some were very, very wide. Along these, branches were cracked and the ground was mulched up. But whatever had created the trails was no longer present. The wood was perfectly still.

The only movement was that of a hunter.

He was following smaller signs. He stooped occasionally to check the bend of the grass, the relative dryness of brown mounds, before moving on. His actions were practised and sure.

It was always difficult to find game here. This far north the ground was hard and the winters unforgiving. Not much could survive for long. There wasn't even any green. Grass was patchy and yellow and leaves were permanently brown. But the hunter had a good feeling about today. He had been unsuccessful for the last two hunts, but he knew there were boars here. He had been closing in on them for a while. He had come back to their trail for two days running and each time it was still fresh. They were just a little deeper into the wood, he knew it. He just had to find them.

When he did he would take them back to his father, who would prepare them for the guests of their way-house. It was the only place of shelter for many days' ride in any direction, situated as it was halfway between Oreln and the distant mountains, and so the guests were all travellers grateful for a meal of boar or venison.

As the hunter went deeper, the nature of the tracks changed. The wood itself changed with them. It felt different. It seemed less friendly. He couldn't hear birds. The vegetation became somehow more angular, more prickly. It became harder to push through entwined leaves. Thick branches held him back. He started walking the opened trails directly rather than tracking alongside, which was what he'd normally do so as not to obscure any tracks, should be need to go back and re-read them.

This was all wrong. He might still be a boy, at least in his father's eyes, but he had been doing this for many years. And this was all very, very wrong.

There was a flash of colour amidst the brown. He crouched and ran his finger over a leaf, tasted it. Blood. Boar blood? Wet and fresh. There were also scraps of fur and streaks of excretion. Signs the sounder had been moving fast.

There were signs of larger game as well, notwithstanding the strange new paths breaking through everything. There were trees almost entirely devoid of leaves, like they had been shaken clean off, and furrows in the soil. He couldn't tell what animal was the cause. What else would be hunting boars out here? These certainly weren't wolf trails, which he would often find near game. These trails were so much bigger. Something new had moved into the wood. He had heard travellers talk of dangerous animals from foreign lands. Creatures twice the size of wolves, tall as a man, with jagged teeth, which could outrun the fastest horse.

He should go back. He could get his brothers and tomorrow they could come out here together. They would return triumphant with the new beast. They would mount its head on the common room wall and forever after strangers would ask about it and his father would tell of how his boys had defeated it.

He went on.

He found the boars. They were in pieces. The hunter was no stranger to the insides of animals. He had dressed many corpses. He had seen partially eaten remains. He had seen them being pulled apart by hungry scavengers. But this was different. Nothing had been eaten here. He could see no bite marks on any of the carrion. As far as he could tell there was no meat missing. It was hard to tell for sure. It was hard even to determine how many boars there had been. There were too many parts torn up and scattered over a wide area. There weren't even any flies. There wasn't the normal smell of decay. The smell was more musky and sweet; sickly.

He shuddered when he came face to face with half of a farrow dangling from a branch. Its blood-shot eyes were wide and staring. It was surely too high to have been flung up there by an animal. But a human would not have done this, and who else could have tracked and ran down these poor creatures? Only a madman would have carried out these acts.

Night would fall soon. He did not want to be here when it did. He turned back down the trail, his mind dark with unpleasant thoughts. He knew it wasn't just the wood that had changed. What he had seen was not something he could ever unsee.

There were sounds now, where before it had been still. They followed him. Sounds of movement; rustling and cracking.

He stopped and listened carefully. When he did so, the movement stopped as well.

He was being stalked. He was being hunted.

He started to run, and the stalking became a chase.

* * *

Herendak felt tired in a way that he had never felt before. It wasn't his legs or his arms telling him to stop. It was his eyelids. They wanted to close.

But Geomancers did not get sleepy. He kept going. He glanced back to check if he could still see the Wrilsch.

It was deep night, and pitch-blue with the moons clouded. The leafy landscape was filled with strange shapes and unusual angles. It was impossible, even staring, to discern the cause of this strangeness. If he hadn't known of the Wrilsch, he'd have thought the landscape itself was playing tricks on him. It reminded him of something, long ago, but he couldn't remember what.

They had made good time from Yurethian. The Wrilsch could not necessarily move swiftly, but they also did not tire. It was a shame he could only move them at night, but to give away their presence too soon would hurt his plan. He had managed to avoid killing too many humans so far. Just some lone woodsmen, some messengers.

How long this could last, he did not know.

There were fewer Wrilsch with him now. There had been many more at the beginning of this advance. He was leaving groups of them behind at highly populated areas, still more where the portals lay. Yet he was careful to keep the balance of them with him. He still needed a sufficient number to win the child, to fight for it, when he found it.

And he *would* find it.

When they neared the Haynian Gateway he went on alone.

He only wanted to ensure it would still function, but when he got there it was gone. Where it had always been there was instead a large building, a cross between a house and a fort. Small, but sturdy looking.

It was occupied. There were lights in the windows, which had bars running down them. It was an inn. It looked safe, and it was cold out here. He had his hands deep within his pockets and his shoulders were stiff and shivery.

He bustled inside. He had to. He had to find out what was happening with the portal. There was, he told himself, no other reason.

The man behind the bar had a mug out for him before he sat down. "Cold night to be out."

Herendak gave no hint of surprise when he saw what had happened to the portal. It formed part of the building. The bar ran across it. The serving staff – which seemed to consist of an old woman and a young man – walked through it as they went back and forth into one of the kitchens.

They had no idea what it was, of course.

Herendak sat on the stool closest to it at the bar. He reached out and touched it.

"Go ahead," the innkeeper said. "Warm yourself."

"Yes," Herendak said. "It is a cold night." There was a fireplace burning high at the other side of the common room. There were people seated around it. Young children played with a dog close to the flames. The dog yapped with excitement. There were tables with benches all around the room, mostly unoccupied.

"Strange isn't it?" the innkeeper said, noting Herendak's hand still on the portal. "But I don't know what we'd do without it sometimes. When the winters are hard and we can't get dry firewood, it's warm enough to get by on. That's why we're the only tavern still out here. No one else has one of these."

Herendak nodded. At the moment there was plenty of firewood burning in the hearth. It looked old. Not the fireplace, nor the hearth, but the fire itself. A different kind of portal, for a different kind of people.

"Yes," Herendak said again, when he realised the innkeeper expected him to say something.

He followed the portal's contours with his eye to where it

intersected the wall. It must have run into the kitchen. Maybe further. Built into these people's lives.

"You hungry? We have pottage. No meat, I'm afraid. But warm." The innkeeper smiled, nodding to the portal. "Unfortunately not hot."

"No," Herendak said. It had been a while since he had spoken to a human. The last time had been with Meryn. He remembered telling her he would find someone to help with the birth. She had said... but he had forgotten exactly. She had said he should go, although her eyes had been saying otherwise. He would never understand her. He could see something similar with the innkeeper now. The man wanted to talk, but Herendak knew if he were to get up and walk back outside he would probably breathe a sigh of relief.

It was an effort to fit in with these people.

"We'll have some meat for the pottage soon," the man went on, breaking the silence, "if that will change your mind. My son will be back with some game soon."

"No. I will be leaving shortly."

The portal was functioning. He could feel it moving, very faintly, and maybe not even physically. It would be ready when the time came. There was nothing for him to do here. There were no soldiers, no one who could fight them, just these peasants. The Wrilsch need not disturb this place; not yet. He should go back right away.

But it was warm here, and he tarried by the bar.

"You're going back out in this?" the innkeeper went on. "You don't want a room? Very cold out at night. Sometimes my son stays out too long. He wants to impress me." Again Herendak saw a contradiction, in the man's evident pride for his son and his preferences for how it should be secured.

The dog was yapping again, and the children were laughing. Herendak watched them. The innkeeper left him to serve another traveller. There was a discussion among the children and a woman, who was presumably their mother. It was about bedtime.

These people are happy, he suddenly realised.

When the portal opened, they would be among the lucky ones, Herendak told himself. They would be ushered into a new world. They would be the new people. It would be better for them, than for those that were not chosen, than for those who were too far from the portals.

"Innkeeper!" he called. He hadn't meant to shout. He ignored the attention this garnered from across the room. He was next to the innkeeper without realising it, a chair knocked over on his way. He yanked the man closer by his shirt. "Get out. Get out of here! Take your son and go. Go tonight!"

"What are you talking about? Let go of me – please!"

Herendak did so. He didn't know why he'd done that. He shouldn't have. He couldn't afford to give himself away. It didn't make any real difference that *these* people were here by the portal. It was an inconsequence. It made so little difference.

What, really, did it matter?

He had just wanted to warn the man who had been kind to him.

"Do you know something, stranger?" the innkeeper was saying, seeing something in Herendak's eyes. "Why should we go?"

Herendak rubbed at said eyes. They were stinging and sore.

"I'm sorry," he said. "I didn't mean what I said. Forget I said anything." He had got up too quickly, was suddenly light-headed. It must have been the warmth and the smoke. They filled the room.

He was aware of eyes on him as he walked out.

As the door closed, he saw the dog scampering up the stairs, to a child calling it to bed.

Yes, he thought again, these people would be the lucky ones.

* * *

There was a commotion back where the Wrilsch were waiting. They had found someone, or someone had found them.

A young man was quivering and crying on the ground. One of his legs was twisted and broken. Bone was visible. His face was covered entirely in blood except were twin lines of tears had run.

The Wrilsch parted at Herendak's approach.

He saw the resemblance immediately.

"You won't tell anyone," Herendak said to the boy.

"Tell? No... No, no. I won't. I promise!" The boy was quick to bargain. Herendak could see questions in his eyes. What were the Wrilsch doing there? How had they organised themselves? How was it that they did not tear Herendak to pieces? Could it be that they were not mere wild animals?

Herendak recognised a smart boy when he saw one.

"You will tell," Herendak whispered. "You will tell. There is no way you will not."

He turned and forced himself to walk away. Each step was difficult. He knew what the Wrilsch had to do. What they knew he wanted them to do. What he needed them to do.

They were so deep into Draldorn now. They had seeped into its skin, crept through its arteries – and Rilenheim had no idea.

But Herendak could not bear to watch how this secret must be kept.

"I am sorry," he said to no one, for everyone, his words emptied out by the ragged beginnings of screams.

Chapter 15

"Are you awake?"

Rilenheim lit a lantern and wedged it between two bars of the cell door. Its light danced over Aldrua's face, but she didn't notice.

She was huddled in one corner of the cell, rocking back and forth, her arms around the book of names. She had pushed the bones into the opposite corner with one foot, some time earlier, apologising to them as she did so. She didn't know how long she had been down there. A week? Longer? It was so quiet, with just the bones and beetles for company, that she had been singing, voice hoarse, to herself. But holding on to the words was difficult; she had never known or had forgotten many of them, and so she corrected herself over and over in desperate mumbles, apologising to the bones, for the loss of words, for her tremulous voice, for everything. She couldn't fill the space. It was too empty. Too few songs. She knew lullabies. Sing them to sleep, sing herself to sleep.

By now she had run out of tears. She was so thirsty. She still tasted salt from when they'd run into her mouth. She remembered someone – Rayant? - telling her that salt was bad to drink in water.

So cold, so lonely, with only the bones and the wind and the memories.

She wanted to sleep, had to sleep. But she kept waking, stomach aching, demanding food, water. Memories of the dead demanded attention. So many dead. Her son dead just like the others. Looking up, exhausted, spent, like now, into the faces of the midwives. Was it murdered?

"Sleep, sleep," she pleaded.

And then her father. Neck glistening, life spilled over the desk. The wonder on Meryn's face.

And dying here, in this cell, her flesh decomposing, her bones blackening, atop a mountain of much smaller bones, consumed by insects.

"Can't sleep, can't sleep."

Rilenheim watched her through the bars.

"You will answer my questions now," his voice cut.

She froze.

"Are you real?"

"Answer my questions."

She nodded, over and over, and didn't mind that he might not be real.

He asked about everything.

He started with her father's death, and about Meryn growing up, and about Rayant, and about the men before him, and the one after. He asked about Ielenia and her likes and dislikes. He asked about Draneth, how the city worked, and Draldorn, and how she understood that worked.

She answered all his questions, staying pressed into the corner, away from the bones and their inhabitants, too cold and tired and listless to move.

He asked her, again, "Why did you help Herendak?"

She couldn't answer. She wanted to. She gabbled a stream of nonsense.

What could she say? She hadn't helped him. How could she make Rilenheim believe her? She should say what he wanted to hear. Something, anything, it didn't matter as long as he let her go. She wanted to reach out to him, as if that could somehow make him understand. To let him know that she was as real as he was. She wanted more light so he could better see her face, and see how very sorry she was.

"Rilenheim," she said at last.

"I will go away," he said, "and you can think on it some more."

"No! Please!" She tried to get to her feet, but her legs were numb and she could only crawl. She made it to the bars. "I don't understand! Why do you keep asking that? I didn't help him. I would never. Never!"

"Never help a Geomancer?"

"What do you want from me?"

"A confession."

"And then... this will be over? Of what? Of what shall I confess? Why are you...? Please..." She thought of Drak, face burnt, scarred at Rilenheim's hand. What would he do if she answered wrongly?

"You would never help," Rilenheim said. "But yet you seek to aid Meryn. Meryn, who is in league with a Geomancer. You declare that you will not assist us, yet you are willing to lend succour through a proxy. You think such lies are not transparent to one such as I?"

"I-"

"Your sister is a danger to you and a traitor to the kingdom. Exiled by the king. Mother of the child of the enemy. Yet you seek her out, after I warned you not to."

Aldrua closed her eyes. Meryn. But it was no longer clear if she *was* exiled any more, since Rilenheim had come back. *Hunted* was perhaps more the term.

"I do not seek her out," Aldrua lied, "and even if I were to, helping my sister is different from helping Herendak."

"I had them both together, my queen," he said. "But I could not undo his work. So I brought her here, to hide her-"

"You need... you need me to hide her," Aldrua spluttered. "You need me to hide Elhrinna, Rilenheim. You need me. Because she looks like me and because I look like my sister. You can't leave me down here-"

"The resemblance is already known," he interrupted. "What happens to you now does not matter. You could disappear down here forever and few, I think, would truly care. You might even prefer it. To fade peacefully away. Would that not be a relief, human?" His voice was dangerously raw.

"Rilenheim." A sudden thought, a sudden hope. She licked her lips. "If you want the truth from me... you have to let me talk freely."

His expression flickered with anger. "So you do know something! I knew you were lying to me! I will make you suffer for this-"

"I'll tell you," she rushed on, "I will. But you're preventing me from speaking of it. You have to undo whatever it was you did. The curse, or spell, or whatever you call it... this blindness of speech. You have to undo it and then I can say..."

She trailed off. He had gone dangerously quiet. He didn't say anything for a long time. She still couldn't see his face. He stood there in the darkness until she could almost believe he was part of it.

"Sometimes," he said, "it can indeed seem like a shadow has settled over our thoughts."

"How old are you?" she asked suddenly.

"Old? You have no point of reference."

He shifted abruptly and she shrunk back, almost falling onto the pile of bones. But Rilenheim merely paced back and forth.

"Very well," he said at last, "you may speak. This once, and only this once, about what transpired that night. But I warn you that I have no patience for lies and half-truths, nor for repetition. I give you this single opportunity to make your peace with me. Do not fail."

He waved a dismissive hand and Aldrua instantly breathed out. An impossibly long breath. It went on so long. She clutched her hands to her throat. She couldn't breathe. She panicked and started to choke. It was as if she had been holding that breath ever since that night in the tower and it would take just as long to let it out. Everything went very bright and white and light and-

But then suddenly she could breathe again, and her mind felt clear and clean.

"I'm surprised you didn't just make me mute," she coughed, looking up at Rilenheim, and realising too late the danger of this being mistaken for a suggestion.

He just laughed.

"That might have been a trifle suspicious, to the one who seeks the child."

She asked the question she most wanted to ask.

"Rilenheim... you blame Herendak. But... was it you who killed my baby? To hide Elhrinna with me?"

She instinctively put her hands to her forehead – it was interesting how quickly matters of pain became instinctual – but there was none. Her hands were freezing, she realised. She put them between her knees. She looked like she was bowing to him.

"Well, Rilenheim? Will you answer?"

"Yes, and the answer is no. I did not kill your child; it was dead when it was pulled out of you. But equally, neither did I expect it to die. That was not something I had planned for. I had to move fast, and the results have been – clearly – less than ideal."

She stared at him. He was a monster. He was wearing the wrong face. Those laughter lines were so out of place. She imagined his face dissolving into something beastly, something with dripping fangs and wild, animal eyes. It would be more fitting, because he was going to take the baby from her either way. It was to have been easy. It goes out of sight for a moment, it comes back different. He could have done it without anyone knowing. But it had died and almost upset his plan. And so the shadow had come.

"What were you going to do with him, Rilenheim?"

"There is a Salo kitchen which takes orphans."

She wasn't sure she believed him. It must have been obvious.

"Your suspicions," he went on, his voice low, "are of no concern to *me*. Believe what you wish, but I see no benefit in strangling the life out of your young one by one. There are," he smirked, "far too many of you."

His smirk dropped when he saw the horror on her face. Wait – did he... did he actually think he was *smiling*? Come to think of it, she had *never* seen him smile, nor laugh, not in a way that anyone human would properly consider to be either. So what *was* it with those laughter lines around his eyes? There was something important there, something that... if only she could understand.

But she could clearly see his face now, as he could hers, and it occurred to her that it would be to her advantage if he thought his smile convincing.

"You were going to take it from me," she said, "and now you want my cooperation? You know *nothing* about us."

"It would not have mattered. You would not have known."

"Yes it would. I would."

"You are wasting my time, my queen. You are here to explain to me your part in this. If it is to do with the dead, then I give you this chance to speak of it. But you refuse to listen to reason. You base your thoughts on deliberate refusals to accept the obvious. You would find a greater degree of clarity if you did not do so much of your thinking with your body."

"Rilenheim, you took my sister's baby, and you would have taken mine." He didn't understand what this meant. She could see it in his blank expression, the sideways tilt of his neck. "You don't seem to... Listen to me, you say you don't understand my involvement. But I cannot explain it to you because neither do I. So let me help you – tell me why you think I'm helping him?"

He was shaking his head, in disregard of her words – but he answered nonetheless.

"It is very simple. Herendak has connected our people, my queen. This must be undone. Everyone involved must undo their part. Everything must be reversed."

"Reversed? So... Meryn could be saved?"

He was silent for a long moment.

"It would be possible to restore her," he said.

"Save her?"

"Yes."

It was Aldrua's turn to be silent. Sudden hope had her heart beating. But her mind was screaming at her, and she grew suddenly angry.

"You're *lying!* You don't care about any of us!" She grabbed the bars. Slowly, she pulled herself unsteadily to her feet. "If you need her to undo this then why did..." She trailed off. Drak had said

Rilenheim wanted Meryn taken somewhere. Somewhere else, not to Draneth. But she couldn't ask the Geomancer about that. She didn't know how much he knew about Drak and the others.

"Why don't I want her found by you?" he was saying. "Why does she need to die? Is that what you are trying to ask?"

"She's not a danger to you, Rilenheim. Let us deal with her. Rayant exiled her originally. Now our own people are looking for her. Let us administer our own justice. She is of Draldorn. She is one of our people, not yours."

"No."

"Why not? Why is it so very important that I not see her? Tell me why! People are dead because you won't explain yourself!"

"Why?" Rilenheim intoned, his face against the bars. Suddenly his arms were wide and his cloak billowed out like he was about to smother the cell and everything in it. The lantern gave up its life with a hiss. "Why?" his voice boomed in the near darkness. Only a distant flaming brand lent any light at all. "Why! Why! Why!" He stabbed his finger toward her. "You are saying *nothing* to change my mind, human. You ask the questions of a child!"

"I disagree," Aldrua said, her voice small. "Why can't I see her?"

"I am finding out. I will find out."

"You don't know?"

"I know you must not touch her!"

"Then I won't. I'll just talk to her!"

"Words are dangerous too, young queen." He was smirking again. "People are dead, little human? That's what you said. What people would they be? You see, I will always manage to squeeze the truth out of you. One way or another."

She clamped her mouth shut.

"You didn't have to hurt them," she muttered at last, giving up on any pretence about the White Ravens. He knew it was her. She didn't know how, but he knew.

"They would not listen," he said, "and they would not have been in harm's way had you not put them there. When the queen of the ants lures her workers into a flame, their fate is not the fault of the flame.

"You may despise me, young queen, but I warned you. I told you what to do. I told you to stay in the Keep, and what would happen if you disobeyed. And what of those men? They are of no consequence. They are men who live and die in a heartbeat."

"You're a *monster!*"

"I am doing what needs to be done. If you were to start obeying my instructions fewer people would get hurt. If you were to stop lying to me, events will progress far more smoothly. Do you understand?"

"More and more so."

"So petulant. You must see that you are to I as a child is to you. Yet you stand before me and ask for explanations for which you are not equipped."

"I just want my sister back."

"I told you before, she is no longer your sister. She may already be changed. She may already be dead."

"But she was alive when you saw her, yes, Rilenheim?"

"That was not recently."

"But she was?"

"She was bloodied and weak. I cannot know what has happened since. For all our sakes she must still live."

"She was hurt?"

"You people give yourselves away to your young."

"What are you saying?"

"A Geomancer would never allow another to feed off of him. She was disgusting, lying there grunting and oozing. Sickening."

"Wait... you were there when she was giving birth?"

"I wonder that the child is not mentally disfigured by the experience. It is a curiosity of your kind that you do not all suffer nightmares of this horror that immediately befalls you."

Her thoughts were racing. She had to keep him talking, had to find out whatever she could.

"So why did you not undo this right then, Rilenheim? You said you needed to reverse everything. But you couldn't do so. Why not?"

"We are going in circles. I have already explained. There was a piece missing. You."

"And – for the last time – I do not know why I am involved!" She took a deep breath. She could make him angry, like she had before in council. Make him so angry he'd forget himself. "It must *kill* you to need me, Rilenheim," she said. But he did not reply. "To need a mere human? You must be *livid*." Still he remained silent in the dark. "Rilenheim?" she whispered, "what if I went away? I could take Elhrinna away. Far from Meryn, and Herendak, from... from everyone-"

"From me?" his voice was slow and thick. "I would find you, and you would be punished, like any disobedient brat would be punished."

"What if you couldn't find us? Not you, or Herendak. Would that be enough-"

"Not find the child hiding under the bed? You have an overinflated sense of your own importance. Oh, dear queen of this small and troublesome kingdom, what am I going to do with you?"

"Just explain-"

"Do not push me, Aldrua." It was the first time he'd used her name. "If you want to keep your kingdom intact and your people alive, you must do as I command. I hope this is clear to you now, and you will no longer be toiling against me behind my back."

"You said something about Wrilsch before, in the Council chamber. But I didn't understand. What exactly *will* happen to Meryn?"

He went silent once again. She wondered if the only thing keeping her alive was the fact that she was in a cell and he would have to bother to unlock it. But then she remembered his command of flame.

He turned and walked away. His bootsteps reverberated around the tiny cell.

She gripped the bars tighter and shook them.

"Rilenheim? Rilenheim, come back! Don't leave me! Don't!"

But then he was right in front of her, his own hands clamped down over hers and squeezing.

"It will be similar," he hissed, "to what happened before, thousands of years ago. They all took on different shapes. Thoughtlessly, desperately. This is what will happen to Meryn. It will be painful. Is that what you wanted to hear? She has no idea what will happen. When it happened before, it was only I who understood. Do you believe that? Not even Herendak knew. They had never taken shapes before; I had. I was always the curious one. I had mimicked the other creatures. That was why Herendak was so often with me; we were both explorers, we both sought boundaries.

"But the others – they did not know which shapes to take. They came out strange; different; twisted. They came into being broken and in pain. They came to be Wrilsch.

"What could we do? Herendak acted quickly – he always acted quickly. He pulled them out of this new world, this broken world where everything is a wall. Do you see that, Aldrua? Everything was open back then. We were free. But now we are *caged*. In these *places* and *forms*." He clenched his hands tighter, and her fingers were crushed into the rusted iron bars. She whimpered. "You are beginning to understand, I think, what this all means, I trust?"

"The Wrilsch," she gasped, "are what is left of you. If you remove immortality..."

"But it turns out Herendak has still been plotting behind my back. He has been guiding you. Growing you. His own pet species.

He thought you were the masters of this new world. Lords of time, where we were lords of space. But now Meryn has lost her power – just as we lost ours. Now she is Wrilsch."

"No-"

"No? No. You are correct. She is only half Wrilsch. And half... something else. Herendak is once again playing at creation."

"Can you really restore her...? Rilenheim?"

He looked at her for a long time. His hands held her steady. She made herself meet his gaze.

"No," he said, at last, shaking his head, and taking all the hope from her. She deflated.

"She is truly lost then," she said.

"If Herendak is not stopped, Aldrua, we will all be lost. So tell me: how is it you are needed to undo this? You were close to your sister. She would have talked to you about this."

"She did not." Meryn of the wondering eyes and the unquenchable spirit. "She told me nothing."

He released her hands and she slumped back.

"Very well. I will find out another way."

As would she, she vowed. Everything he had said was running through her head. If she could find out the truth of all this before him, maybe something could be done. She went over it all, again and again.

She almost forgot Rilenheim was still standing there, stock-still.

"Do you trust me now?" he said. "Will you obey me?"

"Yes," she lied. He hesitated. "Do *you* trust," she asked him, "that I don't know how I'm involved?"

He took a long moment. "When I return," he said, "you are free to go."

"After... all that... you're still going to leave me down here?"

"This time you may keep the lantern. Use it sparingly."

She took it from between the bars. She held it close. Its warmth was feeble.

"Rilenheim?" she said, as he turned to go. "We forget."

He raised his eyebrows, not even bothering to ask her to explain.

"You asked why we did not have nightmares about our births? We forget. We do not have nightmares because we forget."

"You forget because you are weak. This is why you have to write important dates down in books." He gestured to the record book lying forgotten on the ground. "It is just one of your many weaknesses."

"Not in this case, Rilenheim. I think of Herendak, and I wonder. And you, too. What if you could forget?"

* * *

A long time later there was a voice

"Your Majesty?"

Aldrua recognised it.

"Pena?"

"Where are you? I can't see you."

"Follow my voice." The lantern had long since died.

After some scrabbling, Pena was on the other side of the bars. Aldrua grabbed her arm and wouldn't let go.

"It's really you?"

"I have the key. Where's the lock?"

They fumbled it open and Aldrua put her arms around the chambermaid. She started sobbing.

"Come on, Your Majesty. Let's get out of here."

"I can't see."

"No. Rilenheim told me to go find you, but he wouldn't let me bring a light. He laughed at me. I've been lost for I don't know how long. I think he's punishing me for failing him. He... scares me, Your Majesty."

"But we have to do what he says, Pena."

"I know."

"We have to."

"I know."

"But I'm not going to."

Chapter 16

The army left Draneth a week later. Rayant led it, at least in theory. But it was Rilenheim, hunched and becowled on a giant black charger in his voluminous cloak, that the king looked to.

Aldrua also kept an eye on the Geomancer. His long nose was just about visible sticking out of the cowl. She found it difficult to look at him. Only part of that, she was sure, was due to the brightness of the day. And only part of the brightness of the day was due to the actual brightness of the day: her eyes still ached from her time below ground.

A trumpet sounded. Horses whinnied. Armour creaked as soldiers shifted their weight. Otherwise, it was so very quiet. The fields that had been the armies gathering place now squatted sad and empty. A few lonely tents remained, damaged and discarded, or simply forgotten about. Aldrua clutched a hand to her neck, feeling a chill despite the lack of any breeze.

It seemed the entire population of Draneth had come to watch the army leave, which was quite possibly the case. Vast crowds were gathered under the clear sky, on the road, all round the gate, and pressed up against the battlements over Draneth's outer wall; anywhere they could find space and a clear view. They comprised almost entirely of women, children, the elderly and the sick.

Aldrua, of course, got to watch from a special place separate from the common folk, with the nobles for company. She stood in the shade of the ancient sculpture near the gate, with its twin loops of diamond-encrusted stone. It was the same sculpture that hulked all across Draldorn; some kind of primitive tribute. She had always thought it said something about her people's comparative primitiveness that these sculptures were often dented and scored by attempts to remove said diamonds – both in terms of the drive to destroy for personal gain, and the resulting complete inability to defeat the ancient craftsmanship. Her eye was drawn to where the faded filigree which decorated the sculpture's base wove itself into a face. It was almost a human face – but not quite. Like someone unfamiliar with what a face was had taken a sudden, enthusiastic interest and saw fit to depict one.

But even under the sculpture's shade she remained apart from the nobles. Their wildly coloured clothes, their standard means of displaying wealth, seemed so inappropriate after what she had recently seen. She wouldn't have even noticed this was what they were doing before her recent trip through the darker parts of the city. Besides, if what she suspected were true, these distinctions would soon no longer matter.

As she watched, Rayant turned to face his city. He raised his right fist, but did not speak, and the crowd replied in the same fashion, with their own fists to the sky. He gave them a final nod, face set in a non-expression, before turning away. He was not expected to speak; sometimes tradition was set from need.

Aldrua was the last person the king turned to before he mounted. She surprised herself by speaking first.

"I'll be waiting," she said.

His hand moved to touch her, but, as so often the case these days, he stopped himself. He used it, instead, to ensure the crowned silver spire emblem on his tunic was unruffled.

"Don't," he said, his voice gruff. "You've never waited for me before." His mouth moved while he worked out what he wanted to say. "Aldrua, I didn't mean it like that." He turned his head slightly, taking in their vast audience. Many thousands watched, civilians and soldiers. That was expected of the irregulars, but even the highly disciplined ranks of the standing army had dropped their usual protocol of staring directly ahead.

All of them waited for their king to lead them to war.

Rayant's expression was suddenly pained. He curled his lips into a grin but it didn't look right.

He said, "Aldrua, I free you from your duty to me."

She opened her mouth.

"You're going to come back," she said, clipping the words.

"Even if I do... it won't be to you. You have another. You have his child to look after."

"And yours."

"I have not been good around even her," Rayant shook his head.

"I free you."

He ran a hand down his face, clearing his expression.

"I never expected it all to turn out like this," he said, and on his face – for the first time in so long – a genuine half-smile.

"You'll come back," Aldrua said, taking a step forward. "We'll talk."

"About what? You don't love me Ald, you never did. And yet I still can't forgive you for loving another. Isn't that strange?" He was unguarded, speaking simply. She had never seen him like this. Had her words on the archery range changed his opinion of her? But then something occurred to her and she put a hand over her mouth. Did he... did he think he was going to *die?*

He turned and sprung onto his horse. He looked up at the sun, almost fully risen over the horizon. Orange light streaked over the city and its people.

With a final lingering look at her face, Rayant, King of Draldorn, turned away.

He was right about her. How could she love a man who had married simply to expand his lands yet had never even visited them all? And then Kendan had come and been perfect, had done all the right things, said all the right things. Made her feel special and important in a way being a queen never had.

Whereas Rayant... for all his being Draldorn's king was just some *man.* Getting things wrong. Not listening to her. Making her mad. In the brief time they had spent together, all they had done was argue.

She watched him go. The clanking, heaving cacophony from the army was like some vast machine as it tensed to follow, terrifying in its scale and coordination. The ground shook. Dust clouded everything. Aldrua's eyes stung with it, tearing to form a counter, or so she told herself. Over Draneth's gate, the flag of the Silver Spire was slowly lowered, as if in defeat. The king had departed.

Pena was looking at her closely.

"It's very dusty," she told her handmaiden. Pena handed her a handkerchief. Aldrua blotted her eyes.

"He'll come back," Pena said. "They always come back." Pena's cheeks were sallow.

Something occurred to Aldrua. "I'm sorry, Pena, I'm being thoughtless. You have someone, out there?"

"Yes. But he always comes back. If he knows what's good for him."

It was a common refrain. It never quite worked. Neither of them laughed.

Impulsively, Aldrua took the chambermaid's hand. One of the older nobles, standing closest, fanned away dust and scowled perfect white eyebrows in disapproval at this overt affection for a servant, but Aldrua didn't care.

They waited until the last soldier crested the hill.

But not everyone comes back, Aldrua was thinking. Not everyone.

* * *

Almost a year ago now, since she'd last seen Meryn.

Her last memory of her sister was just an image, static and flattened. Meryn in front of closed double doors, palms flat against them, leaning back, like she was holding the whole world out. Aldrua wasn't even sure which doors they were. They were grey and arched and massive, three times Meryn's height. The Council chambers? The Great Hall? It bothered her that she couldn't remember.

If only she had known at the time, she could have made herself remember every detail.

Meryn's last words to her:

"Big sis'... don't worry about me. I'm sorry."

And that was that. The secret of her departure kept intact.

If only Aldrua would have known then, she could have told her sister all the things she wanted to tell her.

Not that it would have made any difference. Not that it really mattered. Later, once Meryn had gone, and it was clear she wasn't coming back, Aldrua had thought back to what her face had looked like in those last moments, and filled in the gaps.

Maybe it was wrong to put words in Meryn's mouth, but Aldrua felt she knew what they would have been, even if they had never been predictable, even if they must now always remain unsaid.

Maybe Meryn knew she didn't need to say anything more than "don't worry". Sometimes words just muddled, and the truth was better left to years of understanding, of friendship – of love. A conversation's worth of words could not change the course of a lifetime together.

But maybe actions could have made a difference.

If only Aldrua had known, she could have hugged her sister goodbye.

* * *

Drak had a perfect chance to sneak out of Draneth. Its people gathered at one edge, leaving other ways clear.

But he didn't.

He'd been on the run, as the amateurs termed it, ever since Rilenheim had "happened" to the Ravens. The fact the City Watch had been mobilised was testimony to the extent to which Rilenheim had the king's ear. The Watch had swept the entire city looking for him. The old Geomancer must have been furious when he'd learned Drak had spoken to the queen not once, but twice.

Drak had resorted to hiding in one of the secret tunnels under the Keep. The Watch didn't check there, of course. It would take someone who had worked for the king to know such places even existed. Drak had been confident he'd got away clean, as would befit a man of his talents, but nevertheless, ever since leaving the Keep he'd been feeling uneasy.

He wore the outfit of a labourer. Loose tunic, belt, ragged trousers and boots. He'd borrowed them from an unlocked house, having unlocked it. To these he'd added a wide brimmed hat, which he'd borrowed from a passing head. And, so outfitted, he was able to join the crowd on the battlements of Draneth's outer wall. It was a decent place to observe the lay of the land. Height advantage, the same amateur might call it.

He carefully scanned the variety of insignias of the rows upon rows of soldiers. He had been military, long ago – what he thought of as his own amateur days. He could name the units from the symbols emblazoned on their surcoats or shields. He was careful to note the presence of a normally non-military group. Their particular insignia consisted of interlocking stonework, in a circular pattern. The City Guard. They had been drafted, seemingly in their entirety. Which left who, exactly, guarding the city?

Rayant was taking with him every man who could carry a sword, every healer who could stitch a wound. He even took the Council. The overly bearded band of old men sat on steeds which appeared far too big for them. They did not look pleased.

With everyone who could possibly be a threat gone, Drak should have no problem just strolling out of the city.

So why didn't he?

He watched Rilenheim ride away, row upon row of metal men clanking after him. It was an odd sight. Drak felt out of place. Normally he would be among them.

Still he made no move. He waited while the crowd dispersed around him. They mumbled and clasped hands to each other. There was a sense of loss spreading, which had them moving slowly, as if something physical had been taken from them. Soon he was alone on the wall, barring a single scout. A strange sight in herself. A young girl, barely a woman, in a tunic made for a man, no doubt chosen for her eyesight, or bravery, or possibly just insistence.

How serious did Rilenheim regard this threat, if he left the city in the hands of children?

Drak was familiar with this kind of move. It was the one made by tacticians who were faced with a threat they could not ignore. The one which would either win them their war completely, utterly and forever – or else obliterate them.

If they did not succeed, what happened to Draneth wouldn't matter.

Drak could see Aldrua down below, holding hands with her chambermaid, under the little open pavilion designated for the superior people. She was a strange one, their current queen, he considered. She'd never done anything interesting. Just turned up at parades, hung around the city, and dutifully went about siring – madaming? - the next generation of superior people. Then, one day, she'd thrown on a disguise and hired the White Ravens, against the wishes of a Geomancer. Very strange indeed.

He watched her talking with her chambermaid. Something else her kind weren't supposed to do. He could see a future with her, if circumstances were different. He liked to imagine it were possible. There were places he could show her, things he could give her a mere king couldn't. Drak was no fool. One day a younger man would turn up who was better at scouting, better at tracking, better at fighting; all beyond the benefits of experience. Drak would retire, and he'd need something to do. It was a shame she'd probably be dead by then. This tended to happen to people he met. They generally lived very dangerous lives, which often started just before hiring him.

The watchgirl moved away along the wall, watching very thoroughly indeed, as if open ground leading to scraggly trees could possibly hide a force capable of taking Draneth. But there was little to look at, and if she wanted to prove herself she only had to look at *him*. Catching a wanted fugitive on her first watch would be a fine career move. But when she did finally glance at him, it was just that, and he amused himself with a tip of his stolen hat. He followed this up with an exaggerated, blind squint in her direction and some pantomimed limping over to a wall, which he leaned on while apparently regaining his breath. Not fit for service, clearly.

All in all, he considered, he should be feeling perfectly safe.

But he wasn't.

In the corner of an eye, he thought he saw movement. He was too experienced a scout to give away that awareness. He just stood where he was for a while longer, apparently pondering the dust cloud which was rapidly taking over the Wide Road, as it snaked into the distance.

But he saw nothing else. He turned and jogged down the uneven steps to ground level. The main gate was nearby. Yes, there were still guards there, but, as was predictable, they were just old men. Possibly old *guards*, but either way they exhibited no recent experience of guardmanship. They might have been given his description, but that was likely the description of an armed Raven, not a harmless labourer, and even if it included his rather distinctive scars – the calling cards of his trade – he could likely talk his way past them, even on a bad day. He could certainly fight his way past them, probably even with his hat pulled down over his eyes.

So why did he hesitate?

He ground his teeth. This wasn't the time to lose confidence. The Ravens did the job. They never failed. Never. Not once. Even if there was only one left, which was a possibility that had crossed Drak's mind. And given what the queen had told him, this would not be a good time to start.

He wasn't sure if he believed her suspicions. The end of mankind seemed a little extreme. But he did believe she was on to *something*. Rilenheim with his geomantic feud and Meryn the exiled princess were clearly related. And then there was that whole thing with much of the population of Draldorn marching to war.

There – movement again!

Drak slowed. He tilted his hat down, casually scratched the back of his neck. He glanced over his shoulder. Seeing no-one, he ducked into an alley.

It was empty of people. An elderly dog snuffled around a pile of sacks by a door a little way down it. He walked briskly towards the door.

* * *

Rilenheim's shadow slipped into another shadow. This was a

more mundane shadow, that of a middle-aged woman trudging, eyes downcast, in the desired direction.

It rode with her to the alley entrance, where it slipped up to a drainpipe. It liked drainpipes. They were always dark and cool.

Below, the Raven had his ear to a door. Checking left and right – but not up – he turned its handle and leaned on it hard, bursting the feeble construct inwards.

The shadow slipped through a gap in a window frame, then had the freedom of a shadowy room.

It took position in a corner of the ceiling.

There was no one else in the room, except the Raven, who stepped over long splinters from the door, and frowned.

The shadow watched. It had tracked humans before, of course. It had been Rilenheim's helper for a long, long time. And this one was different. Interestingly different. It was what Rilenheim would have called an irritation.

The shadow wasn't concerned though.

It was, after all, only a shadow.

It waited, and waited. After that, it waited. Time didn't matter to it, as long as there was contrast; whether between light and dark, or action and inaction, or something and nothing – just so long as there was *difference.*

Though it was surprised the man it followed was so patient. He stood mostly stock still in the middle of the room, not looking at anything in particular, as if trying to see with his entire body, which the shadow knew he couldn't do.

Then, with remarkable abruptness, the man strode across the room into a hallway, straight out the front door, and proceeded to march over to Draneth's arched gate and on through as if he was Rilenheim himself.

It was still a bright day, and tracking and trailing was difficult for the shadow on bright days.

Especially with the Eye near. It didn't look much like an eye, but the shadow thought it as one. It always seemed watchful. Those two rings of ancient stone gave off waves of brightness, pale waves, possibly unnoticeable by the humans, but they made the shadow feel grey and faint. They had once been to Geomancers what contrast was to the shadow.

But it was fortunate for the shadow, and unfortunate for Drak, that this was the precise moment that Aldrua and Pena and a selection of colourful nobles happened to be returning into the city, bringing with them a mess of twisting flickering blots of darkness as their cloaks and hats and scarves shifted darkness about them.

The shadow slipped up the thin aisle created by a flag pole, and fluttered through the newly created clothes paths, then wavered through the pavilion's dark spots safely into the haven of trees. It liked trees, woods, forests. Somewhere where it would always be safe from becoming trapped or obliterated by a sudden burst of light. There were always dark places beneath trees.

It had little trouble in following Drak as he hastened away down the road, and even less so when he ducked into the brush and made his way cross-country, avoiding known paths. The Raven's attempt to stay unfollowed only made the shadow's task easier.

* * *

The army went north. Like some vast, amorphous beast, it surged along the Wide Road until it reached the Pentaret crossroads, then spilled onto the Kalastrade Back, where it bulked up and trampled the thorny ground into mush as it made its way in the direction of Haylen. Behind it there was left a trail of broken ground, spent provisions and refuse, and a few deserters who had hid in the merchant caravans that were run off the road.

Rilenheim was the beast's brain. He rode at its head and set a fast pace. He was still hunched in his cloak, still becowled, and he rode alone, distinctly apart from Rayant and his generals. The Geomancer remained silent, almost brooding, and didn't join them when they stopped to rest and eat. Rayant hadn't seen him or his horse consume a single morsel in weeks. Rayant was beginning to doubt that the thing he rode *was* a horse. At night, Rilenheim would disappear with it into the darkness, only to return at first light.

It grew colder the closer they got to their destination. It began to rain. Almost pleasantly, at first, just enough to cool them. But it was unrelenting, and soon they were clutching their coats close around their necks, blinking droplets from their eyes, and watching rivers spill down their noses; and one day they woke to find themselves enveloped in mist.

"We should remain encamped until it clears," Rayant said to Rilenheim. "We cannot see the path."

"You do not need to see, my king," Rilenheim replied, gazing into the mist. "All you need do is follow."

They did as he commanded. Rayant didn't see that they had much choice. He strained to see the Geomancer's hazy outline out ahead of them, just a single bulky shape, a ghostly shadow in the whiteness. He could not shake the impression of a silent spectre leading them to some inevitable doom.

Draneth's soldiers were noticeably subdued. Normally a lively group, they trudged with their eyes cast down to the mud under their feet. There was nothing else for them to see. They couldn't distinguish each other's faces, which made it difficult to hold normal conversation, and the mist was thick enough to make their voices sound thin and eerie; and so they marched on in silence.

* * *

One day the sun itself seemed to vanish from the sky. That vague, misty bowl of orange disappeared and did not return. The men muttered to each other and cursed the day itself, and began to wonder what it was they would find at the end of their ill-fated march.

Rayant once again asked Rilenheim to delay until they could know where they were. He was worried for the men, he told the Geomancer. Imaginations were beginning to fill in the gaps created by the mist, and an imaginative army was one which could look into the future and be afraid.

Rilenheim just laughed at him. Rayant couldn't see the Geomancer's face when he did so. The laugh seemed to come from all around.

"You said you would obey me," Rilenheim said, "if I were to deliver your kingdom. And that is what I am doing, my king. Why should I be concerned with the human predilection for make-believe?"

Rayant had no answer to that.

It was only on the fourteenth day of blindness that a chill wind rushed down and over them and washed all the mist away, and their position became clear. They had made better progress than Rayant had guessed, but not quite in the direction he thought they were taking.

Directly on their left were the vast, snowy forms of the mountains of Yastran. The range stretched as far back and forth as he could see, its spiky edges sliding into the sky amidst hazy blizzards. To their right were the wide open spaces of the Haylen plains, which stretched all along the range, its constant companion until the mountains sunk into the ocean at the peak of Kilsmouth.

The Beast paused, clanking to a standstill.

"Rilenheim?" Rayant asked.

"There, up ahead, is the path we must take," Rilenheim said.

And Rayant stared at what the others were already staring at. He had never been this way before. He hadn't even been aware there was a path here. It wasn't on any map. Sometimes even history forgot such things. He blinked repeatedly, but it didn't change what he saw.

It was as if someone had simply taken a knife and cut out a slice of mountain. A path right through Yastran, right up to the sky. A narrow pass of perfectly smooth, white, unblemished rock. The stonework was perfect. Whatever craft was at work had not succumbed to weathering. It must have taken years, decades – possibly centuries – to carve such a way through a mountain, or at least it would have if it had been made by humankind. There was no sign as to what had happened to the excess stone. Neither sign of any settlement nearby, nor that there had ever been such a settlement. There was simply a gap. It was almost casual. Just some oddity left behind by something passing this way, a thousand years before.

"Behold the Rorlan Divide," Rilenheim said. "We can be through before nightfall. We can attack before Herendak is even aware we are here."

Rayant just stared, in awe.

"What could do that?" he said.

Rilenheim just chuckled. But there was an ominous tone to it.

"One day," the Geomancer said, "before you die, I'll take you to Ilris."

And he rode on, without seeming to give any instruction to his mount.

"Was that your mist, Rilenheim?" the king called after him. "The plains are normally windy places. Mists do not last!"

There was no reply. Rayant exchanged looks with those around him. Battle hardened colonels of many campaigns were ashen-faced and hesitant.

Nevertheless, they let the Geomancer lead them into the darkness of the unnatural pass.

* * *

Drak climbed the crumbling steps of the slope. The sun beat down and the sky was clear. It was almost midday. Almost *exactly* midday. He slowed down his ascent. The path, once wide and magnificent, was long overgrown. At places there were no steps at all, and he was forced into a kind of four-limbed scramble.

The hill was steep, massive and old. Not old in the way that all hills were old, that everything was old, being ultimately made of the same stuff. No, it was old as a place, as a location known to humans, named a long time ago by the people who had built the steps.

Drak scrambled ever higher. He pulled at vines, used them to help him bound over the branches of fallen trees, and climbed with his sword as a piton where necessary. When a gap opened up through the foliage enough for him to see the view, he could almost understand the Builders.

He knew about the Builders. It was an oddity of what the Ravens did that, in their travels, they sometimes came across scattered remnants of the past – though it was not at all an oddity that they then sold these remnants, or at least the knowledge of their location, to those who sought to study what had been. It was these people who had called the ancient peoples Builders; as they had left so much behind.

Drak stared at what had always been visible below. The Ralman running through craggy hills, skirting vast ruffled fields filled with wild, spiky cow-like creatures. The great bowl of Orthal Lake. These were stunning enough vistas, but the eye was caught by more extreme sights.

To the east, the Onyx Plateau, though Drak had been there and it was not made of onyx. A giant, town-sized slab of... something. Something which was entirely flat. It gleamed a deep brown and was home only to a strange kind of lumpy creature which moved about on suction cups, much like an octopus. It wasn't clear whether they, or the plateau, had come first.

All around, but mostly to the west, there were the Pits. No one had come up with a better name for them, though some of the larger ones had the honour of being named by those who'd been there first, or at least who had the biggest mouths in taverns. They were difficult to get to. The ground around was torn, jagged and steep. Auerton was the biggest, named after Erton Auerton, the explorer. It was awash with a strange kind of fungus, which glowed visibly even from Draldorn on dark nights, and which hissed when it rained.

Erton had wasted away and died within a month of his return to Draneth, a sunken and ghastly wraith of a man.

And as far south as the eye could see, just on the limits of vision, the Sea Wall. That far Drak had never been. Sailors who had tried that way had made it no further. They had found no way over, and those that came back spoke strangely of what they'd seen. Drak had no desire to go see for himself. He wasn't much prone to superstition, but there was something very real about the way previously bold men were unable to meet his gaze.

Yes, all in all, he could see why the Builders had done what they did.

In the days when the sky was free of rings, they must have looked upon the world and been thankful. They had vast trees to shelter under, bright fruits to eat, a warm sun. It was only natural that they devote themselves to those who gave them such. Drak had no trouble understanding that. To look upon the works of Geomancers, when even fire was new and mysterious, would make even a Raven humble.

Historians had unearthed a reasonable picture of what had occurred. At first the Builders had praised the magnificence around them. They had lit tiny candles to the great ones, built little mounds. The Ravens found them still, sometimes, these mounds, in the wilder parts of Draldorn. Some still contained little offerings of shiny things. Bits of rock, gemstones, fragments of silver. Often little engraved boxes of ground diamonds, which seemed to hold a certain significance. And with such the Builders had given their gratitude.

Drak was nearing the top of the slope. The sun was rising ever higher in the sky. He slowed. Despite the terrain, he was still moving too quickly for his purpose.

He passed the poles, then, still there, after so very long. They jutted into the ground on either side of the path, at even intervals, with the odd gap where one had succumbed to fallen debris, or rain and wind, or a careless traveller.

They were mostly missing, these days, the skulls which had once adorned them.

Then had come the days of awe. The world was a place of bright moons and burning sun and savage rains. Forces they could not understand had battered and bruised the Builders. Floods and earthquakes and pain and death, and Drak could understand that these did not seem to be just natural events. The masters must have been angry with them. Coincidence and randomness were advanced ideas to these people – hell, in Drak's opinion, they were *still* sophisticated ideas, even to the people of Draldorn. Meaning was too easily assigned to that which had no meaning. It was a rare person who saw things as they were, as things which happened because of things which happened. Drak had seen such cause and effect time and time again, most noticeably on the battlefield. Why did one friend live while another died? Was it because of fate, or the act of a deity – or was it because one muscle was faster than another?

But to a Builder nothing happened without a will – and there were such powerful wills in the world.

They had learnt the concept of barter. They had started to offer gifts no longer in thanks, but in exchange. An illness hit a village, they would offer grain. A poor harvest, they would give up their finest spears. A storm might be worth mounds of treasure delivered to as high a place as the brave would carry it. But still storms hit, and still diseases ravaged, and newborns still died, and communities were still savaged by wild beasts. Rings of blue had begun to appear in the sky. The Builders moved beyond awe, to fear. They offered livestock, opened throats, spilt blood, drenched alters in it. Pigs and sheep and deer were cut up and emptied and burned to tell the masters that they were willing to do whatever was necessary – if only the storms would stop, the beasts would leave, that they would be left alone to live.

And so, inevitably, in the last days, had come the temples.

Drak saw evidence of walls as he came higher, just lone, scrappy sections of tumbled stone that had not been reclaimed by the natural world they had tried to defy. The lost parts of them now belonged to moss and insects.

And, finally, he reached the hill's apex, and the temple.

It was a dome, squatting at the top of the hill. It was remarkably free of invading vegetation. A layer of ash – fresh ash – surrounded it, slowly being whipped away by wind. It was made of something which looked like silver, but which had not tarnished with age, and was as bright as it ever had been. It stung the eyes.

The massive doors, also silver-like, opened at a touch. Drak entered, stood in the doorway for a few seconds – judging that just long enough – and pulled them to behind him. They boomed.

It was almost pitch-black inside.

For now.

It must have been a particularly painful way to die. The temple consisted of a single, spherical chamber. The dome visible from outside simply continued into the ground. The room echoed with frightening loudness when he stepped forward. Everything was solid and sure, hewn from massive blocks of the same strangely shiny material, and fitted together with little in the way of creasing. The construction was a remarkable example of metalwork, given the sophistication of the people who had built it. They may well have had help, or had very closely observed the works of the Geomancers. Or maybe much of it was stolen.

The focal point of the chamber was four manacles in the floor at its centre. A rail ran around a man-sized area. The curve of the floor was only broken in four places, where it had been built up into seat-shapes.

Directly above centre there was a gap for a sloped opening, currently curled shut. A chain ran from it to one of the room's edges.

Drak stepped over to the manacles, with care not to slip. Casually, he pulled out his waterskin, and drained it. He had built up quite a thirst, and the sun was almost at its highest point. He dumped it to the ground, in the centre of the chamber, and spun it idly with his boot.

His timing had been perfect.

The sun finally reached its highest point. Gears ground. A mechanism sprung into life.

He leapt forward.

Light shot into the room – but quickly became more than light. It scattered through hollow pathways in the metal, focussed by mirror-like surfaces, and blasted out into the centre of the chamber, filling the place with ghostly silver light.

Obliterating every shadow.

Except one.

Drak leapt for his waterskin, still discarded in the middle of the chamber. Before he could be fried, he twisted on the cap with fingers already sizzling. He hurled a piece of cloth around it, which started to smoke, and wrapped it tight as he darted away.

He heaved the door open and fell away from the furnace, narrowly preventing himself from sliding down the sheer path outside. Without delay, he secured the cloth in place with twine.

He lay panting on the cool ground. The waterskin was bulging, at one end, then the other. It bucked and writhed and at one point managed to leap up off the ground.

"I am Drak of the White Ravens," Drak mocked at it, his smirk making his eyes bright. "And you are Rilenheim's shadow, aren't you? Trying to be *my* shadow. Trying to find Meryn for your master, I would wager. Is Rilenheim really that desperate? Or perhaps he regrets not tying up loose ends?"

He stood. The shadow continued to writhe in its container. Drak looked down at it.

"Got you, you bastard," he added.

Chapter 17

The chase through Homefire wood lasted two more days and two more nights. Progress was slow. Meryn did the best she could with the makeshift crutch, but with little feeling in either leg, it was left to Drael to support her weight. Whilpan wasn't much use with his arm the way it was, and Brogan refused to even go near her. So they all struggled on in silence, barely looking at each other, each busy with their own thoughts.

They got little rest. They stopped marching only for minutes at a time, and only when Meryn told them they could. They would slump to the ground, dropping right where they'd been standing, grateful for any kind of respite. Meryn would stand staring back the way they'd came, until she'd prod Drael with her crutch and tell them, "I can feel it near," or, "It's found our trail," or, "Drael, I don't know where it is and I'm afraid."

Eventually the wood thinned into fields and Drael clasped Brogan's shoulder and shook Whilpan's hand. He nodded respectfully to Meryn.

"Almost there," he said. "Just a little further. We're out of the woods."

Nevertheless, free from the shelter of the trees he felt exposed. They seemed to be only crawling along the massive fields of once carefully tended crops towards Eyhold. The condition of the fields was a worry. These crops were the lifeblood of Eyhold, and the many farming communities which surrounded it. That the fields appeared neglected did not bode well for what they would find when they arrived.

The chase became almost surreal the next day.

As the sun rose, Whilpan cried out. The rest of them looked where he did.

Behind them, barely a speck on the horizon, was the Wrilsch. The reason it hadn't yet caught them was clear, at least to those with the eyes for it. This group didn't include Brogan. Drael explained it to him.

"You really hurt it, Broge. You crushed its leg with that mace swing. Its leg is... mostly gone. It's dragging the rest behind itself, moving in kind of a bearlike crouch."

It was doing so slowly, but relentlessly. Any other creature would have long since given up its prey. But this wasn't just any creature. It had an intelligence to it, a purpose. A purpose given to it by, according to Meryn, a Geomancer.

Being able to so judge their pursuers' position clearly was what made the chase so bizarre.

It was slow, but didn't need to rest. They moved faster, but had to pause to rest and get what sleep they could. They'd stop to sleep with it out of sight, and awake to see it in a distant field. Its pace was constant, its stamina unyielding. It gave no hint of frustration at being so often so close to its prey, but never quite able to catch them. At one point – and this was certainly only his imagination – he could have almost thought it stopped to wave at him.

On two occasions they stopped long enough to salvage food from the overgrown vegetable gardens of deserted farms. They pulled up tomatoes with the Wrilsch a tomato's throw away, its presence so constant they could regard it almost casually – if it wasn't so entirely terrifying.

They munched on the tomatoes as they walked. They were soft and maggoty, yet greatly welcome given how long ago it had been since their last meal.

"Doughty little bastard, isn't it?" Whilpan said one night, of the Wrilsch. "Tempting to go back and finish it off."

"Be my guest," Drael said.

"Or maybe split up. See who is goes after," Whilpan went on, getting at what he really wanted to get at.

"We already know," Drael said.

They marched on without further comment.

The little group arrived at Eyhold just as it started to rain.

The foreboding grey walls of the castle rose up against the shimmering lake behind.

"This is where we leave you," Drael said.

"Wait," Meryn answered, squinting ahead. "There's no one on the walls, and the drawbridge is lowered. I see no firelight, no smoke.

No movement."

Whilpan started cursing.

"There'll be someone home," Drael said.

"Yes, yes, of course," said Whilpan. "So go. Good luck."

"There's no one there," Meryn said. "Somehow, I knew that. I..."

"There must be somewhere else-"

"No. This is where we must go. I can see all ways, and this is quickest."

Brogan must have been thinking what Drael was thinking. He put his hand on Drael's shoulder, adding force to his memories.

"We better take a look," Drael said, to more cursing.

* * *

They hobbled into the courtyard. It was completely deserted. Vast, silent and empty. Drael had lived at Eyhold for a long time. The courtyard was normally a busy place, lively with labourers, cobblers, coopers and hoopers. But the kennels were empty, as were the chicken coops; there was no familiar barking or squawking, no hum of voices or footsteps. Where were the trappers and hunters, bearing meat on spiked rods? Where were the servants going back and forth with buckets of water?

"Wait here," he told the others. He walked across the courtyard, trying to ignore his sense of unease. He went into the nearest entrance to the castle proper. The kitchens, normally so bursting with life, were empty. There were piles of ash still in hearths, some blown out across the floor. The fires had burned out long ago.

He made his way through the rest of the ground floor. His bootsteps were loud and lonely. Not a single sign of life. He stopped at the armoury to pick up a sword. There weren't any. The weapon racks were empty. The hooks from which crossbows had hung were bare.

He should go back for Brogan, he thought, but didn't. He took a winding staircase up to its end, stopping to check each floor – though skipping the first floor – all the while expecting more of the same, but nevertheless hoping for some sign of life, no matter how small.

But, as expected, all deserted.

Coming back down to the first floor, he stood for a moment looking down the desolate grey hall at the painting at the far wall. It had been turned around to face the wall. He could only see its back.

He went and checked every room. At Ethi's he froze outside for a long time. He still thought of it as her room, even though this had stopped being the case two weeks after the accident.

Finally, he pushed the door open.

The room was very tidy. The rug was straight and uncreased. The old chair was pushed under the little desk. The desk was clear. The bed was made. It all looked as it had always looked. It was cold though, and silent, and smelt of mouldering wood.

Two weeks she had lain there, in that bed, not speaking, not moving, with not even her eyes open, except that one time he had opened one of them by hand, lifting the lid so very gently, and seen...

nothing.

He had only ever been allowed in by night, very late, by the duchess, when the duke was elsewhere. The duke had wanted him dead immediately.

Ethi had died slowly. They couldn't make her eat or drink. Her skin had sagged. Her lips had deflated. Her hands were no longer soft, at the end.

Somewhere past these memories was the rest of her, but they were too difficult to get through, too painful to think past.

He went on to the duke's room.

Empty, deserted, the same as everywhere else.

He went back down.

"They've all gone," he said. "There's no one here."

They took Meryn into the kitchen. Drael lit one of the hearths with flint and tinder and searched the cupboards for food which hadn't spoilt. Brogan and Whilpan went to raise the drawbridge, which, judging by the sounds that floated across the courtyard, consisted mostly of Brogan winding the winch mechanism while Whilpan continually informed him that the bridge persisted in its rise.

They ate a meal of stale bread, salted ham and much water from the well, while the evening drew on and the sky dimmed. They didn't talk much. The fire crackled and smoked and unleashed from somewhere the smell of goose fat. Drael could barely keep his eyes open. They kept eating long after they normally would have stopped. The others were so hunched and shadowed and slow as they chewed he considered they were like what hungry statues would look like.

Waiting, Drael thought. Waiting for the inevitable.

* * *

Whilpan sat in the firelight, watching the others. Mostly watching Meryn.

He had to do something. He knew he had to do *something*, he just didn't know what.

He had known moments like this before. Just before he'd first snatched a stranger's bag counted as one of them. Knowing that he *had* to act as he was being watched – and judged – by the crowd he had fallen in with. Dared by their eyes to be just like them. Later there was the time when he had lain in wait in an alley, watching as a shopkeeper left his store, carefully locking it behind him. And later still there was the hesitation in the clammy dungeons of this very castle, fighting the urge to just run, but instead kneeling to pick the lock on Drael's cell door.

Right here, right now was one of those moments. He had to do something. He had no choice. He knew it would change things. But he didn't yet know what it was he had to do.

He wasn't one for planning, never had been.

He felt the outline of the dagger he kept strapped to his sleeve and kept watching Meryn.

For the good of all of them, he had to *do* something.

* * *

The Wrilsch came at the walls that night.

Chapter 18

The world moved around the shadow. It could feel it. The world was flowing, where it could not. It had flung itself around its prison of skin until all its memory of colour was leached away. Without light, it had nothing to define itself. Now it took the shape of its surroundings, expanding and contracting with the fall and rise of its captor's footfalls. A kind of frustrated lethargy was building into an ache.

At some point, the outside movement stopped. It was replaced by noise, crunchy and distant. Digging. Hard ground. Hard mud.

Weightlessness. A fall. An impact, which spread it out as far as the leathern material around it allowed. More noise, similar to before. Slowly, pressure built upon it.

Buried alive.

The frustrated ache called for action, for fight, for anything. But it had nothing, could do nothing – and the pressure built.

So it waited. There was nothing else it could do. It could not move; there was no light.

Soon the weight was steady, and even vibrations ceased.

Time passed. It lost track of how long it was in the dark. It became unsure if time even continued to pass. There was no way to mark its passage. There was no sun, no moons, no rings, moving across the sky. There was no candlelight or lanterns. No fires, flickering light at those who had mastered life.

It was like the beginning. The beginning of everything, when time was new, before humans had come and named it. The shadow had not really *Been*, until that very first light. A simple spark; and it *Was*. Later it learnt from humans the concept of a Creator, but it had not seen one. It had just *Became*.

It would have been angry at a Creator, if it had known what one was. For a long while, there had been nothing. Just darkness. Nothing for it to know, nothing for it to witness. It did not know its purpose. It *Was*, but that was all, and it did not know why.

It could still recall the details of this old existence, though it did not like to. It had learnt a lot since then, learnt not to dwell, to keep ever moving, ever lively. It now knew the human word for its condition at the time.

It had been *lonely*.

It did not care much for life, in general. It never had. It had no time for animals and plants. It did not care for their company. These things had only arrived much later, and were uninteresting, worthless, grey, uniform and bland. With them the sun and the moons and the stars and for these the shadow was glad, because they gave it the contrast to move about, but it had never found solace in those living things which crawled and consumed and died.

But humans. Ah, humans. Only for a tiny speck of time had humans *Been*. But they had come, just lately, when conditions were right, when all had formed and settled, and they had brought with them light, in all forms. Wondrous forms. Fires, both small and large, and tame and wild. Made of burning wood and wax and oil, night and day and always moving, ever moving, never ceasing, shadows flying, whirling. Everywhere there was light and shadow and movement and life and then the shadow had known what lonely was; what it had been and no longer was.

It lived to witness the lives of humans.

Now it was trapped by one. In the dark, all alone. It could not be this way. Not again. Not for millennia. Not now that it understood what time and loneliness were.

It could not bear it. This had to end. It needed to end. It called out, to the only one who could hear it.

Rilenheim.

Help me.

I am here.

It didn't care who heard it.

It could not know that Rilenheim was far away, too far away to hear its cry.

But Herendak heard.

He was much, much closer.

Chapter 19

The Wrilsch couldn't get in to Eyhold. But it made a lot of noise about it. Growls and wails, mostly.

Drael stood on the battlements and let relief wash away anxiety. He had been prepared to fight. No matter how that would end. There was simply nowhere else they could run to. But they had bought themselves some time. The Wrilsch was unable to break through Eyhold's defences.

Whilpan jeered at the thing, and managed to put two arrows in it, despite his arm. It bellowed at him, almost taunting, daring him to come down and fight it face-to-face. It did not seem hurt in any way.

They went back to the kitchen. Whilpan scratched at his beard and muttered to himself as they walked. He finally grabbed Drael's shoulder, just outside the door.

"I can't just stand by any longer," he said. His voice was low and urgent. "We *could* leave her here, Dray. No, listen to me! You were planning on doing that anyway when we got to a place of safety. And here we are. Let's not complicate things."

"No-"

"Yes! She'll be perfectly safe if she stays inside. You've done your good deed. Well done! You've saved one of your betters. Maybe now you'll forget that nonsense with-"

"Shut up."

"Dray-"

"I mean it. Shut up."

Whilpan did so. But his face went red. He spluttered for a moment.

Finally, after all this time, he snapped.

He pushed Drael so hard he almost fell.

"Maybe I should do what you couldn't! Maybe I should do what the king needs to do! Maybe I'm the only damn person in this kingdom willing to do what's right for the good of everyone!"

"Calm down! What the hell are you talking about?"

A voice from behind the door.

"I *can* hear you, you realise."

They glared at each other for a moment.

"What I'm talking about, Drael," Whilpan said, loudly and clearly, "is taking a knife to her."

"I'm warning you-"

"I'm not an idiot, Drael. I know you thought about it. Brogan told me. She's a traitor! She was an exile! She obeys the whims of a Geomancer! The king wants her dead! What are we doing protecting her? She's a danger to us all!"

"Listen to me-"

"Not this time, Drael!" Whilpan had a knife in his hand. His hand shook.

"What are you doing?"

"Something is happening, don't you see? Everyone is gone! Everyone we knew here! A Wrilsch has come south! She had Herendak's baby! She already admitted she's part of all this!"

"But she was with us when we got here, remember – how could she have done this? Be reasonable. We can't afford to turn on each other!"

"She turned on us, first! She sided with the Geomancer!"

"Put that down!"

"Stay back, Drael! I'll stick you too!"

He was through the door in an instant.

Drael grasped for him, but was too late. Always too late.

Meryn sat on the floor in front of the fire, her ruined leg stretched out in front of her. It was too close to the flames, but that didn't seem to bother her. Her eyes were closed. Brogan was frozen mid-action, in the act of piling up more firewood by the hearth, his mouth open. All was dark except where the fire shivered.

"I do this for mankind!" Whilpan cried.

Meryn opened her eyes. They were black mirrors. Whilpan stopped short. In them, he saw his own face, twisted and distorted. He saw his knife, curved and broken into angles. All was dark, and severe, and nightmarish.

It was his hesitation which broke him.

* * *

Her voice entered his head: "You are a thief, a robber, a murderer."

He heard the knife clatter to the ground, but he didn't have a knife, and there wasn't a ground. Her eyes were everything. They were unblinking and all-encompassing.

"There are more of them, now," she said, directly to him, to him alone, so quietly he had to strain to hear. "Do you understand me?"

"I-" he tested his voice. It echoed, in whatever this place was. Inside his head? Hers? "Yes." He could feel her surprise, her uncertainty. She hadn't meant to do this. He had threatened her, and she had reacted.

"There are more coming south," she continued. "They are coming for us."

Whilpan tried to turn his head, to break from her implacable gaze. He could feel sweat dripping down his forehead, but couldn't move his hand to wipe it off.

"What is happening?" he stammered.

"I..." She was suddenly right in front of him. "I could live inside you," she said. "For a time." He felt her excitement. "This must be what... I think I see at last. They are coming for all of us now, whereas the one he sent first was for me and me alone. Do you see? To keep me alive, just as to keep them alive. A joining. His way to restore them all...

"But... but he underestimates me. He has underestimated humanity. I will not give in. I refuse to die. I refuse to change! So try to take a knife to me; try! You will see how I bend to the wills of others!"

For a moment she filled him, and he thought she would do as she said, that she'd stay, and he would be locked away, a prisoner in some small corner of his own mind.

But then she tensed, and was gone from him.

He fell to his knees; he had knees again. The floor was cracked under them.

She was gone from him, but he felt different. She had washed out like a tide, leaving uncovered detritus behind. He thought long buried thoughts, felt long buried pains and regrets.

He heard her voice again, but it was normal this time, coming in by the ears.

"Perhaps you are right, Mister Whilpan," she was saying, dreamily. "Perhaps you have been right all along. Perhaps you should all go, and should not have helped me in the first place. For it is indeed I who has given the Geomancers this way back in."

* * *

"Don't say that," Drael said. "You didn't mean any of this to happen. That means something."

She just shrugged.

Whilpan stood there, shaking.

"What...?" Drael trailed off. "Did I miss something? What just happened?"

Meryn looked away. She reached for the poker, and leant forward to prod at burning timbers. The fire caught flat and colourless in those strange eyes.

Whilpan was staring at her with his own eyes wide and brimmed with tears.

"Whilp?" Drael asked.

Whilpan shot him back a look he couldn't decipher.

"Whilp, if you want to go..." Drael shrugged. "I think Meryn's right, Whilp."

Whilpan coughed, and swallowed, and looked like he was holding back sick.

"What? You'd stay with *her?*"

"You don't want to be here, Whilp. You helped us get this far, but now I think you should go. In truth... I'm surprised you came with us at all."

"You... I..." Whilpan coughed again, hard, and wiped away something with his sleeve. "So that's it, then, is it, Drael?" he said. "Just like that? Well, whatever you say! Don't know what I was thinking wasting my time anyway! Come on then, Brogan. Let's get out of here! It's dangerous here. Let's get as far away as possible from this dead-eyed *thing.*"

The big man, inevitably, shook his head.

Whilpan looked to him, then to Drael, and finally to Meryn. At this last he shuddered.

"Bah!" He spat at the fire. He missed; it hit the floor, slid down a crack between the stone slabs. He jutted out a finger at Drael. "I'm not a coward, just you remember that! I rescued you, remember? I rescued you from the very dungeons under our feet when the duke dumped you down there!"

"To save your own skin too... don't forget that."

"You still owe me," Whilpan said.

"Then go."

Whilpan grabbed a sack and started shoving food into it.

"What a waste of time," he said, "I pull you out from right under the duke's nose, from certain death, and now you just throw your life away. Might as well not have bothered."

Whilpan paused by the door, poised to say something, but eventually, didn't. He went out shaking his head, his cheeks sallow, his eyes filled with fear and confusion. The door swung closed behind him.

* * *

Drael let out a long breath. He stepped forward to get a better look at Meryn's face, now turned to the fire. He leaned on a long table with feigned casualness. The table was scored with a variety of shades of brown where cooks had been lax with their instruments. Why he noticed this, he had no idea. He ran his fingers over the cracks.

"You may also go if you wish," Meryn murmured, not taking her eyes off the fire. "I'll be safe here. From two, or three of them, maybe, if they are the same kind of thing as this one. And this is where I should be."

"I don't think Herendak would send more of the same thing that had already failed," Drael said.

"Did you see its necklace?"

Drael nodded. "Same heraldry as your ring."

"My sister has a necklace just like that."

"Do you think-"

"No."

"Then-"

"It is not difficult to make a necklace."

"I guess not. Meryn, what do you mean by 'where you should be'? You've said that before, but never explained."

Her brow creased. "I am closer here. I know it doesn't make sense. But I have to find my daughter and, somehow, this place is closest. This is the way. This is the path. But the path is yet to open. We – I – have to be ready when it does.

"Don't look at me like that, Drael. It makes no more sense to me than it does you."

Drael just shook his head.

"I still don't understand where everyone is," Drael said, after a time, deliberately changing the subject.

"The soldiers would have been called to Draneth," Meryn said. "The summons has gone out, even to small outposts such as this one."

"Not everyone here was a soldier."

"I'm sure many were. At any rate, we can look for clues in the morning. I don't know about you, but I'm looking forward to sleeping in a bed tonight."

It did seem like a good idea to focus on practicalities. He helped her up the stairs to the living quarters on the first floor. They made their way down the hall he knew so well.

"Here's a bedroom," she said, clearly in pain, at the first door.

"No. Not that one."

"It's as good as any."

"No, further along."

"It'll *do* Drael," she said, pulling toward it. He helped her in, refusing to acknowledge who's room it had been. It was the one with the best view, the room of everyone's favourite.

He left as quickly as he could.

Drael couldn't bring himself to sleep in any of those rooms. He dragged some blankets out and instead slept in the hall, by the stairs, on guard.

They spent the night restlessly. The Wrilsch howled at the castle, didn't sleep itself. Drael got up three times and went out to watch it. It was roaming up and down along the walls, testing them for weaknesses. He mirrored its movements from the battlements, silently observing. Once it stopped and scrabbled at the base of the wall, before growling up at him, and moving on. He couldn't shake the idea that it would find a way in. It was beyond relentless. If there was a way, it would find it.

The castle seemed even more silent at night.

"Where are you all?" he asked of it.

* * *

He was woken a final time by Meryn stepping over him to get to the stairway. She was wearing one of Ethi's nightdresses. She was spindly and haggard, almost insubstantial, like Ethi had been at the end. He had come straight from his nightmare and so for a moment he didn't know where he was or *when* he was and he could have almost believed...

But when Meryn leant open the stairway door she rested against it for a moment and he saw her face; he knew then where they were and what was happening and he was suddenly horribly awake. There was a sheeny pallor to her that was almost ghostly. She entered the stairway, making heavy use of the railing. Her eyes were briefly closed while she apparently gathered her strength. She looked so young with them closed. He should tell her to go back to bed, he considered, to rest while she could, but something stopped him. It took a few moments for him to realise what it was. He was frowning as she closed the door behind her.

He lay there, thinking. It was still dark outside. It was cold, but he was warm and comfortable enough to not want to move. Listening carefully, he could hear little above the light rainfall. He wasn't sure why he thought there was a chance of him hearing the Wrilsch. His eyes were drawn to the frame of the backwards picture at the end of the hall. He wondered why it had not been moved elsewhere.

Wait. Why had Meryn taken the stairway *up?*

He got to his feet. He threw on a tunic, wrapped his blanket around his shoulders and went after her.

He couldn't find her on the next two floors, but the door up into the belfry was open. But she wasn't there either. He made his way around the bells so as to reach the ladder leading further upwards. There were two bells in total, half his height each, their clappers tied safely out of the way, otherwise the wind might have been able to move them. The wind was alive in the tower, thrumming against the gears and pulleys. It made the bells even more silent, and the castle even more deserted.

He climbed the ladder out into the open air. He had only been here at Eyhold's highest point once before. The timekeepers had shown him how they did what they did. He hadn't stayed long. There was only a waist-high lip around the wide expanse of the roof to prevent accidents, and the stonework became slippery in the rain.

This was where the sundial told the timekeepers when to ring the bells to herald each new day, or to indicate the start of a festival, or where they could simply look out all around the castle and know to ring the bell in warning, to tell everyone to run and take shelter inside because the drawbridge was about to be raised.

The flagpole ran even higher, of course, though no flag on it at all now, and the pole itself was keening at a strange angle, like it had been hit by something.

Meryn was lying flat on the ground, staring up at the stars.

"Meryn?" he whispered. She didn't answer. "Are you hurt?"

For a moment she lay there on the wet stone like she was waiting to be entombed within it.

She said, "You should be resting," though not in a whisper. Her voice put to rest any thought of ghosts.

"Difficult to sleep," he said. "Meryn... what are you doing?"

"I am navigating."

"Navigating?"

"Yes. Navigating. Plotting a course."

"I know what navigating means. I sail. Or I used to, anyway."

"Well then. That is what I am doing."

He watched her as she navigated. It appeared to consist of lying very still in the damp, while squinting at her little finger as she dragged it across the sky one finger's width at a time. The wind played with the edges of her nightdress, where they weren't sodden. He should probably look away.

She was using her finger to *measure* something, he realised.

He drew his blanket closer around him. The height of this place seemed suddenly insignificant compared to what was above.

"Are you planning a trip to the moons, Meryn?"

"Herendak," she said, "once told me," she waved both arms for emphasis, looking for a moment like a deeply confused swimmer, "that certain things above are as the things below. Mirror like. The Geomancers made them that way. They had to..."

She trailed off. Clouds drifted overhead, obscuring her view of the sky.

"I don't understand."

"Lie with me." She splashily patted the stone next to her. "Here.

Come on."

"I'm not going to..." but he was already there, and she was pulling him down by his blanket, which she then took and pulled over herself.

He lay down next to her.

"I see clouds, Meryn."

"Wait a moment."

"For it to rain?"

"Why is everyone so afraid of rain? It's just – there, look!"

Through a gap he saw stars, just ordinary stars, though then her bony hand was overhead, guiding his view.

"Do you know your constellations, young Drael?"

"I used to."

"There are the *lycel* and the *teyrs* and the *kyrintars,* in the old languages, though of course they are much more bland when rendered in the new." She chuckled to herself. "Rendered? I may have spent too much time with Heri."

"I don't see what-"

"Straight up above us, Drael, is the shadow of Eyhold. Where is Draneth from here? Two days march? That is *so* fingers. See? If I measure it out? Are you following? And here is Orton, just as so, and... I could go on."

She skipped across the sky with her fingers, and his heart beat faster as the pattern became clear. How had he not noticed this before? The constellations were shaped from the places below.

But it was impossible for anyone to notice, because they didn't match *all* places.

"What is going on up there?" he murmured.

"I told you this was the path. These are the roads the Geomancers left so very long ago. These are the places that will become portals when Herendak begins the end. So now you see. When the time comes, I intend to know the way.

"If you thought the way *we* were chased was strange, wait until you see how we do the chasing. We simply wait until he opens the door for us. Now, I don't know what the door will look like when he does. Or even exactly where it will be. But if we act quickly, we can get to Herendak before it is too late. I know where he has to go. He told me. And he will find me there with him once again. If Herendak ever mistook me for a fool, he will be finally made to understand that..."

She crossed her arms over the blanket.

"Now shut up and let me concentrate."

Drael did so for as long as he could. He spent the time tracing the places above, wondering why some places were paths and some were not, and considering that right now it didn't matter one bit, let alone back then when things were different. Paths only had a very short lifespan. You had to wait to take one. And then you could never take it back.

"Meryn," he said, when he couldn't hold the question in any longer, "why did you help Herendak?"

She didn't hesitate. "Have you ever been in love, Drael?"

It was almost an accusation.

He looked at her sidelong. She was still intently examining the sky.

"I know you have," she went on. "Brogan told me what happened here. Now... imagine... what would it be like to watch the *entire world* decay in front of your eyes?"

Chapter 20

Aldrua had a way out. The solution had come to her in the middle of the night, two nights ago. She hadn't slept since.

She sat in the banquet hall, surrounded by people. The smell of smoky roast pheasant filled the hall. A minstrel played a pleasant tune. There was much discussion, about the war, about past wars, about the king. Aldrua said not a word. She would not be drawn into conversation. She barely heard the conversation. Her face was grey.

Pena was watching her carefully, concernedly.

By her belt, Aldrua couldn't even feel the presence of her new dagger, but she was so very aware of it.

She closed her eyes and imagined the Keep crumbling around her. Wall by wall, until nothing was left. Everyone crushed. The chatter of her subjects cut short. No more talk of war. Maybe some still alive, being slowly crushed until they could no longer draw breath.

Is this what would happen? If Herendak got to Elhrinna? Was this the final culmination of her line? He had been planning this for so long. What would happen, at the end, if he got what he wanted?

Now, stretch to a little more. Draneth. A flood. The city sinking into the ocean. No survivors. Not one. So much death, so much pain. Every single member of every family water-bloated and still, their accusing eyes bulging at her.

Could she could stop this? Could she stop Herendak right now?

Because what if- what if she went upstairs, this very moment, with her dagger, and-

Took it to Elhrinna? And- and- took it to Ielenia?

And then – with relief – took it to herself?

Rilenheim could do what he wished with Meryn.

More. There was plenty more beyond Draneth. The kingdom itself. How many subjects did she have? How many people lived in Draldorn? How many were there to die? Just how damned many?

Enough to weigh against Elhrinna, against Ielenia, against herself?

"Your Majesty?"

She opened her eyes. The hall had fallen silent. She wasn't aware of having said anything. Maybe she hadn't. Maybe anguish had found wordless release.

If only she could be sure. If only she could know, for certain, that this was the only way. Oh, if only it was ever truly possible to be sure, about anything!

Chapter 21

Ambush. They were all thinking it.

They marched through the gap in the mountain shoulder to shoulder, five abreast. Rayant found his gaze constantly shifting upwards, wondering what could be up there, gathered on the mountain's top.

The reverberation of their bootsteps was deafening. The wall's shadows were chilling. The narrow slit of light above had no way of making itself felt. They were scurrying ants stuck at the bottom of a fissure, the earth one quake away from closing up on them forever.

"Ambush, Rilenheim?" he said again to the Geomancer.

Rilenheim just shook his head.

"He does not know we're here. I can sense when Wrilsch are near, and we are quite safe. The few that are here are no threat to us."

"But there are some here?"

"Not many. Some are close. But if they are here, they are not with Herendak. He has not got to them all. Lone Wrilsch will not attack a force such as ours."

They marched on. There was nothing else for them to do.

"Do you know where Herendak is?" Rayant asked, after a time.

Rilenheim took a moment to reply. He appeared preoccupied.

"He is not near."

They gained the northern wastelands without incident. There was no ambush. Stretches of dead, ashen ground spread out to the horizon, hewn in dreary hues of brown and yellow, pitted with scars. The air was dry and stuck in the throat.

They marched into open ground and circled into a vast camp. Rayant posted watchful bowmen around their perimeter. The only Wrilsch they saw were giant slug-like creatures, the size of cows, which came to look at them for a while, before loping away.

They spent the night there. They hadn't dared to rest on the long march through the secret pass. Rilenheim had given the mountain's name as Niri, and told him the pass was known as Niri's Cut, or Yastran's Wound. Neither name did much to lift Rayant's spirits. He was exhausted. They were all exhausted.

That night, Rayant lay in his tent and stared up at the canvas. He listened to the faint camp sounds, murmuring voices carried by a faint wind, until they washed over him. Every sound seemed muted, even the harsh tearing of swords being sharpened, as if his men thought if they were just quiet enough they could avoid a battle.

He stared up at the canvas, tinted blue with moonlight, and thought of the future, and remembered what he'd said earlier to Rilenheim. Thinking of a future would not be a comforting thing to do. He thought of the past, instead. That, too, had its unpleasant aspects. He found himself thinking of Aldrua. He ached, somewhere deep in his chest. He folded his hands over it.

She had wronged him. She had gone with Kendan and in doing so had rejected everything he was. She had said to him, without saying a thing, that he was not needed, nor wanted.

In the darkness, he took all the bitterness and held it close and let the hurt well up. He thought of her face, those solemn eyes – those so often worried eyes – with that unknown thing shifting behind them.

What was it, that thing, that was there wherever she was? Behind her eyes, whenever she smiled at him, whenever she shouted at him, whenever she spoke? A foreign thing which could fill him with wonder – the kind of wonder he'd known as a boy, but never since, never as an adult, except when he was with her. That forever unknowable, mysterious and sometimes frightening spark.

He knew, of course. It was obvious, he'd just never stopped to think about it. It was *her*. It was Aldrua.

He thought, as hard as he could, of what it would be like to be behind those eyes.

What had happened with Kendan wasn't completely her fault. It wasn't completely his. They had both made mistakes. She could not wait for him forever. He had been busy running his kingdom – and she had not.

It didn't matter now. None of it mattered now. He was silently crying, he released.

He was sorry. It was a painful sorry. He wished he could see again that glint in her eyes, her smile, the brightness of the things she said and was. He missed her terribly – which was strange, as he hadn't missed her at all before, on those many previous occasions on which he'd left her behind at the Keep. These last few weeks had collapsed everything down to what really mattered, and this woman he was married to, whom he barely knew but felt so much for, was someone he really should have taken the time to know.

But he hoped – there was still that – that maybe, just maybe, he would get to tell her that what she'd done didn't matter, to tell her that he didn't judge her. To tell her that he had let it all go and it was all beyond the need for forgiveness because none of it really mattered any more. Just to say, quite simply, that he understood.

It was too much, far too much, to hope for. He lay there and thought about how she must have felt, how she must be feeling right now, and he let the hope wither. For a time he clung on to one thought: that he might see her again. Just see her face, one final time.

He thought of Rilenheim, and Herendak; two Geomancers playing games with him and his people. He thought of Meryn, and how so very different she was from her sister. He thought of the Wrilsch, and how this must all end.

He let it all go. He let it all drain until all that was left was the thing they had to do. The ache went away. He felt empty, but strong. He hoped he wouldn't die.

After a time, he discarded this last hope as well.

Numb to everything, he lost himself to a dreamless sleep.

He woke sometime around midnight. It was pitch-black.

Moonlight had abandoned his tent. The ground was shaking.

It had begun.

He was up in an instant. He buckled on his mail tunic. His heraldic surcoat went on over it, and he was pulling on his gauntlets by the time a scout appeared.

"Report," Rayant demanded, striding out into chaos. Men milled about, waving weapons at shadows, crying out warnings to each other. The horizon had vanished around them. The edges of a new darkness shifted with vague shapes. "Where is Rilenheim?"

The Geomancer was nowhere to be found.

"Form a perimeter!" Rayant ordered. He pushed the scout aside. "Get me archers. Get General Frin. Now! And somebody find Rilenheim!"

He had flaming arrows fired out from the camp. They landed in the dust. The outlines of beasts were highlighted for a few seconds before the arrows burned out – or were stomped on and eaten.

"Bring the pikemen up!" he ordered.

"Your Majesty, I am here," General Frin stepped up beside him. The General handed him a sword, still in its scabbard. It was Rayant's; in his haste he'd left it in his tent. He belted it on.

"Any recommendations, General?"

"We need more light, Your Majesty."

"More light."

"Yes, Your Majesty."

Rilenheim rode out of the darkness, a silhouette until mere paces away.

"There's no one out there," he grunted.

"There are Wrilsch. We saw them."

Rilenheim waved an arm. "Not in numbers worth mentioning. They are not out there. Herendak is not out there. Rayant, you don't understand. No one is here!"

"I-"

The ground shook again. This time fiercely enough to knock them off their feet. They struggled to get back up.

Rilenheim seized Rayant's arm with a grip that threatened to splinter bone.

"Rayant! Have your men light up Yastran's Wound!"

A volley was unleashed. Flaming arrows skipped about the pass. Movement flickered in the light, and there was a cracking, creaking, but it wasn't a normal creak. A creaking door could make the spine tingle. This was the spine being grated. This was a door with hinges a mile thick. Niri shuddered around its cut. Clouds of rock billowed out. There were other sounds, clicks and crunches and booms.

"Archers! Archers!"

"More light!"

A second volley opened up further pockets of light. The mountain was scored with Wrilsch. They tore at Niri's side with mandibles. Their gullets were thick with mashed stone. The booms were pitch-black boreholes collapsing in on themselves. Rayant stared, open-mouthed.

"Weroms," Rilenheim hissed. "Herendak has found a way to control the weroms!"

Rayant ordered the archers to expend everything they had. Arrows peppered the mountain's side. A werom went up with a whoomph and let out a screech, high-pitched and terrible, as it rolled and writhed and died.

Then other Wrilsch were upon them, coming out of the darkness; tearing and biting, pulling men into the black.

"Hold circles!" Rayant cried. "Back to back!"

The general took up the cry. Other officers followed. The command relayed out to the rest of the men.

"This is not an ambush," Rilenheim spat. His face was ashen, and twisted into sharp lines. Rayant recoiled at the sheer magnitude of the hate outlined on the Geomancer's craggy features. He had never before seen a face he wanted to flat out run from. "It is a feint," Rilenheim went on. "Herendak knows! He holds us here to get to Draneth!"

"Draneth? Rilenheim, Draneth? Why there?" Their eyes met. "The thing he seeks, Rilenheim – you hid it there? You hid it in my own city!"

"Yes, my king. He seeks to hold us here, until it is too late!"

Now Rayant's face, too, was twisted with rage. He had failed. He had failed his kingdom. He had failed his people. He had failed Aldrua.

And, so they stood, Geomancer and king, and together watched as Yastran's Wound began to close. Niri began to topple. The peaks of the pass shivered against the sky. Rayant could only stare, as around him men died. One peak tilted into the other, gracefully, like it was weightless. Its head cracked from its shoulders, and plunged as a meteorite.

Rilenheim was moving.

"Ride, ride!" he cried. His horse – the thing he rode – jolted into a gallop.

He disappeared into the darkness, re-emerged leaping over a flurry of broken rock and flaming bodies, then was again swallowed by the night.

Rayant made an instant decision. He grabbed at the nearest horse, swung into its saddle. It was a scout's horse, and fast. Nevertheless, he couldn't catch Rilenheim. He shot after him, tearing through knots of Wrilsch and men, as the ground shook and the air swam with dust, and arrows plinked and burned and the world fell from above.

"Go back!" came Rilenheim's roar, or so he imagined. He didn't obey. He spurred onwards into a mass of choking dust until, in a shocking blur of impact, he was floating. There was screaming and he hit the ground, hard. Something kicked him. He shielded his eyes with a sleeve filled with ground rock. His horse was in half. Its mouth foamed as it screamed. As he watched, a pile of rocks slid over it.

He gained his feet. Gritting his teeth, still trying to protect his eyes, he ran. Something snagged his face, and he stumbled. He got to his feet only for a block of stone on his back to knock him down again. He crawled on. There was something stuck in his cheek. He wrenched it free, and felt blood pour.

There was a looming shape ahead. There was a hand. Rilenheim grabbed his shirt at the back of his neck and scooped him up bodily. He was flung over the back of the thing pretending to be a horse. A sense of coldness came off the thing in waves.

They galloped. Faster than the fastest horse possibly could. Maybe faster than anything. They streaked through the dying of Niri until the dust thinned enough to see. The walls slid past like silent shadows. The ground shook all the while.

Towards the other side the pass was still mostly intact. At the highest point the two peaks touched foreheads, as if to urgently whisper secrets kept hidden for a world's lifetime. But cracks were running down them and flakes were peeling off and it would not be long.

Rayant clung to Rilenheim and roared as they rode.

Chapter 22

Whilpan hurtled through the rain in fits and starts. It was a pounding rain, the kind which battered down leaves and trembled branches. It threatened to floor him into thick mud. He took shelter under the thicker branches as it got too much. When it relented, he ran as fast as he dared.

He traced the sodden bank of Orthal Lake, letting himself be guided by the patches of water reeds, grey in the light. They curled over each other, all in the same direction, away from the lake, as if it held sights they would rather not see. It was difficult to run. There was not enough space, and everything was too slippery, too dark. He stumbled and staggered instead, and pushed himself blindly off trunks as he went, grateful for their solidity, even if they seemed hunched, and solemn, even if they seemed to sense something coming, something from a future that bore him ill-will; though all they could do was wait.

When he lost his bracer to a tangle of undergrowth he didn't stop for it.

There were eyes following him.

He would have taken off through the wood if he thought he had the slightest chance of staying a straight course. But he was a city boy, always had been, and what he knew about navigation was about as much as he did about herding cows or milking sheep. Figuring a direction from the position of all those taunting stars was for people who kept pigs in the house for warmth, not for those who knew what street names and maps were for.

So he followed the bank, as fast as he could, and as he coughed and wiped his nose he shaded his eyes and stared up at those dim, white stars and pleaded with them to show him the way, to form into a giant arrow and point the shortest way to Draneth. Instead, they shimmered on the other side of the rain like so many more winking eyes.

Those that followed him were green and bright.

No matter how fast he went, they stayed with him, until his chest was heaving and he couldn't tell whether the water down his face was rain or tears.

He crouched down behind a bramble patch, and stared back the way he'd come.

And there it was. Looking at him, just as he looked at it.

Very slowly, under cover of bramble, he unslung his bow from his shoulder. His shoulder twinged. His injured forearm ached in anticipation, though it was now much stronger than it had been, and he didn't think the break was as bad as he'd originally thought. Admittedly, there had been a certain amount of exaggeration – for Drael's benefit.

The eyes blinked at him.

Another Wrilsch? Or was this just an animal of some kind? Was it an animal that would know what a bow was, if he lifted it up and took aim? Would it run – or maybe attack?

Bah. It had all been so much easier before he'd run in to that no good do-gooder, Drael. Though still better out here, free to make sensible decisions, than trapped in that castle of ghosts with a walking target. Of course, here there was no one around to cover his back – but he was well used to that.

The lake was gurgling at him. He risked losing sight of the eyes for a moment. The lake was lower than it should have been. He hadn't noticed that before. He hadn't paid the impossible much mind.

There were dead fish splayed out over loose stone where the water had receded. And now that he looked, some of the leafy branches that had caught on his quiver were seaweedy – or, possibly, lakeweedy.

The lake was also brighter than it should have been. It was softly lit, as with the light of an old stub of candle. He knew of the light. There was something in Orthal Lake, circles of stone, something very old. The light came from these, from both of them – from the middle of both of them.

As he watched, they flickered, with such an intensity that for a second it was day.

He cursed and clutched both hands to his eyes, the flaxen string of his bow coarse against his cheek. Now the stars were inside his head.

For a moment he saw distances, places – many places. He saw Wrilsch, still and silent, gathered at each place. Waiting. He blinked them all away. He couldn't see a damn thing any more. He crouched down and waited for his vision to adjust.

There was movement nearby. He scrabbled backwards. His clothes ripped through clinging thorns, his skin tore. He brought his bow up, but not enough room to get the string back. He waved it wildly. He couldn't see what was causing the movement.

And then the flickering became solid and he stared into the lake, blinking furiously, and saw what had become of the people of Eyhold, and from where the Wrilsch came.

The thing pounced. Whilpan tried to duck, but lost his balance. He fell into the thorns, and it flew past his head. He got up and ran, without looking back. He couldn't hear it. He couldn't tell if it was behind. But he kept running anyway, on and on, until his throat felt torn open from raspy breaths.

He ran for a long time. Finally he stumbled out onto clear ground. He dropped to his knees on the road, the sweet, sweet road. He could almost kiss it.

There were others on it. Two men stumbled past him with unblinking eyes.

There were sputtering fires in the distance.

He started forward, thinking they must be camps, but the flames were darting too high for that. He stopped and considered his bearings. He must be near Nulwhey... what villages were by Eyhold? One bit of road looked like any other to him, especially when it all looked like rain.

He frowned when he noticed the outlines of buildings in the flames.

A knot of people rushed past, barely visible, just shapes, like a moving tableau.

"What-?" he tried to ask.

He stared after them.

He managed to stop a lone older man, lagging behind the others.

"What's happening?"

The man's eyes were rimmed with red.

"We need to hide," the man said. "Go somewhere they won't go."

"Hide? What's-?"

The man was gulping, over and over, words locked in his throat. He grabbed the lapels of Whilpan's coat.

"Wrilsch! So many! And – and the one who is with them..."

"They're here?"

"Why didn't we stop them? Where is the army? The call went out... where are our men? The Wrilsch are here and we cannot stand against them! I – we never thought they'd come this far. And now they're everywhere. They're taking the babies. Sniffing them out. We weren't able to hide them. Once we found out what they wanted, when we tried to stop them... they tore us apart. They..."

"Where are you going now? Draneth?"

"Where else can we go? We can't hide. We tried and they found us. There's nowhere else."

The man let go of him and hurried away.

Whilpan looked up and down the road. He looked back. Behind him, the sky was practically humming. That ghostly bright whiteness coming from the lake threw the wood into sharp relief; a vast, spiky, angry other world.

The path. Was that the path Meryn had spoken of? Was it really through those lake-bound rings?

The ones surrounded by the bodies of the people of Eyhold?

What if Meryn and the others had tried to take that path?

He looked up and down the road. Fires and screams. This was it. Another moment of change.

But he knew what he had to do.

For a moment, Whilpan turned his face to the sky. He closed his eyes and let them be soothed by the drops.

He shook his head.

Even as he stepped back into the wood, he knew it would be the end of him.

* * *

Drael checked their situation again from the gatehouse in the morning. He rushed out through the rain to stare out over the sodden landscape. The Wrilsch snarled at him from below, its misshapen yellow teeth glistening.

He then went to check on Meryn. She was still in *that* room.

"Drael, it's spreading," she said, without preamble, as he walked in. She sat on the bed, her legs stretched out in front of her. The black ley-lines were inching above her ankle, which was now nothing but black, blistering blotches, like her skin had been bubbling. It looked very much like the poison she had snatched out of Brogan.

Drael sat next to her. With a grimace, he hesitantly touched his fingers to the dying – transforming – tissue. It had the texture of burnt sand. He ran his hand up to where he felt the warmth of *human* flesh.

"I think," he said, "if you wouldn't have twisted the ankle, it would have found another way. I think it's just a weak spot, somewhere to start."

Meryn nodded.

"I think so too. Somewhere to start. I am finding it more and more difficult to concentrate, Drael. Sometimes I close my eyes and I see myself from above, as I drift away."

Their eyes met.

"We need time," she said. "Cut it off." Drael shot to his feet. "I know what you're going to say," the princess continued, "but let's skip the histrionics. You have no idea how much it hurts. No – not hurts. How much it *takes* from me. I'm pretty sure I'll be far more of a person without it. And I also think you know I'm right."

She had that look to her again. Chin stuck out, eyes challenging. No sign of the manner of someone about to lose a foot. "Come on, Drael, don't waste time on pointless rationalisations. I don't think I can afford a delay." She made a feeble attempt at a smile. "So. Chop, chop."

It wasn't the least bit amusing.

"What does histrionics mean?" Drael said.

"It means you're going to do this right now before it gets worse." She pulled herself into a more upright sitting position, and dragged up the appropriate trouser leg as far as it would go. She watched her ankle impassively.

Drael opened and closed his mouth a few times. It finally set into a flat line. He took one further look at her face, then went and fetched some bandages, a belt for a tourniquet and his dagger.

* * *

Drak waited patiently, lying face down in the dirt, ignoring the insects which scurried past his nose. His plan had been to remove Rilenheim's ability to track him, but then the shadow had screamed – he could think of no other way of describing it – and his plan had changed.

And so he had expected Rilenheim, if anyone at all. He had expected – no, hoped – a chance to take off the Geomancer's head. Sure, his objective was to find Meryn, but killing off the competition always made that kind of thing simpler.

It perhaps wasn't so likely Rilenheim would come himself, unless the army had made particularly poor progress, but he would surely do *something*, after hearing the shadow scream. And then Drak would capture whomever came, find out what they knew. Maybe follow them. Any lead was better than none. As a Raven, any and all avenues would be followed.

Drak had heard that scream, at first at least, as a knife to his brain. Which had then smothered out into just a... kind of a sense of something, an awareness that set the back of his neck tingling. The scream had gone on, but after the initial shock he could no longer hear it. Maybe it had stopped, or maybe it was a different kind of scream, with a life of its own, which moved on ever outwards, rustling through the grass, disturbing rodents and startling birds, until it reached the one who needed to hear it.

So Rilenheim would know. The shadow and its master had been together a long time. Rilenheim had come to its aid before. Perhaps he would come now. This was the advantage of attempting to outwit a legend: his deeds were legendary.

But what would Rilenheim do this time? How far north was the army? How necessary would Rilenheim deem it to stay with them? And how quickly could he travel, these days? In the tales, Geomancers were the masters of geography. They could be everywhere at once. They could move faster than a thought. Their powers had faded, of course, especially in needing an army of humans to assist them – an army which moved far slower than they could – but nevertheless this was one avenue definitely worth pursuing.

He waited the best part of a day, thinking this would be long enough, but no Rilenheim.

Instead, what he got was a slim, unassuming man, dressed like a nobleman who'd got lost in the woods. No pack, no satchel, no travelling equipment whatsoever.

The man burst into the clearing so suddenly Drak was too surprised to be startled.

The man stopped directly in front of the burial place of the shadow, almost on top of it. He was breathing heavily. He squatted down and placed a hand, palm down, on the freshly turned over dirt. For a moment, he cast narrowed eyes around the clearing.

Drak stayed still, breathing evenly, avoiding the mistake of holding a breath which would only need to be expelled later all the louder.

The man returned his attention to the shadow's resting place. He stayed there for a while, fingers gouged into the earth. After a while, he took a long, slow breath.

"Tell me," he murmured, and Drak tensed, but the words were not meant for him. "Tell me and I will free you from this."

Drak clenched and unclenched his own fingers around the hilt of his sword. As soon as the man started digging...

But wait.

What kind of man could talk to a shadow?

And there was no digging, just silence. Drak did his best to ignore a growing sense of unease. He was being excluded from some deathly silent conversation, and could not help but think it was at least partially about him.

The man was suddenly on his feet. His face was flushed. Drak almost drew his sword in reflex.

"I will return for you when it is done," the man said. "I promise." But his eyes were already absent, and staring distractedly away into the distance. "You devious bastard," he said, shaking his head.

He walked away, which quickly became a march, and then he clearly thought better of even that and started to run.

Drak clambered to his feet. He had to think quickly. What should he do? He ran his hands through his half-burnt hair. There was only one other person he could think of who would know of the shadows of Geomancers. Only one who would know how to communicate with them.

He knew what he had to do.

He waited a judiciously short while before following, staying not in eyeshot, but earshot, hanging back and stopping to listen to breathing and out-of-place rustles and the scratchings of branches and using these to guide him.

It soon became clear that the man – Herendak – was going to Draneth.

Drak went with him all the way.

He would just have to hope Meryn would stay out of trouble until Herendak was dealt with.

After all, if something happened to his employer he'd never get paid.

Chapter 23

The rain somehow got worse. The castle thrummed with it. It ran down the walls as if fleeing from something high above. Eyhold looked almost spectral in the moonlight.

Whilpan edged around the walls, some distance from the drawbridge. He couldn't see or hear the others, but nevertheless he shouted up at them.

"Hey, Brogan! Drael! Lower a rope!"

But there was a limit to how loudly he was willing to shout.

He didn't think he had been followed, but there was still their archenemy loitering around here somewhere – unless the others had made a run for it. He almost thought he could hear it growling. He froze to listen, keeping as quiet as he could. The rain had given him a cold, so he had to muffle sneezes on his sleeve. The rain was also making nearby branches creak and sigh and he couldn't help but keep glancing over his shoulder.

He stood shivering and sniffling until he was certain he was alone.

And then he knew what he had to do. He didn't know how long he had, so he moved quickly. Taking his dagger, he shredded his coat and then part of his shirt into strips, as fast as he could. In his haste he cut a finger, deep, and gave a cry – which died somewhere out in the wood.

He didn't wait to see what would come. He worked even faster, recklessly fast, cutting into his hands time and time again. Then he tied the strips together with numbing fingers. His hands shook as he tied the knots. Blood streamed down them, and he cursed the knots and the walls and the others and especially Meryn. What the hell was he thinking trying to get back to her? But he had to tell her what he'd seen. He had felt the extent of the danger when she had pushed into his mind, and now he had seen that it had already begun. He had understood that she did not understand everything – and if he did not let her know where the path began, how would she be able to find it in time?

Finally he tied the makeshift rope to the base of an arrow. Even at such close range it took three shots fired into the top of the wall before the arrow both didn't shatter and dug deep enough to hold fast. He tested his weight against it, and it still held.

This time, when he heard growling, he was certain it was real.

He heaved himself up as fast as he could. There were few useful handholds and his hands quickly cramped. His boots slipped and slid about.

He felt movement. He felt heat. He risked a glance and there the Wrilsch was, its hot breath snarling out as it leapt for him.

A surge of exertion and he tumbled over onto the battlements. He lay with his chest bursting and head swimming. It couldn't follow.

He rolled over and got up.

The others were back in the warm kitchen when he burst in.

"I found the path," he said, without preamble. "I found your path, Meryn. You're not ready. You still need to get to it."

Drael had his sword immediately half-drawn. Whilpan glared at him, and it almost seemed like Drael hadn't recognised him. Whilpan looked down at his ragged and bloodied clothes. He must look like hell.

"Wha-"

"And I found *them*," Whilpan said, voice flat.

"Found who?"

"The people of Eyhold."

Whilpan pushed his way inside, and stood in front of the fire, his torn shirt hissing.

"You won't believe what's happening out there."

* * *

Whilpan grabbed Drael's arm and dragged him up to a lake-facing window on the second floor.

"There," he said. "Look close."

Darkness cloaked everything but the glowing buoy, which was not quite so submerged as it had once been, though the lake was re-filling quickly. Closer to them, just visible by the walls, the Wrilsch paced back and forth, its mangled leg trailing. It was generally as close to Meryn as it could get. It had proven it knew exactly where she was, just as she knew where it was, if she stopped to concentrate.

"Well that's new," Drael said. "The brightness of the buoy, I mean. But what should I be looking at?"

"It ain't all lake," Whilpan said.

Drael finally saw. The entire lake had tilted. Curled around the buoy, underneath the surface, was something massive, something almost shapeless, swaying with the water's movement.

Some kind of... Wrilsch.

"See how it's bulky? See them knots?"

"Yes, I see them."

"What do you 'spose they are?"

The faintness of Whilpan's voice drew a glance at his face. He usually looked bedraggled and unkempt, but right now he looked like he was back from the dead.

"Those are people, Drael. *Were* people."

"They were...?" Drael stared for long enough to see that Whilpan was right. The knots were bodies, broken and tangled within the Wrilsch. It looked to have simply enveloped them. He hoped they had died quickly. He hoped they hadn't been straining for breath even as the thing filled their throats and slowly pulled their limbs from their sockets.

He turned and vomited onto a hat stand. "No," he said. "No, no, no."

Meryn placed one hand on his shoulder. It had taken her this long to get up the steps. She held a crutch in a fist as tight as her face.

That she had managed the steps at all said something for both who she was and what was happening to her. She was a wiry thing in the gloom. She pushed Whilpan out of the way. Her eyes glittered a reflection of the twisted thing in the lake.

"It's waiting," she said. "But for what?"

"It's a guard," Whilpan said. "It blocks the path."

"The path?"

"Meryn..." there was a tremor in Whilpan's voice. "*That* is the path you were talking about, out there in the lake. But there's Wrilsch behind each door! I saw through – just for a second."

She stared out over the lake. The twisted metal and diamond rings were so very bright now.

"Yes," she nodded, after a time. "That's it. You are correct, I'm certain of it. That *is* the path. Right there. Herendak told me there were anchors strewn about Draneth, anchors to try and contain the thing he had done to the world. I never thought they were right under our noses. They truly are everywhere! Whilpan, thank you. We now know the way!" There was triumph in her voice, even though it came out of a face that looked half-dead, its rictus grin and flat eyes resembling a painting of a corpse.

"You told me they needed us," Drael croaked, "so why did it kill my... why did it kill the people of Eyhold?"

"I don't know. Maybe to clear the path for others. I..." She shook her head, suddenly laughed. "It occurs to me that I was never really with Herendak. I wonder what he used to look like, before all this? I wonder what any Geomancer looked like? Nothing like us, I imagine. I wonder who the person was that he looks like now?

"It doesn't matter, of course. All that matters is that Herendak is making his move. The Wrilsch are moving. The gates are ready. Here, everywhere, all over Draldorn – maybe beyond – so they can get to us all. But we *can* also get to him."

"But," Whilpan murmured, "you ain't getting to the path. S'posing you even could, as I say, there's Wrilsch waiting behind each door."

No one had anything to say to that.

* * *

Later, Drael circled the courtyard restlessly. It was only by chance that he saw it. In one of the warehouses at the castle's rear. It was under a tarpaulin, covered in dust and cobwebs. He almost walked right past without seeing it. He'd thought the duke had destroyed the only one that was left. But not this one, not the one that had been retrieved, smashed, from where it had washed up on the shore. But here it was. It had even been repaired.

They had a way to the path.

Now they needed to get rid of the Wrilsch blocking the way.

* * *

The flaming mass of wood and cloth flung high over the walls of Eyhold, over the Wrilsch – which was now waiting a distance up the road – and over a great expanse of field. It crashed through the wall of a barn and came to rest.

The Wrilsch didn't move. It hadn't moved for a while. The shiny silver necklace it wore turned into a noose of fire as the flaming shot tore overhead. A red-to-yellow rainbow of embers and smoke trailed in the shot's wake. But the Wrilsch itself made no move to break up the darkness.

They watched the barn catch fire with a whoomph.

"Nice shot," Drael said, dryly.

"It was a ranging round," Whilpan claimed. He seemed in better spirits now that he had a siege weapon to play with. "Still slightly too long. You couldn't have done better. Wind it back, Brogan."

Brogan did so, heaving the wheel of the trebuchet's winch mechanism around, spoke after spoke, his face red, his arms bulging. They'd found the thing on one secluded edge of the courtyard, near where the boat had been stashed, where it had been too dark to see on previous rain-filled nights. It was stained with weather and a thin patina of rust clung like mould to its iron parts. But it still functioned nonetheless, at least after they'd restrung the sling, or whatever that part of its mechanism was called. Meryn had supervised this, and seemed to find ordering the others about thoroughly calming.

They'd also found two ballistae inside an open wareroom. These looked to have been moved out of position very recently, same as with the trebuchet. The stone floor was discoloured where they had lain for a long time. They were both missing drawstrings. Whatever had happened here had clearly called for their use, but there just hadn't been time.

Whilpan reloaded the trebuchet's sling with firewood, a couple of ornate vases, some forks (as they'd already used all the knives) and a painting of a dog. He added oil from a pot, stopping and starting, like a cook trying to get a recipe just right. Finally, he threw on a burning brand.

"Fire!" he shouted and yanked the release lever. The pivot arm arced up, but immediately exploded to one side with a teeth grinding tearing of gears. Brogan leapt aside, covering his head with his hands as flaming detritus rained across the courtyard. "Too short this time!" Whilpan called. "Everyone all right?"

"This is ridiculous," Drael said. He could hear Meryn laughing, which annoyed him. She was one floor up, inside the castle proper, level with him, leaning out a window. Or maybe he was just disguising worry with annoyance. How was she able to laugh after what she'd made him do to her leg?

"Do you need more ammunition?" she asked. "There are plenty more vases and paintings up here. And I'm sure I could find some dolls."

Shaking her head she disappeared inside.

Drael kept one eye on the Wrilsch as the others put out pockets of burning grass.

His sense of wrongness was growing. He scratched at his arms. Other than the mess they'd created, the courtyard was pristine. Until right now it had looked like it had been thoroughly swept. There was nothing anywhere to say people had left in a hurry. Had not a single person dropped something as they tried to flee? And the missing ropes from the siege weapons were the only loose parts of them. Were they stored this way? Maybe there had simply not been time to set them up? But there wasn't even a loose strand of hay near the stables, and the sconces around the outer walls were missing their brands.

Nothing loose. No people. Had that massive guardian in the lake simply scooped up everything that wasn't nailed down? The only loose items they'd found during the search for trebuchet ammunition had been in windowless rooms, or where windows were sealed. Inside a child's toy chest they'd found a small wooden mallet, now propped against the trebuchet by Brogan's side. It probably wouldn't be any use, but Brogan wouldn't part with it.

The Wrilsch in the lake had come and taken everyone and everything and no one had been able to do a thing about it.

And there it still lurked – and they were making far, far too much noise.

Drael shook his head. No time for this now. They needed to deal with the *other* Wrilsch first. Then they could worry about sneaking past the lake's guardian.

He stared at their pursuer, still hulked motionless into a large, dark mass, its face to the ground, as if resting. Was it so disinterested in the possibility of them hitting it with a siege weapon?

There was movement out there. He caught it through the corner of an eye. Something four-legged, moving across the fields, low to the ground. He leaned out, as if that would somehow result in a valuable improvement of what he could see.

It was a wolf. It was very thin and its fur was scraggly. It stopped and cocked its ears, presumably at a sound Drael couldn't hear. Then it moved on, sniffing along one corner of the field, circling back and forth.

He watched as it abruptly concluded this business, and trotted away across his view. Right by the Wrilsch.

The Wrilsch did nothing.

"I-" Drael frowned. "Hey, something's... something's wrong!" he called down to the others. Brogan and Whilpan looked up with blank expressions, and seeing him making no urgent moves, continued to douse the small fires they had created. "Meryn!" he called to the window. "Meryn!"

Why didn't she answer?

A silhouette danced against the window where she was, but he couldn't get her attention by waving.

He stared up the road. Maybe the Wrilsch was more injured than they'd thought. Maybe it had died from the wound Brogan had inflicted. Because while it itself may not have been interested in the wolf, surely a wolf would have been very interested in keeping distance from it. And it wasn't exactly inconspicuous. It had the kind of wet death smell not even a human could miss, let alone a wolf.

Drael scrabbled for a stone to throw in the Wrilsch's direction, but, of course, there was nothing loose anywhere. At any rate the distance was too great for his arm.

Something occurred to him. His heart didn't leap. It went too slowly from uneasy nervousness to fast panic.

"Open the gate! Open the gate! Broge, go check on Meryn!"

When he finally got out to get a closer view of the Wrilsch, it became obvious very quickly what it was. A mound of poorly sculpted mud ringed awkwardly with a necklace. A pile of rocks, looking to have been taken from the wall, made up the head.

He scraped up the necklace. Its centrepiece was a pendent, with an emblem engraved delicately onto it.

Silver spires. Definitely the same as on Meryn's ring.

What the hell?

A cold chill settled on his shoulders. It quickly turned to fire on his neck.

Stone from the walls! Stone from the walls!

* * *

Meryn barely had time to bar the door. The Wrilsch thumped against it, knocking her back across the floor. The crutch rolled from her outflung hand.

The door curved inwards, its hinges screaming.

She'd heard the thing mount the stairs, but had thought nothing of it. She'd thought it was Brogan, but it had been too slow, there had been too many pauses, and that dragging sound, as of an injured leg. If anyone should have been able to recognise that sound...

She should have been paying more attention.

No matter.

Hide.

In the closet. Under the desk. But that was a foolish first instinct. This wasn't a normal foe. It knew exactly where she was. In the same way that if she closed her eyes and focussed, she knew exactly where *it* was. If only she had done that very thing!

How the hell had it got over the wall?

Another foolish, irrelevant thought.

The door returned to its normal shape, a crack riven in an angry line through its middle. Rasping breathing seemed to envelop it, seeping through each edge, each crack, like the door itself was alive and angry.

She dragged herself away. She found a weapon, a dull letter opener, in a drawer of the desk. Woefully ineffective against a creature such as this. She pulled herself up to stand uncertain behind the desk, it between her and the door. The stump where her ankle used to be was searing with pain.

The door burst into splinters. The Wrilsch rushed in. It flung aside the desk with one arm and took one loping lunge forward. She fell back. She held up the letter opener in a tremulous hand.

Go for the eyes, one chance, go for the eyes...

She met its gaze. No. It met her gaze. She gasped. She felt again that vertiginous instinct to let go, give in. So very, very easy to just sink into the peaceful torpor suddenly promised. Its eyes were vast inky blots deep within the bulging crags of its saggy face, the pupils filling them, and in them she saw understanding, intelligence – and something more. An abyss of madness. Thoughts swirled behind them. She slipped into the pull of them, with a shock as of ice-cold water, and everything spun. The room became a great yawning dark, the Wrilsch its centre, into which everything pooled.

"What do you want?" she wanted to ask it, but she couldn't make her mouth move, nor her thoughts form. "I will fight you." But this thought, too, slipped away.

She fell into its eyes.

Around her, space, vast space. She was floating, high up. Very high. Dots of brightness. Stars. She was standing on something, in the middle of nowhere, but connected to everything. There were passages through the sky itself. Rivers of silver in a world stark with youth, unsoftened by time.

A wash of thoughts had her gasping. The Wrilsch's thoughts. They stung through her brain. Drowning in needles. It was a she, this Wrilsch – but in a different way. Someone who had known Herendak, long ago. Someone close to him. And there was a feeling of belonging and acceptance, kinship. A warmth. Love, but shared, for one thing; no, one person. For Herendak. Not hers, not all of it. A merging.

Herendak's mercy wasn't what she'd thought. It was not his entire motivation. His reasons to send this thing after her were more complex. But she had been right about some things. His people – what was left of his people – would become what was left of her people. The Geomancers would live again, in the forms of those who had come after.

And this was the one chosen for her.

This explained the necklace. It wasn't her sister's. It hadn't killed her sister. It hadn't killed any of her family, any of her ancestors. It *was* one of her ancestors. Herendak had tried this before but had not understood the force of his new form.

He would not lose her, after all, despite the change he'd forced on her.

This wasn't what he had promised. This wasn't what he'd told her. This wasn't love, as she understood it.

"No! I-"

Meryn still had the blunt knife in her hand.

Slowly, she turned it on herself. The blade jutted from the ball of sweat that was her fist and shook violently. But slowly it turned, forced around like she was wrestling a mountain.

She cut into the palm of her other hand, and with the pain gasped back into the room.

The Wrilsch growled, filling it. Outside, through the window just behind her, she could hear cries and running feet. Daylight fell over the Wrilsch as it closed the gap between them. Light made it look even more wrong. Its twisted form and rotten grey flesh were something of the night. She was close enough to hear its thumping breaths, the rotten stench of them. It didn't belong in daylight, didn't belong here anymore. She could see the seams of its drooping face, the lines around those deep eyes. She could see that it *knew* it didn't belong.

It growled, one final time, so loudly Meryn fell back against the windowsill.

"But it can't happen yet," Meryn said to it desperately, "he doesn't yet have our child... it's all still closed..."

Except she was wrong, she knew immediately. The change had already happened to her. She was almost as broken as any other Wrilsch. This is what she would become.

She was crying, she realised. She stopped herself. She raised the knife now to her own throat.

The Wrilsch hesitated.

It opened its arms in an embrace.

"Jump, Meryn! We'll catch you!"

The window...

The others were below. She didn't hesitate. She dropped the knife and with both hands heaved herself to a sitting position on the windowsill. She half-rolled, half-threw herself through backwards, even as the Wrilsch came after. A jolt of pain and she was on the ground in a pile of limbs, not all of them hers, in the courtyard.

A crash and a roar. Face to face with a cracked, rotten leg; fragments of broken mace still jutting out. She tried to scrabble away; felt claws on her shoulder. She saw Drael pulling at Brogan, who was trying to get to his feet.

A soft thwump and something flashed over her head.

She felt pain – a dreadful and ancient pain. Rusted and terrible and thick as tar. The world shifted back into focus.

She looked up, the pain gone.

The Wrilsch was impaled to the wall with a javelin through its neck. Slowly, gravity detached the rest of it. Just the head remained, pinned to the wall.

Drael leant with his hands on his knees, breathing hard. He slumped down next to her

"Nice shot, Whilpan," he said.

Chapter 24

Herendak wasn't recognised at the gates of Draneth, only at the gates of the Keep, and not by a guard, but by an old steward doubling in this duty.

"You know who I am," Herendak said to him.

The steward nodded. He wasn't sure what to do.

"Wait here," he said, and Herendak smiled, ever so faintly, and sat on a barrel by the door. People using the street glanced his way, but bustled past without knowing him. It was up to Herendak who would recognise him. It always had been.

The steward fetched his walking stick and clicked across the courtyard as fast as he could. He passed the message to a faster serving girl, who ran up the spiral staircase, around and around, taking three steps at a time. The message was breathlessly passed on to Pena, who answered the queen's door.

Leaving the serving girl to watch the children, Pena went and found Aldrua in the bower of the Keep's sky garden. It was a high and lonesome place, extending far out over the city the Keep was built to protect. The queen was sitting within an outbreak of books.

Some of them looked to be very old. She looked up as Pena came in. She looked distant.

"I'm beginning, I think, to understand," she murmured.

"Your Majesty," Pena said. She swallowed before continuing. "Your Majesty, Kendan is back."

Chapter 25

"It's time," Meryn said. "He's close."

Drael nodded. He offered Brogan the chance to take his own chances. Brogan just stared at him, as if Drael had turned into a sheep, and so together they heaved enough rollers into place to get the boat moving, and pushed and rolled it into position by the rear gate. It would be a short run through sodden mud to reach the water. Another advantage of the storm was that it would be less of a run than normal: the lake was now flooded. What had been flung out into the wood had rushed back with reinforcements. The little pier was only discernible as a different shade of shimmering.

Drael left Whilpan rigging the sails, the work made near impossible by the weather's incessant buffeting, and went back for Meryn.

She waited directly above the main gate, standing tall but not quite straight, uncowed. She was leaning less on a newly constructed crutch than he would have expected.

"Ready?" Drael asked.

"We have minutes," she said. She had that faraway look in her eyes again, but seemed less distant than before. She had, Drael considered, accepted this new part of her. Around her neck she wore the Wrilsch's necklace.

"Why minutes?"

"Can you see them, in the storm? *There* and *there* and *there?*"

She pointed into the wild cascade of glittering rainwater. "The others. They are minutes away. They are different shapes, different sizes. One of them is very large indeed. This gate will not hold. They won't even need to come in through the ruined wall. That one, there, can fly, Drael. But not very well. It almost seems like it's an accident that it can. Its wings are stubby and one has a hole in it, and I know you cannot see them, because *I* cannot see them, but I know they are there, Drael."

He pulled her away by the arm. The Wrilsch would sense her moving away from them. They would sense her limping through the castle's corridors, all the way to the other side of the Hold. Then, when the time came, she would be moving faster, faster than they had become used to, as he hoisted her up and ran with her, and then she would be outside the stone protection of Eyhold... and then the Wrilsch would know.

Drael didn't waste time. He spared enough only to, optimistically, pack a small bag with stale rolls as they passed the kitchen, just in case they lived long enough to eat.

In an outhouse at the rear of the castle, they waited.

"Five minutes," Drael said. Five minutes for Brogan and Whilpan – mostly Brogan – to roll the boat down to the lake. He could just about make out their rain-hazed movements through the cracked door. The rest of Eyhold was so still it was barely discernible.

He would never see it again, he knew, at that moment.

"You should know," he blurted out, "that I killed her." Meryn said nothing. He didn't wait to allow her to. "I don't know what Brogan told you. In the end, I mean. I clamped my hand over Ethi's mouth, and her nose. I held her until she sighed. She didn't even struggle."

It was too dark to see Meryn's face. She said nothing to say she understood, to say she cared, to say she was even listening.

He heard the unmistakable solid burble of a boat being birthed into water.

"Time to go," he said.

They ran. And hobbled. Through the castle's corridors. Through all those memories which Drael couldn't shake. Through the rear gate. There they were met by the distant shapes of Brogan and Whilpan in the gloom, both standing knee deep in the lake, beckoning them to move faster. Drael lost his footing and went down in the mud. Meryn tried to drag him. They sprawled and staggered on for the final stretch.

"Wait!" Meryn called a halt. "Where is it? The guardian! It's moving. It's time! Herendak! It knows it's almost time!"

"There!"

The guardian had spread out and risen high. It was near the far bank, but heading their way. It seemed able to alter its shape, able to shrink and expand, and encompass what it wished, spilling over its enemies like an erupting volcano. Malleable enough, it would seem, for it had hidden, flattened, at the bottom of a lake for a long, long time. Where else could it have been? They hadn't seen any sign of it on their flight from the cave, and it was too massive to have escaped notice. It must have always been there, lurking in the darkness, even as Drael would sail overhead. But now its time had come. It had smothered the castle, taken whatever yielded to it. It had snatched up torches from their sconces, and blotted up hay, and taken the drawstrings from siege weapons. And, of course, it had taken the people.

"What do we do?" Brogan asked.

There was a boom, and a crash. The sound of wood and steel rending. The other Wrilsch had arrived. The gate was being torn asunder. Their pursuers wouldn't even need to go around the walls.

"Well, we can't go back," Meryn said.

Drael said nothing. He spat out a bright, mirthless laugh. It would have to be on a boat, wouldn't it?

Brogan clenched his fists around his newly acquired mallet. He raised it and held it ready.

Whilpan spoke, his voice low.

"I can get its attention."

They all looked at him.

"Whilp?"

"This is a good bow." Whilpan bared his teeth into a grin and held it up for them to see. "And I am a very good shot. Always have been. The one thing I was always good at. It can't chase us all at once."

"No. Give me the bow. I'm faster."

"I've got this, Drael."

Whilpan didn't break his gaze. He was staring out over the lake, sizing up his opponent. "Besides, you can't shoot for shit."

"I-"

"Get ready to go, as soon as I have its attention."

Without looking back, Whilpan splashed his way to the end of the submerged pier, looking like he was walking on water, not once taking his eyes off the guardian.

Wordlessly, they watched him go.

Chapter 26

They met, finally, in the sky garden which looked out over eastern Draneth.

Herendak stood at the balustrade, facing the view. The arched white rooves of Draneth's homes undulated away, like frozen waves, to merge with the real waves at the busy harbour. Distant boats were moving about, tiny and silent, absent the sounds of crashing waves and raised voices with which they were fuelled. Closer to, in the city directly below, more voices; always voices.

Aldrua rushed into the garden, out of breath. She stopped short on seeing Kendan. She stared at his back. She ran her fingers through her hair, almost undoing Pena's hasty end-tresses, and rechecked the fit of the clothes she had changed into just as hastily. She had kept the dress he'd always liked. Bright, flouncy, taffeta. And of course the bodice with the cunning decoupage work on the chest. Not that he'd know what half those words meant. Herendak's own clothes were torn and muddied.

What she didn't notice was what was now so suddenly wrong – that she stared at him past wilted wisteria, shrivelled peony and unrecognisable bottlebrush, all newly drooped and taupe and dying, where minutes before they had been thriving.

She cleared her throat. He turned.

He looked exactly as she remembered. He hadn't aged one day. It was as if he'd never left. She didn't know why he was back, couldn't think of any reason for it after all this time. What did he want? Was it because Rayant was gone? With him out of the way, did he think it safe to return?

"Hello, my love," Herendak said. In his hand he held a flower she didn't recognise, its petals sagging, clearly long since picked. He proffered it to her with a smile, but right now she didn't care for flowers.

"You came back," she said, smothering a smile which she deemed would come out far too girlish.

"Of course I came back," he said. "I heard about our son. Can I see him?"

He didn't know, of course. How could he have?

"Daughter," she said, "not son." She thought she caught a flicker in his face. "Though she's n-" but she was choked off again. The secret of the baby's origin was again protecting itself.

"Daughter," he smiled. "Of course, I simply assumed. Can I see her?"

"But..." Aldrua stepped closer, to get a better view of his face as he turned again to check what was happening below. "Why did you go? Where have you *been?*"

"I will tell you all about it. But first let me see my child – I came all this way."

"But to see me, too? I- you could have seen her anytime. You- I- you could have come back months ago!"

"I had to go away for a while. But I'm here now." He was looking at *her* face, now, with an intensity. "I missed you," he said. He stepped forward and put his hands on her shoulders. "I missed you and am here because I love you."

"Oh. Oh!"

He opened his arms wide, and she put hers tremulously around him. He squeezed her tight, ever so briefly, and patted her back.

"There, there," he said, pulling away. "May I see her now?"

"Yes, of course."

She led the way to her quarters. Herendak followed briskly, close behind, his hand on the small of her back, almost pushing her along.

And Drak, unknown to all, followed them both.

"Is that her?" Herendak said. The cot was still alongside the bed. Pena stepped back, discreetly, letting him sit down on the covers. He stared at Elhrinna for a long while. Finally, he stirred, as if from a long way away. "May I?" he asked, almost in trepidation.

"Of course," Aldrua said. "But be careful!" She looked at him and thought of Rayant, but – it was all so complicated.

Ielenia was tugging on her dress.

"Mummy?"

"Hey there." Aldrua put her hand on her *real* daughter's shoulder. "Look who's here, Ili!"

And Herendak leant forward and lifted out Elhrinna.

In that instant he felt the truth of her, despite Rilenheim's disguise. He had known she was in Draldorn, once he'd neared the city, but that was as accurate as he could have been. If Rilenheim's shadow hadn't given away the secret, he would still be searching even now. She was still muted, but this close, holding her, he knew for certain. To hide her as one thought dead, one thought not to have been able to live, one who would have looked so very similar, felt so very similar – had it lived...

Rilenheim was indeed one devious bastard.

But Rilenheim hadn't realised that Aldrua's child would never – could never – have lived; that its life was needed elsewhere.

He had his daughter back.

It almost didn't seem possible.

He did not need to delay. He needed only do one tiny thing to start the process. Turn the world back, just enough, to what it had once been. To return enough of his strength. Rilenheim's, too, of course – so he would have to act quickly.

Then to Ilris – and the finish.

Rilenheim could not stop him now.

Something was wrong with his eyes. He put his hand to them and frowned. He was *crying*. But this was not something Geomancers did.

"I-" he looked up, and caught Aldrua's gaze. Her eyes were moist as well, though she was smiling. She looked like Meryn in this light. He forced himself to be still. He willed the sudden wave of conflicting feelings away. They did not befit an immortal. He bid his chest stop heaving, forced his face into plain composure. It was difficult, and he shook.

"Are you alright?" Aldrua asked.

"Mummy, mummy, mummy!" Ielenia was yanking at her arm.

"Not now!"

"Aldrua," said Ielenia.

Aldrua looked down, her smile going uncertain

"Did you just call me by my name?"

Ielenia's mouth was set in a determined line. Aldrua had a sudden premonition of what she'd look like as an adult.

"What is it, Ili?"

"I have to show you something."

"What?"

"Come with me!" and she tugged hard at Aldrua's dress until it almost ripped.

"That's enough!"

"Mummy!"

Aldrua looked at Kendan, who appeared to have made peace with himself. He was no longer crying. He was utterly, utterly still.

"Very well – what do you want to show me? Quickly – can't you see I'm busy? This better not be one of your games."

She followed Ielenia to the doorway, where the little girl paused to put her finger to her lips, all with the utmost sincerity, and then they were in the hallway, and there was Drak, with his sword in his hand.

"Your Majesty," he said, in the lowest of voices. "He is not who he seems! Or perhaps he is exactly as he seems – I do not know what happened here a year ago. But the man in there is-"

"Drak! What are you doing here? You're supposed to be finding my sister! Did you-"

"I don't know what I can say that you'll believe," Drak rushed on. "But on my honour as a Raven, the man in that room, with your daughter, is not who he seems!"

Aldrua laughed a fluttery laugh.

"Shh!" Drak hissed, but she looked back through the doorway and saw Kendan was still entirely engrossed with Elhrinna.

"Drak? Is this some kind of-"

Drak had his eyes shut. His face was streaked with dirt, and his wounds still hadn't healed. Sunlight through the half-moon windows gave his burnt and blackened cheek and ear a ghastly hue.

"Your Majesty. Aldrua. I followed him – Herendak – from where he spoke with Rilenheim's shadow. I saw it with my own eyes." He stared into hers. "What will it take for you to listen?"

"I *am* listening, but you're not making much sense!"

"Mummy?"

"Not now!"

"But Mummy!"

"Drak, is this some kind of game to you?"

"Ma'am, I do not play games. I am a Raven."

"Aldrua!"

"What!"

But then Aldrua saw it too.

Through the window, the sky was falling.

The rings were shimmering and dissolving.   They turned to glitter and shredded through cloud.

Near Draneth's main gate, the ringed sculpture was glimmering black and white, black and white, as if made of harnessed lightning, and then it went solid white and the colour of a lake.

Geomancy, she thought, distractedly. A portal. A lake, and a castle. And through this portal there was another, a circle of blackness, taking shape. Through that – walkways, ledges, pillars. And then there were other images, other places. So many.

Through them poured an army of Wrilsch.

"Drak?" Aldrua said, tonelessly.

He was already moving. He didn't say anything, didn't shout any warnings, no "Stop you fool!" or "Get away from the child!". He simply barrelled into Herendak, knocking him back onto the bed.

"Elhrinna!" Aldrua shouted. Drak came away with the baby, fell awkwardly into a corner of the room, taking the fall to protect her. Herendak was on his feet, his hands outstretched, as if to unleash something terrible.

"But-" the Geomancer said. His hand shot to his forehead. There was blood there, red and flowing. He stared at it on his fingers.

"Kendan?!"

But it was Herendak who looked back at her. She didn't know how she knew, but in that moment she just *knew.* It was something beyond the falling sky, something that came from inside.

"Herendak?" she whispered, mouth dropping.

He looked at her impassively, then turned his gaze to Drak.

As he did so, Aldrua jumped on his back.

"Run, run, run!"

Drak, sheltering the child in his arms, did as she commanded. He blundered for the door, knocking Ielenia aside as he ducked out and disappeared.

Aldrua clung hard to Herendak, her arms over his eyes and around his neck, pulling him back. Pena hit him in the stomach with a serving tray. He threw himself back against a wall, crashing Aldrua into it. He grabbed her arm and twisted and threw them both into the dressing table. It toppled and spilt its contents across the floor. The impact took her breath and Herendak broke free. She blinked away pain and staggered to her feet but Herendak was gone, after Drak, after Elhrinna.

Through the window she saw the sky had frozen into icy blue particles. They shivered and vibrated. They gave off tones like a finger around the brim of a wineglass. Whatever was happening, Drak had slowed it – for now.

"Mummy?" Ielenia was crying. There was blood on her face.

"Stay here!" Aldrua said. She shook the girl. "Stay here, no matter what, do you understand? Bolt the door." She put her hands to Ielenia's head, kissed her forehead, once, then got up and started to run.

* * *

All across Draneth, from Orton to Arenfold, and over the seas, spanning to Murfold and the Gilen Isles, all eyes turned upwards, human and animal.

The sky changed, as it had once before.

Anything flying veered away, screeched and dropped to safety. Predators stopped mid-pounce to stare upward, alongside their prey, lion and wildebeest and hawk and mouse all still and staring. And the long-lived among them, the reptiles and lizards of a thousand years, and with memories as long, knew it as it once had been.

The rings overhead were cracking, crumbling, falling to earth as blue stars.

The earth shook, trembling in anticipation.

At Orton, the ships bucked and tipped over. Sailors failed to keep their feet and plunged into the cold waters. They scrambled for land in a sea which was a twisting reflection of the chaos above. The marble pier of Morgram shattered.

The towers of Arenfold crumbled, until the streets were strewn with stone and corpses.

The island of Murfold broke in two, and one half begun to sink.

Very quickly, there were no more Gilen Isles.

At the pass of Yurethian's cut, Rilenheim skidded to a halt, Rayant almost flying from their mount, which skittered and danced just to keep them upright.

Rilenheim started to laugh and scream.

His people's essence sunk down from the rings, one by one. Starting as just flickers in the sky, each one of them grew larger, bolder, as they fell, taking on wispy forms, recognisable forms.

Time almost up.

He felt his power returning. He felt himself expanding with a breath which made him feel as unstoppable as he had once been.

The horse looked less like a horse than it had ever had. It was the same colour as Rilenheim's cloak, to the point where they appeared to be made all of one thing.

Rilenheim raised a fist to the sky, then tore a hole in it right in front of them. Through it, Rayant saw a city of spires and walkways and impossible heights.

They stepped through.

* * *

Drael pushed Meryn unceremoniously into the boat, then seized the side and pushed. Brogan had the other side, and the boat started to slide. When they were thigh deep, they fell inside and Drael saw to the sails. Meryn sat in the back with an oar, wondering how rowing could possibly help in such conditions. She settled for holding it crossways for balance. The storm was bad, the boat difficult to control.

Brogan had little experience as a sailor. He followed Drael's instructions as best he could, and then hunched down in the rear of the boat, sheltering from the storm. Lightning crashed overhead. The whole sky flashed with it. Meryn told him everything was going to be all right.

Meryn was right about the other Wrilsch. They came within

minutes, and one of them was massive. In each flash of lightning it became a shadow looming over the castle behind it. The one that could fly was flying. It lurched overhead, the size of the boat, dragging its torn wing behind like a broken sail. Brogan took the oar and tried to see it off. It screeched at him and snapped its cracked jaws.

The other Wrilsch howled at them from the bank. But they were too misshapen to swim. Instead they began to skirt the bank, to be able to catch them when they returned to land.

Drael did not allow himself to be distracted. He worked tirelessly at the rigging. He worked until his arms burned and his back felt about to snap. He kept their course straight, even as the wind tried to tear the boat apart. He knew how to do this. He had always been good at it.

And this time it wasn't hubris that had him here. It wasn't foolishness. It hadn't necessarily even been foolish before, all those years ago. How could he have known? The others had argued, but none had refused his challenge. And Ethi had wanted to go, he knew, even if she had been doubtful. Even later, when she was frightened, she had followed him – because he had asked her to and she had loved him. She had paid for this, and he hadn't. But he hadn't known and how could anyone have known, and how could anyone who took risks, who gambled and so catastrophically failed, manage to carry on?

He gritted his teeth and fought with the sails against the wind and rain. He did not bend to them. He would not.

The weather coalesced. Above them in their tiny boat, the sky writhed and solidified with a shudder.

"Look!" Drael pointed, as if that was necessary.

The blue rings overhead had brightened. As they watched, they began to split, and dissolve, and started their fall to earth.

The torn-winged Wrilsch dived away with a screech. The other Wrilsch running along the bank, about a dozen of them now, stopped still. They sat on their hind legs and watched.

Meryn, slowly, pulled herself up.

"They are coming back to themselves."

There was a circular sheet of sky sliced into the middle of the lake, vertical, half above and half below the waterline. It was crinkled, like it had been balled up and imperfectly rolled out. This was the portal, and around it the ancient device glowed.

As they watched, it patterned itself with a thousand images, which rolled and bubbled and then...

They stared.

The sky became a river, then a wood, a swamp, a desert, a forest, and a city, a vertical city, burning with golden light, grassy plains at its base, furrowed by the lashes of wind.

Beyond the opening the shore was visible, and was getting closer, because the lake was falling into the tear, and dragging them towards it. The waters roiled into a kind of whirlpool, swirling into the gap, draining the lake. Closer to Drael he could hear the under buoy vibrating, almost like it was calling out to him.

He panicked.

"Meryn!" he shouted. "Row! We can make it to shore!" The Wrilsch didn't matter any more. He had to get out of there. He had to get Meryn out of there. He didn't care that this was where she wanted to be.

"No! No!" Her forehead was suddenly against his, her arms on his, squeezing hard. "Shortcut!"

He glanced at the portal, then back to her. He could see she was sure. Her eyes were reflecting the sky and the lake and he saw his own terrified face in them.

He went still. For a moment, so did everything else. He drew a deep, slow breath. He let the current take them.

They neared the whirlpool. A gust of savage wind thumped over the boat, throwing it onto its side. Water filled it. Very quickly, they started to drown.

They held on to the boat's hull until it splintered. Then they held on to each other. Nearby, Brogan thrashed hard, struggling to keep his spluttering mouth above the foam.

Brogan was first through the opening. He thrashed wildly as he passed through. It took seconds, then he was gone.

Drael was next. He instinctively threw his arms around the diamond-encrusted ring as he was swept through. He held on tight. It was warm against his chest. His legs were already through. He could feel them against something solid. But he couldn't see through the water, and the bright searing light was saturating this close, overwhelming all sight and sound. He could feel Meryn holding tightly on to him still, but then her grip loosened, and he knew she was to throw herself free onto her path.

At the last moment he put his arms around her, and let go of everything else.

The riotous whirlpool drew them through the bright light.

They slid fast and hard into thin mud. The emptying lake had created an instant marsh. Fish flopped and sucked at the air and died around them. Deposited fronds clung to everything.

There were also Wrilsch. Drael faltered to his feet. They were all around, their malformed faces encircling him, mocking and sneering. They had backed away as the water flooded in. But now they skittered back like some strange new tide.

"What now?" Drael croaked, his voice tiny.

"Stay close. I know this place."

"Meryn-"

"This is Ilris. We were on our way here when the baby came. This is the place where Herendak cracked everything."

She walked forward, in a kind of crouching limp. Her shorter leg did not appear to be painful. She used it exactly as she would if it were uninjured and complete. She jolted up and down, and then dropped to all fours for a few steps; then back upright. Her crutch was long since lost but, in this place, she didn't need it.

Her eyes reflected back the Wrilsch's gazes.

* * *

Drak ran. He gave up the Keep's secrets now. He had sworn to the king to keep the hidden passageways to himself, but what did it matter now, when in his arms he sheltered the future? He pounded through the Keep, taking the shortest route he could think of to get out, to get away from Herendak, to buy the world what time he could. His heavy bootsteps crashed in his ears. His teeth were gritted, his dark eyes deadly. His long coat threw deep shadows around him.

In the king's study, he unhinged a trapdoor of seamless stone, hidden under a bear-rug. He half-fell, half-rolled out of an alcove onto the floor below. He flung wide an ancient trick wall, overthrowing side-tables and their contents around the feet of shocked servants. He barrelled recklessly through the mess. Another hidden passageway he ducked out of through a hearth, dislodging smoking, flaming logs into a hall full of minor nobles eating a late meal. They thought to stop him; he scattered them with a growl. He leapt from a high window into the upper branches of a sturdy tree, Elhrinna almost slipping from his grasp. She giggled and burbled and burped at the danger, in a manner which made him shudder, even as he held her closer. Climbing and sliding and crashing down to the ground, he staggered up and was away. He pounded toward Overton Bridge, leapt over its side and skidded and rolled down the bank to the Ortman.

He came to the tall door which led into the city's aqueduct and burst through into a vast airy chamber, full of turning wheels and gurgling water. The pulleys and vats and bucket-vats on chains were mostly still and unmanned, their workers off to war. But then the ground started to shake again, and the workings chinked and howled. One of the pipes shifted and he fell back from a jet of scalding steam.

No sign of Herendak, but he didn't dare stop. Whilst he had more recent experience of the Keep's secret ways, Herendak's knowledge was more intimate: the Geomancer had walked them as they were built. And it would be a grievous mistake to underestimate Herendak's ability to track the child.

He stopped for a moment to check on Elhrinna. She stared back at him placidly. She had been watching him all the while he ran. His heavy breaths fluttered the blanket around her neck. She hadn't cried, or struggled in any way, and still did not do so now. She just remained still, and calm, and kept those clear eyes on his. It was like she understood her importance, and did not want to break his concentration. He shuddered. What exactly *was* she?

Must not delay. He followed the pipework, followed the flow of water, let it lead him to another door, through which all was dank with the smell of fresh rain, though it hadn't rained here since the aqueduct was first sunk into the earth.

And then he was rushing down steps, which shivered and almost threw him off his feet, until he was jogging along the thick, stone, underground bank of the Ortman. The machinery, which farmed the water, cast blocky shadows from light which oozed in from rows of light-wells sunk into the aqueduct's roof.

For a moment Drak recalled being younger and hearing the tales of a baby in a basket being floated downstream on a raft of reeds –

and he would have done so now if he wasn't convinced such tales were for idiots.

As he jogged, the stone echoed every sound he made, the scrape of his feet, the rasp of his breath. The curses *under* his breath. These came and went as ghostly whispers. He stopped and started down the bank, peering out through the low, filtered light, looking for a workboat, or one of the smaller goods barges, something to let him rest even as he fled. He couldn't see any – or much of anything – and wasn't helped by the path's increasing narrowness the further along the tunnel he hurried.

Every so often he paused to see if there was any change in Elhrinna. At one point, he demanded of her, "Why aren't you crying? Why don't you ever cry?" She didn't so much look back at him as look back *into* him. The safest place for her, he considered – for all of them – would be in the middle of an ocean. Possibly at the bottom of it.

This wasn't much of a plan, he reflected. Running away was something that grated against everything he believed. But what alternative was there? Rilenheim, who was the only person who could know as much of this matter as Herendak, had decided that hiding the baby from him was the only sensible plan. So what else could he do other than the obvious? Or that *other* thing.

"Drak! Drak!" Aldrua's voice skittered down the halls. Drak hesitated for a moment.

Damn her. How had she been able to follow him? She would give him away. He turned away from the main of the river. There were branching tunnels leading away, engineered to feed different areas of the city. He echoed along one of them until he was seeped in damp.

Aldrua called again, and again, her voice sometimes near, or sounding so, sometimes far, sometimes cut off abruptly as he turned into a new tunnel.

Then she started shouting Herendak's name, from a completely different direction.

Was he here? Was he close? Drak stopped to listen hard. But nothing.

He could go back for Aldrua. He wanted to. She could take care of the child and he could take care of her. But what he wanted and what needed to be done had not been the same since he'd met her, on that bright day at their camp. She would, he could not deny, only complicate things.

No, he must keep on. The river would lead out of the city and he would follow it, boat or no boat.

In another dingy passageway, which ran alongside the narrow bank, he came to an abrupt halt. The bank ceased, and the stream flowed onwards alone, foaming under the wall through a thick pipe.

Dead end.

He turned around. He started back. There was a light, a flaming torch. It was coming towards him. Nowhere to hide.

He stopped.

"Aldrua?" he asked of it. No answer. "Herendak?"

He listened intently for a second, thinking to discern who it was from their footsteps, but the roaring waters drowned out any possibility. He squinted into the darkness, but couldn't make out anything more than the distant light. Yet it wasn't wavering. The torch was held high and steady, and was moving slowly but inevitably toward him.

And he knew it was the Geomancer who bore down on him.

Drak knelt quickly. He still had time. He placed Elhrinna on the ground, still wrapped in her blanket. He drew his sword. He did what he did before every fight, accepted the steel of his sword as part of his arm, accepted his arm as part of his task, accepted his task as something that had to be done. She was looking at him, just as before. Always looking at him. Every instinct screamed at him to keep her safe, to protect her.

He held the sword poised over her tiny chest.

It should be easier, he considered, to take a life when it wasn't fighting back. But somehow it was harder. It's not as if it was even much of a life. A baby had no memories, no personality, was nothing but the potential for these things. Nothing that existed right now would be lost.

He could do this, he knew. He could do anything if his need was suitably great. But what other effects would killing her have? There had to be a reason Rilenheim had not done so already.

And there was also a difference between considering he had the nerve to kill a child, and actually doing said thing.

He glanced at the flaming light. He had no choice. If Herendak got hold of her, if Herendak finished what he'd started up there in the Keep, and the sky fell...

This wasn't a choice.

Hunched in the dark, he stabbed his sword through the baby's chest.

Chapter 27

The blade shuddered. Something gave.

The end of Drak's sword went missing.

Its new end was ragged and flaky, almost like it had rusted away, or like it had decayed over a long period of time.

Elhrinna watched him with calm grace.

Herendak came at him, hands red with flame.

"Get away from her!"

No more options. Drak stood over Elhrinna. He held his ground. He levelled his newly shortened sword at the Geomancer. Its end smoked. Slowly, he drew a fresh sword over his head from his baldric. Only when it was safely trained on his opponent did he discard the smoking blade to one side, offering the Geomancer a wolfish grin as he did so.

Slowly, they circled each other.

"Stay back, Geomancer, or I finish her!"

Herendak said nothing. The cut on his forehead still bled down his face. He betrayed no emotion. There was nothing but a deadly concentration behind the blood. The Geomancer edged forward, circling Drak in the dark.

Drak kept himself over Elhrinna, not giving ground.

"I mean it!" he growled. "Get back!" But still Herendak remained silent.

This was it, Drak realised. Right *now* was what people would talk about. Around campfires, when his name was brought up in song. This very moment. Raven versus Geomancer. A fight to decide everything.

And the Geomancer was already bleeding.

Yet there was something about Herendak's intent expression...

"You're making this too easy," Drak taunted.

He realised his mistake a few seconds too late. He had let Herendak lead his footwork. He had stepped too far from the baby. He was outside the bubble of the Geomancer's concern for her.

Herendak unleashed a bolt of fire. Drak threw himself flat. The heat seared overhead. Before he could move, Herendak shot out another. Drak shielded his face with his arms, but...

Somehow, the flames spluttered and died.

From the ground, Drak looked out through his fingers. Herendak was frowning. His eyes were on the baby.

Drak was on his feet in an instant. His sword rung as he scooped it up.

"Something not as you figured, Geomancer?" he growled.

Herendak drew back, and hunched into himself. Drak closed. Herendak grunted, and the next blast knocked Drak off his feet. He slid and rolled against the wall, breath gone. Embers popped off his tunic, smoke twirled away. The crackling of singed clothes and flesh filled his nostrils.

"I will, always," Herendak was saying, through strained breaths, "be more than a mortal."

Drak fumbled for his sword, once again lost to his hand. He heaved himself up, staggered onto his feet.

"You're bleeding," he said, trying to buy time with talk.

"Get out of my way, fool. You have no chance here!"

"Ah, Geomancer. But you never fought a Raven."

He was quick. Oh, he was quick. Everything Drak had ever done, every battle fought, every feint, every parry, every blow had all been for this. He twisted, leapt and was before Herendak, keeping his balance by swinging his sword *hard*. It cut deep into Herendak's arm, brought up quickly to block the blow. The Geomancer's face twisted in pain. Then his hand clenched around Drak's throat. He slammed the Raven into the wall so hard dust jolted from the tunnel roof.

He twisted Drak's sword hand until bones cracked. Drak screamed as Herendak ripped at his chest, opening him up.

And Aldrua drew her concealed dagger and plunged it deep into Herendak's back.

He jerked around, gasping, almost wrenching the dagger from her hand.

Drak slid to the floor.

The Geomancer bared his teeth and hissed at the queen. She fell back. He lunged for Elhrinna. He scooped her up off the ground in a flurry of sparks, which came off her as if in greeting.

He held her under one arm while he reached out with one silvery hand to rip the air into two. It flapped open, leaving a hole. A red wind rippled his clothes. Through the gap another place was visible.

And he stepped into the gap with Elhrinna, and they were gone.

Aldrua looked to Drak, her eyes unblinking with terror. He coughed, and spat. "Go! Go, you crazy bitch!"

It took a moment to realise what he meant. For another moment she just gaped at him. But no time now for hesitation, or consideration, or fear.

She flung herself through the closing tear.

She stumbled and fell. Herendak was a few paces ahead of her. They were in a hall. A hall as big as Draldorn's keep in its entirety. She stood. Its walls went on so far they were curved by the horizon. There was a ceiling, but it was made of light.

Herendak raised his hand again and stroked a shimmering from the air. He stepped into it and vanished. Aldrua's heart leapt as this new tear began to heal. Before she could be left behind, she stumbled after.

This time they were on a hill. Wind ruffled her hair. Below was a city. She would have called it Draldorn, except it was only half-built. Scaffolds of silver arced over the Keep.

Herendak was turning, frowning. He wasn't where he'd expected to be. For a moment he looked into the baby's eyes. Then he abruptly raised his head and again tore a breach through empty air. He stepped through.

Aldrua staggered through after, felt the air shift but lost sight of him. It was dark, pitch-black. No – were those stars? They were balls of fire, and they were raining down. She dropped to the ground and shielded her face. When Herendak appeared, bathed in light pouring through from another opening, she scurried after him on her knees, her dagger clenched tightly in a bleeding hand.

And a desert with a searing sun, and then somewhere low, so low she felt heavy, her stomach and head pulling her down, and sheer rock faces up all around, and a place of water, and one of space and...

A high place, so very high, a vertical city, of walkways and slopes and curved passageways and Herendak, walking away, upwards, not looking back.

Aldrua vomited onto the white stone of Ilris.

* * *

She stood and looked out, shivering hard against a bitter wind.

What was this place?

She knew the answer as soon as she thought the question. She knew from fairy tales. Ilris – Herendak's home. This was where he had come from.

A stone's throw below was an army's worth of Wrilsch. And she understood that this place was also *their* home. They were gathered around what she now knew was a portal, and it was already open, and through it water rushed with a roar. The torrent surged around them. They were forced to brace against a tide of mud.

The water brought with it wooden detritus, broken twigs and branches, and sodden leaves and ferns and mosses, and fish dying.

And there were curved fragments of wood, in segments, as if from a boat, and there were – people?

And she recognised one of the people.

"Meryn?" she mouthed, not believing. But it *was* her. Though her sister looked different. She looked hurt. Part of her was *missing*.

Ignoring Herendak and the baby, Aldrua hurtled down the ledges and platforms.

"Meryn!" she shouted. "Meryn!"

There were others with her sister. Two men who had come through the portal with her. Aldrua watched some hurried discussion between them, words shot back and forth. She couldn't make out what was said.

One of them took Meryn's arm and began to run with her.

The Wrilsch were also moving. They shook themselves free of water like dogs. They closed in.

The bigger man had a length of smashed boat in one hand, a mallet in the other. He brandished them at anything that came near. He backed up toward the first ramp, protecting the others.

The Wrilsch threw themselves forward. The big man blocked their path. He broke his mallet on the first of them. He shoulder barged its bulk back. Unbelievably, he kept his feet. A smaller Wrilsch, scrawny and stick-like, clamped its jaws down on his arm. The big man took its head and twisted it off. There was a spray from its neck, but it wasn't red.

Aldrua didn't stop running until a terrifying bellow stopped her short. It was a very human bellow. It roared above the cries of the creatures.

As she watched, the big man ripped another creature from his back, cast it to the ground, and stomped on its neck. Impossibly, he had four Wrilsch down, their bodies broken at the base of Ilris's first step. He would let none pass.

He bellowed again, his arms wide, taunting his opponents, and for a moment – for just one brief moment – they hesitated.

But he had already given too much. Blood dripped from him.

He took a single step backward, and faltered on the stonework, only just keeping his feet.

Then they were on him, and Aldrua turned away with a cry of her own.

* * *

Her sister was close now.

This was all too fast. She hadn't planned for this. She didn't know what to think. Meryn was the cause of everything that was happening. Meryn had run away with *Kendan*. With *Herendak*. Who had been selectively murdering their family for generations.

Herendak who had killed her baby.

"Stay back! I can't touch you!" she told Meryn. "Rilenheim said it would be dangerous to-"

"Dru, what are you doing here? I can't – I don't-"

"I followed him, Meryn! He's got – he's got..."

But something was happening. Meryn was...

Aldrua reached out her hand and her fingertips blurred. Rainbows swirled around them.

"What?" She looked up. "Meryn?"

The rainbows were bending towards her sister. Something was trying to *leave* Aldrua's fingers.

Meryn was just skin and bones and her pupils filled her head. Parts of her were blackened.

"Meryn-"

And Aldrua recalled the black liquid that was all that was left of her baby. The same colour, the same glaze, the same sickliness as Meryn's eyes.

Aldrua's own eyes brimmed.

"He *took* something from you," she gasped. "The same thing he took from... if he hadn't – Elhrinna would be..."

"She needed part of us *both*, Dru, or she couldn't be."

Aldrua felt her knees go. She would have collapsed if not for a sudden flash of knowledge.

"You *knew*."

And *she* knew the answer to Rilenheim's question. Her own part in all this. She knew because of the tug of her blurred fingers, because of the feeling of loss she felt now that Elhrinna was being taken up and away from her.

Herendak had taken them and their children and cut them apart so he could mix up something new.

"Meryn... how could you? How *could* you?"

She looked into Meryn's sunken face. She remembered it as it been that last time. She remembered those last words, except only now did she truly understand them.

I'm sorry.

* * *

"Time to go," Drael croaked. "He slowed them, damn him, he saved us – but they're still coming. Move. Upwards, upwards, unless you want to face an army of them! Run, you fools!"

Aldrua did so. She felt numb, and dazed, like she had hit her head and floated away. She drifted higher. The others scurried behind. She kept her distance from the two of them, leading, for want of a better word, constantly glancing back. Meryn looked so different. She was a mess, where she'd never before been a mess, and her eyes were so funny and her leg was... her poor foot! But she looked as determined as ever, and despite looking like she wasn't quite in control of her body, despite it all, she looked... strong.

"Keep moving," the man said again, through gritted teeth. "Keep moving; they're still coming, always still coming!" He was holding back tears.

And although the Wrilsch were wary now that four of their number had fallen, and although not all of them took naturally to the narrow walkways, they were still gaining. And she and the others had to move faster, but she couldn't help Meryn with her injury, couldn't help take her weight, and, for that matter, couldn't even ball up her hands into fists and punch her sister in the face for being so *cruel* and so *stupid*.

Aldrua stopped short.

The Wrilsch were going to catch them. There were hundreds of them rushing up the ramps. It seemed suddenly inevitable.

"We keep moving!" Meryn shot.

"I-" Aldrua started.

Herendak screamed down from high above. "Go back you fools!"

But he wasn't talking to *them*. Why wasn't he talking to them? "March!" his voice boomed. "Animals," he added, almost to himself, or maybe to Elhrinna, who was still in his arms. "Just animals!"

The Wrilsch hesitated. They shirked back, and slipped down a way. There was a brief commotion, as they pushed and shoved and something was decided. Some of them – very few – started back down the ramps.

"Fools!" Herendak cried, and turned away.

At the base of the city below, the furthest back of them pooled and surged together. Their dark shapes formed a writhing knot. Trampling and fighting each other, they were making for the bright portal.

Why, why, why?

"They need *people*," Meryn said in explanation. "Elhrinna is Herendak's map to combine them and us."

Rilenheim's line ran through Aldrua's mind once again. Swirling half-formed thoughts came together in a rush that made her gasp.

If you remove...

"We must sacrifice ourselves?" she said. "Is that his plan for us? We must sacrifice ourselves so the creators of our world can live again?"

"I... I thought we would share everything with them. I didn't realise... but he did not intend for us to share *just* the world.

"He just needed that final thing he was missing, and he got it from both of us. *Time.*"

Aldrua stared at her sister.

"I never could say no," Meryn murmured. "Could I Dru?"

"Rilenheim," Aldrua said, "was not lying. He does need us. You and me and Elhrinna. To undo all of this."

"They are *still* coming," Drael said.

"Dru, Listen to me. I am sorry. I promise you I didn't know about this. Not all of it. And... even now I am not sure that what Herendak wants is wrong. But he didn't even ask us, didn't even ask *me*. He doesn't regard us as equals. So we have to get Elhrinna away from him. You can stop what's happening to everything – and to me, I think. Get her safely away. I'm too slow. You have to do this. And you have to do this now. Drael-" she pushed violently at the man. "Go with her. Go with her, Drael. I'll only slow you down."

"What? No, Meryn – I won't let the Wrilsch take you!"

"They won't." Her teeth were gritted. "I'm one of them now."

"I'm not going anywhere."

"Dru can't do this on her own!"

Aldrua let out a brief, sharp sob. It hung in the air.

"None of us can do this! What are we thinking? Herendak is a-"

"Shut up, Dru! You have to stop him. Shut up and run!"

Aldrua shook her head, over and over. She wanted more than anything to stay with Meryn. To either punch her or hug her; she wasn't certain which.

It didn't matter anymore. Nothing mattered. She shouted up at Herendak to stop, but didn't know why, didn't expect him to. He was single-mindedly making his way up through the maze of walkways with Elhrinna. He didn't even look down.

And she was beginning to understand. She understood now that there were some things that *should* be done.

Sometimes, for the children to live, the parents have to die.

She started to run.

* * *

Meryn and Drael chased after her, but it was difficult for Meryn to move fast, especially upwards. The remaining Wrilsch, all differently twisted and misshapen, would quickly run them down.

They did their best to lose themselves among the dense pillars and ledges and walkways. They tried feinting in one direction only to double-back. They tried dropping out of sight and crawling away. They tried dropping onto lower platforms and changing direction – anything they could think of to throw the Wrilsch off. All the while a bitter wind tore at them and heaved them to and fro. The shattered sky helped hide them. Drael tried to reach out and touch it

– the cracks and falling stars looked so very close. But always out of reach.

Drael had spent a long time hiding from the duke, learning how to evade pursuit, and he put these lessons into practice now. Lessons on which the future of everything now hinged. He had lost Brogan and Whilpan. But he would not lose Meryn.

They stopped dead at something that fit in so well they almost didn't recognise it. An ordinary – for this place – walkway, but encircled within two rings of diamonds. It was strange to see something extraordinary in context. It looked like it belonged.

"I guess we shouldn't be surprised," Drael said, sounding surprised. "There are likely many of these here."

"Does it work?"

Drael stepped closer. Condensation covered it. Without hesitation, he stuck his hand through.

"Yes."

"But we have no idea where it goes."

"I don't suppose what you saw mapped in the sky helps us out much here?"

"What are you saying?"

He didn't reply, merely thought for a moment.

"Meryn," he said, "the paths that led us here... that led both of us here..." He looked out over the city. It was all so clear. The Wrilsch coming at them had split up, were coming from different directions, from different levels. His subterfuge had worked thus far, but there were so many of them, too many to hide from forever. He looked up at the remains of the rings, ragged and torn, bleeding an ancient people into the world.

And he laughed.

"Ethi would have loved it here," he said to Meryn. He smiled, faintly, complicatedly. "But if I hadn't one day gone out into a storm, you would already be dead. And if I hadn't one day gone out into a storm, I would be standing somewhere else while the world ended.

"Instead?" He turned and put his hands on her shoulders. "I stand here with you. Because you also went out into a storm. We cannot know what will be, can we, Meryn? Not ever. We can only gamble, and sometimes lose. I learn the lesson of my friends: it falls to me to make sure you get that chance. I will lure the Wrilsch away. I am of no importance now."

Meryn reached out her hand, and shook his.

"Thank you, Drael."

He nodded.

"That's it?"

But she hadn't let go of his hand.

"I think we understand each other," she said. For a moment they let that understanding pass between them.

Abruptly, she looked up. "Clouds," she said. "I can lose them in the clouds."

He nodded. They began not far above. They were grey and dense and writhed around knots of wind. Aldrua was somewhere inside them, running through another kind of storm.

"Just keep after the queen," he said, "and I'll... catch up with you when I can."

When she released his hand, the flesh of his palms was seared and flaked angrily away. He bled where her nails – claws – had pierced his skin. He could, with an effort, still see her as she used to be, but in reality her limbs were skeletal and her hair was losing its colour. It was white against her pale skull.

"Goodbye," he said, and ignoring her black lips he put his arms around her burning body and gently kissed her on her left cheek.

"Just one more mistake," he said, and flashed a smile which came from nowhere.

And he darted across an open walkway and bellowed a barrage of insults at the Wrilsch below.

With a cry, they took up the chase.

Chapter 28

Aldrua forced herself higher. She followed the Geomancer, and he himself followed some hidden path, some secret design that wound to the very top of the world.

She saw similar – or perhaps identical – structures, again and again, as the pursuit circled around and around and around. The stone beneath her feet taunted and spun. Around its sheer edges she could see Draldorn. Not its details. Not its people and their homes, but its vast landscapes; the shape of it, the sculpted outline of its valleys and peaks and green places.

Ilris seemed to be shrinking. The higher they went the less city and more sky there was. Maybe it would all end at a point. A single pinnacle, where even Geomancers reached the end of the road, and there would be just her, and him.

She couldn't see Herendak clearly, but the shape of him was moving like a man exhausted. He was hunched and slow. They had somehow hurt him, she and Drak, in the aqueducts beneath Draneth. Geomancer or not, the darker patch on his back was surely blood.

Everything was becoming hazy. She couldn't tell if she was catching up, nor had she any idea as to what she would do if she did. Time seemed to be moving differently, like it was disconnected, flapping loose. These were stolen moments. They moved through portals, more plentiful now, and they shifted from place to place, higher and lower, here and there.

They got so high the crystal snowflakes that had been part of the rings glittered on her arms. The air was so thin it was pulling apart, and sometimes she could have sworn she could see things moving in its gaps. Her rasping breath split the air. She felt light-headed, but this somehow spread to her limbs, and she managed to put on a final, fluttery burst of speed.

Herendak was so pale now, as pale as the empty air. She had to catch him before he disappeared completely.

The path ended. A perfectly circular platform. It shook, vibrated. Above, there was only what was left of the rings, and nothing else. She almost felt like she could reach out and put her fingers through them. The faint crystals danced over everything. This was not a place for a human. This was all of something else.

Herendak stood before her. He held Elhrinna clutched tightly in his arms. Elhrinna's face was grey. She looked in pain, but still she did not cry. In sudden recognition, she feebly reached out her arms for Aldrua.

Herendak was grinning, but there were tear lines down his cheeks. He spoke in a low, cracked voice, scratched up by the wind.

"I never thought you would be the one," he said.

Aldrua stood her ground.

He was a Geomancer. Who was she to face a Geomancer?

"Herendak. Kendan. I-"

"I thought there would be others. Soldiers. I thought there would be battles. I was ready for battles. I did not expect *you*."

"After what you did to me?"

"I always cared for you, Aldrua. I did. I have always cared too much. But – Meryn. I think, maybe, you finally understand. Because if *I* don't fight for my people, who will?"

"Are you Kendan, or Herendak?"

"It does not matter." He shook his head. "Go back and be with Meryn, Aldrua. Spend your last moments with your sister. Tell her I am sorry." He closed his eyes. "Even if neither you nor she believe me."

"Stop this. Please."

"Tell her that I love her, and that no matter what happens now, I always have and always will. And, on that thought, I arrive, finally, after all this time, at the very end of the road."

"It doesn't have to be-"

"Such a long, hard road. But, despite this, somehow, oh so short! But it finally comes to this, Aldrua. My final goodbye." He looked up, eyes wide. "Forgive me."

The sky, once again, began to fall.

"Wait!" Aldrua cried. "Wait! Don't do this! Tell Meryn yourself! She is just behind me. Talk to her before you do this-"

"I sent a Wrilsch to save her. She could have come with me."

"Herendak –"

"But she did not wish it. Now go."

But instead she stepped forward. He did not back away. He was very pale.

"One more step," he said, "and I will kill you."

But he was swaying, and his eyes were dull.

And she was willing to die.

"You are already part human, aren't you Herendak?" she said. "You already tried this once, when you saw what you had done, all that time ago? But something went wrong. And you could only save yourself... and Rilenheim?"

He shook his head, but he wasn't disagreeing with her. "So many more of you now," he said, "and in Elhrinna I can finally see how it is to be done. I can, finally, save everyone. I must."

Aldrua took a deep breath.

"No," she said. "No, Herendak," and her voice carried over the lonely city, and onwards, like some endless thing that could fill all the sky. "This is not your world anymore." She put her hands on his shaking forearms. "You had your chance. The Geomancers had their time. You know I must do for my people what you would do for yours. I am the Queen of Draldorn and I speak for humankind. Enough of this. Give me Elhrinna and *grow up*."

He didn't respond. He didn't even seem to be able to look at her. He was still shaking.

Perhaps that *was* his response. He could not do this without her help.

Very slowly, she unfolded the baby from his unresisting arms. He collapsed to his knees. His tunic was so red. He had lost so much blood.

He was dying.

"I'm sorry," she said, and turned away.

"No." His voice was choked up. "*I* am sorry. You are too late, Dru. It is already done."

She held the baby to her as the sky shivered and creaked and then – with a boom which really did fill the world – shattered.

* * *

Drael lost the Wrilsch again. He lay flat until they moved on, before crawling through another portal. It led higher. He wasn't sure for how much longer he could get away with this, for how much longer he could outrun his taunting. He had long since lost sight of Meryn, and any idea as to where she might be.

He got up and kept going under the cover of cloud, until there was a boom. It seemed to come from inside his head. It dropped him back to his knees. It took the clouds and in an instant obliterated them. He was instantly soaked.

And instantly visible.

The complex lines of the intersections and supports glistened around him stark and harsh; like everything had been cut up and folded before being straightened back out.

It was all unfolded below him, and on it, on almost every level of the city, were...

People.

So many people.

He saw a woman running, and at first thought: Meryn! She was somehow below him. Wrilsch were on her tail. He tensed. He could reach her – he could jump. Maybe drop a couple of them, if he hit them square on. But it was far, and-

But the woman screamed, and he knew it wasn't Meryn. The first of the Wrilsch reached her and knocked her down and its bulk blocked his view of what happened next.

So many people. They were everywhere. All over the city. Many were also running from Wrilsch. Others milled, lost and confused, around the portals through which they had arrived. More were coming in all the time. But the milling groups didn't mill for long. Wrilsch rushed through after them, ran them down and pushed them to the ground. They weren't harming them though – at least not physically.

A different kind of harm was evident, however, in their cries and screams.

This must be happening all over Draldorn, maybe all over everywhere. Because now everywhere led to Ilris. All was opened up to Herendak and the Wrilsch. A crossroads. But the people who came through seeking shelter would find none. The main part of the Geomancers was freed from above, and from their corrupted forms as Wrilsch they leapt to shapes that could sustain them.

Herendak had won.

* * *

Meryn was struggling. There was a deep pain in her stomach. Her head felt stretched. When she leaned against a stanchion she left claw marks.

She just had to hold it together a little longer. She was almost to the finish. She was close to Dru, she could feel it. She was so close to Elhrinna. So close. This could all be undone.

But there was a growl behind her, and she gritted her teeth and turned to face it.

A single Wrilsch stood there. Drael had not managed to draw them all. It took a moment to look her up and down.

And a boom shook her vision, filled up everything. The city shook and a slew of stone plunged down to one side.

She opened her mouth, and a growl of her own purred out.

"I guess I'm out of time," she said.

The Wrilsch tensed to pounce.

"Come on then, monster," she hissed.

And then she leapt.

* * *

Aldrua found Drael below. He waved at her frantically when he saw her, and gave up a shout when he saw she had the child.

"What happened?" he said when he reached her. "Did you stop him? Is it finished? Are we safe? Wait – you must have passed

Meryn on the way down?"

"Where is she?"

"She was right behind you. I led the Wrilsch away, before all these others came. She must be near. Aldrua – were you in time?"

Aldrua shook her head. "Look around you."

"But- you have the baby-"

"I was too late."

"No!" Drael put his hands to his head. "But it can't..." He stared out from Ilris into the strange new clarity of everything below. There seemed not even air left to impede his view.

Wrilsch everywhere. Dead Wrilsch everywhere. Those still alive pinned people to the ground, then toppled over, lifeless, to join the other carcasses, leaving those people to slowly stand, and look up and around and at themselves, and to lift their hands to their eyes as if to discern for the first time what they might now do with them.

The sky was so clean and empty it looked like it had just been made. The sun and both moons were startlingly vivid.

The end of everything looked so new.

"So what do we do now, Aldrua?"

She wasn't listening.

She had seen Rilenheim below.

She was running.

* * *

She raced down the ramps as fast as she dared. She held Elhrinna tight – maybe too tight. But as always the baby gave her no signs of distress.

People were dying, changing – right now. She couldn't afford to waste a moment. These were *her* people who were changing. For the very first time, she understood what this meant. What else did it mean that she was queen? Rayant could not help them – so it was up to her.

"Meryn!" she called. "Meryn!"

She had to get to her sister before Rilenheim did.

It was disorienting enough among the ledges *before* the portals were functional. Now she found herself turned around again and again. Sometimes she was hurled back to right where she had just been before she realised and righted herself.

"Slow down!" Drael shouted after her. "You'll fall!"

She almost did, when the ground fell away in a sharp arc. She was panting and aching and not overly steady on her feet. She forced herself to stop and take stock. Drael caught up.

"What," he gasped, "are you going to do?"

"Find Meryn. We threaten to do what Rilenheim told me not to do. We have to try."

But it would be a costly bargain, she knew. Otherwise, Rilenheim would not have lied about his motives, would not have obscured the truth of them, would not have tried to turn her against her sister. So she would offer him what he wanted. But she would get something in exchange. She would bargain for the lives of her people.

There was no one else to stand for them.

Rilenheim was moving fast. He rode a shadowy creature, which swirled around him like the blackest of cloaks. It was the shape of a horse, but otherwise bore no resemblance.

"But what can Meryn do? Aldrua? Hello?"

Aldrua didn't hear him. She was thinking: *I am still human. I am still the thing that has been taken from Meryn. It happens to have not been taken from me directly, but from my son instead. He was changed. I was not. Can I restore my sister with a touch, at the cost of my own life? Or perhaps share half Meryn's transformation?*

She shuddered.

Drael clicked his fingers in front of her face.

"This is no time for daydreaming. Your Majesty!"

She blinked.

"You're right. Let's go. Do you see her? I don't see her. Come on! But keep an eye out for Wrilsch – we are so very close to losing everything!"

"Come on then," Drael said. "She has to be... Let's try this way."

He led them back up and around. They moved more cautiously now. More and more people were flooding in through the portals. More and more Wrilsch also. When they stumbled upon such a group, Drael quickly ushered Aldrua back. They ducked away before they were seen.

At every outflung point, they craned their necks for some sign of Meryn, but saw nothing.

They turned one corner, and came within arm's reach of a Wrilsch. Drael tried to pull Aldrua back, but suddenly she wouldn't budge. He saw her face and the horror he saw there stopped him short. Then he saw what she saw.

The Wrilsch was Meryn.

* * *

Meryn was covered in blood. It was thick around her mouth, and dripped from her fingers. Her breathing rattled and her eyes were dull. There was a dead Wrilsch at her feet. It was torn apart. She crouched amidst its remains, blankly swinging her head this way and that, as if in a trance.

Aldrua was frozen to the spot.

She wanted to shout out her sister's name, but didn't. Because what if it wasn't recognised? What if Meryn did not look up and back at her? This is what Rilenheim had warned about. About Meryn being a danger to them, being lost to them. But to see it – to see her like this...

Abruptly, Aldrua sat down on the ground, cross-legged, right where she had been standing, placing Elhrinna on her lap. Her face felt like it was somehow unfolding. The sob, when it came, was so wrenching and violent there was no sound but a long hissing breath.

It was Drael who spoke the name.

"Meryn?" he said, in a voice which doubted itself.

But Meryn *did* still recognise... something. She looked up at him, though with the blankest of eyes.

"I did the best I could. I'm sorry," Drael said. "Is she... one of them now?" he asked Aldrua.

Everything the two Geomancers had ever told Aldrua jostled through her head.

"No," she said, "I'm certain she's one of *her* now. Geomancers never had *time* to begin with. They had *space*. I guess those things were never meant to be removed from either of us."

"Aldrua... she's coming closer." The Meryn creature was hunched to a fraction of normal height. It – she – seemed oblivious to her surroundings, unfocused and lost.

"What are we going to do?"

"Nothing has changed." Aldrua forced herself to her feet. She felt light-headed. She felt numb. But she had enough now to bargain with Rilenheim.

"Meryn?" she called out, softly, like talking to a frightened pet. "Can you hear me, Meryn? You need to come with me. Do you know who I am?" Aldrua did her best to keep her voice steady and calm and non-threatening, but she was slipping, and it was cracking. "It's me, Meryn," she said. "It's your big sis'."

She could barely see through her tears when the portal behind Meryn flickered with a blinding white light and shattered with a terrible crack. And there was Rilenheim, on that horse that was a cut-out of darkness, and behind him, slumped and unconscious, Rayant.

* * *

Rilenheim took a moment to observe the situation. His gaze washed over the city. It was returned by many. There were many thousands of people now, from all over Draldorn, and just as many Wrilsch – and many that were now both Wrilsch and human – whose collective concentration immediately focussed on the Geomancer suddenly in their midst.

"Aldrua," Rilenheim said, with a sharp nod. "Put down the child, and back away."

Aldrua also took in what was happening throughout the city. She thought she recognised some of those below. Some were people she had seen on the streets of Draneth. Others she could place by their style of dress. The woollen tunics of those from Arenfold. The Kilsmouth fisherman with their stabbing spears.

"No," Meryn said, to Rilenheim.

"Come, Meryn," Rilenheim said. "Come and take my hand." He reached his hand forward, staying mounted. "Wait – what do you mean 'no'?"

"Meryn – stop," Aldrua commanded. "Stay where you are. Rilenheim? Do you know what has happened?"

"Of course I know – the world is open again. Now allow me to undo this disaster!"

Aldrua resettled Elhrinna so she was held to her chest by one arm. With the other, she beckoned to Meryn.

"Meryn? You come to *me*."

Meryn looked from her to Rilenheim, and then back to her. Rilenheim seemed to sense something. He started forward.

"Stay back, Rilenheim!" Aldrua cried, and thrust out Elhrinna with both hands. "Or I will pitch little Elhrinna over the side!"

"You – you would not dare! You would not do such-" but he saw something in her eyes and fell silent.

Meryn watched this impassively, huddled still, her breathing guttural and uneven.

"You are still of us," Aldrua said, quietly, "you always will be."

Drael murmured a word to himself. It might have been "balance".

And Meryn turned to them and began to crawl.

"No!" Rilenheim shouted. "You must *not* come into contact! I warned you about this! You must not touch her!"

Aldrua allowed Meryn to collapse at her feet.

"Stay back!" she commanded. "Rilenheim, it is time for you to speak clearly! It is time for you to explain your intentions."

"My intentions? I will do just as I promised the king." He indicated to the prostate Rayant, with a certain pointedness. "My intent is to *save* your people. It always has been!"

"I don't believe you. It's yours or mine, Geomancer. Why would you choose mine?"

"Why am I even-" Rilenheim's mount dissipated under him. It became almost smoke, but a smoke which moved into him. He seemed to grow larger. Not so much in *size*, but *substance*, like there was so much more Rilenheim than there had been before.

He looked like he could break through solid rock.

Rayant sprawled awkwardly on the ground behind him. Aldrua

couldn't tell how badly he was hurt.

"I have no need to negotiate with *you*," he said.

"But you *do*, Geomancer." Aldrua's voice was small, but clear. It again carried over the city, and all that were there heard every word, Wrilsch and human alike. "You do. You needed my help before, and you still need it now. Otherwise you would have killed me long ago. Do you think I'm stupid?"

"We don't have time for this. Give me Elhrinna, before it is too late!"

And Rilenheim came for her. A massive, spectral shape, he raised his arms and flames began to form between his fingers.

Drael threw himself forward – but Aldrua shouldered him back.

"Rilenheim?" She backed up, but only to buy a little time.

In an instant Drael found himself holding Elhrinna – and Aldrua stood on the very edge of the walkway. She peered down over the toes of her shoes, her weight on her heels.

"You're right," she said. "I won't harm her. But what wouldn't I do to protect her?"

She glanced from certain death to Rilenheim. He froze. He was just too far to leap for her. A strong wind flung his cloak about him. Aldrua's dress rippled as she teetered over nothingness. She barely held her balance.

"It is," she said, "quite a way down."

When Rilenheim finally spoke, it was almost a growl. "What is it that you want?" he said, simply. "I am the very last of my people, Aldrua, and you are wasting what little time I have left."

His words hung in the air, and in that moment she knew what it was that drove him.

"You want to live forever, Rilenheim?"

He just smirked at her.

Somehow, it made him seem... smaller.

"You've lost all the others, haven't you, Rilenheim?"

She felt a shadow fall over her. Herendak's shadow. He was a few platforms above. He was barely keeping his feet. She didn't know how long he had been listening. His brow was knitted.

Rilenheim went pale when he saw him.

"Run!" Rilenheim said to her, not looking away from Herendak. "Get away from him-"

Herendak shouted, "Stay where you are! Stay where you are!" And he started back down towards them, bounding recklessly from platform to platform, staggering and slipping. He fell and cried out. He had difficulty getting back on his feet. He looked surprised and lost and hurt, like none of this was happening the way he'd planned. Like being hurt by a mere fall was astounding in some way.

But he had decided something, Aldrua could see.

She raised her chin to Rilenheim. She raised her hand and once again pulled her dagger. She pointed it between Rilenheim's eyes and looked along it as she spoke.

"I think I understand, Rilenheim," she said. "I know why you need all of us. Herendak has joined us. Your people and mine. They – we – will live out our lives, and die. You too, Rilenheim. You didn't want this. You want to go back to before you were as you are now. Before you looked like one of us. Before you could *die*."

"You would end my entire race?" he said. "That isn't up to *you*. It never was. You are not even supposed to be involved, except that was the only way he could do it! But given such, you must understand that this is all that you wished for! Do you not see? No more Wrilsch, and no more threat to your kingdom. I will undo them! For you! No more decisions to be made! You will become the new Builders, except this time there will be only one Geomancer for you to worship! If there can be only one of us, then let me be at least as I once was. Now... enough! Stand back from Meryn! And I will put everything back in its proper place!"

"You're not even lying, are you? You're just leaving out the important part. As you've always done. And you're not even going to acknowledge that I'm right. But I will no longer be dismissed by *you*. So tell me what you are still hiding. I want to hear you say it. It must have been so galling to pretend you were on our side. To have to beg Rayant for help. To *need* us. Why do you need us, Rilenheim?"

"Because you are the by-product!" Herendak screamed. He was directly above her now. He was gasping in pain, on his hands and knees. "You are the best he could do!"

"Shut up, Herendak!" Rilenheim bellowed, striding forward.

"By-product?" Drael murmured. "We-"

Aldrua stared at the Geomancer.

"Rilenheim," she said. "You *are* us, aren't you? The best you could do. You are our creator. You *and* Herendak."

Blood dribbled from the mouth of one of the creators. His face was grey. His words came only with effort.

"No longer," Herendak said. "Your turn, Dru." He closed his eyes. "Meryn," he said, simply, and somehow it was both a command and so much more.

And he toppled from the ledge onto Aldrua. She barely had time to duck away from the edge.

He hit her with a thunderclap.

* * *

Meryn heard him say her name. She knew it was her name. She knew what it meant to the one who had said it. She understood that they had succeeded – both she and Herendak. She understood that it had cost them both everything. She wished he had trusted her enough to have explained that it would cost them both everything.

She was unravelling, but from the outside in. On the inside everything was clear, but there was a haziness the further out she went, and it was becoming denser. But she still fought it. She couldn't help but fight it. Stubborn; that's what she was. It was what Aldrua had always teased her about and it was what had always annoyed Rayant.

It had always interested and confused Herendak.

But no matter how hard she fought, soon she would forget. *That* was the price of immortality. *That* is what had happened to the Wrilsch. They were timeless, but in physical bodies which could not keep so many memories intact – they had needed to be preserved elsewhere. Above.

As for her? Her time was all gone, to her child, to Elhrinna.

Which meant there was only one thing she could yet still do.

* * *

"My turn?" Aldrua echoed.

Herendak's last thoughts had been about Meryn. He *had* loved her. He had.

But he had been talking to *her*, not Meryn.

Elhrinna giggled in Drael's arms.

"My turn," Aldrua said. She looked up. "Make way for something new, Rilenheim?"

And at her feet Meryn rose.

Meryn placed one lingering hand to her daughter's cheek; then she and Aldrua clasped each other's wrists.

Meryn did so with a smile so wide and so deep that when she channelled the time from Aldrua and turned to black liquid dust, she did so with a deep sigh.

Herendak's thoughts filled Aldrua's head. He had given her everything he had left. She had all the pieces that Rilenheim needed.

"Rilenheim?" she said. She knew a secret now that only he had known. Herendak had given the world time. With the power he had given her, and with the map that was Elhrinna, Aldrua could take it away again. Like Rilenheim wanted. Like he would do himself if she just gave him the chance. But she now knew what Herendak had done originally. What he had done to accidentally destroy his people.

And she could do it again.

She and Rilenheim faced each other wordlessly for the longest time.

And then she stripped a further dimension away from the Wrilsch.

* * *

She could not put them back in the sky. She had not the power of Geomancers at their peak.

She flattened them. Timeless and depthless, they were absorbed into everything around them. They became as of paintings, simulacrums, embedded into the stone, into clothing, even into the sky and into flesh.

They became emblems and symbols; were tattooed flat into the world that they had once ruled.

It happened all across the world, and it did not take long. They did not even have time to scream.

Finally, the city – everything – went still. The world went silent, as if itself could mourn the passing of a people, the ending of an age.

Very gently, it started to rain.

Rilenheim had nothing left to say.

For a moment, he raised his hands, and it seemed he would strike her down. But, in the end, he simply stooped. He went to Herendak, whose broken form lay twisted by her side, still – barely – breathing. He tarried only long enough to put his hand to his friend's brow, and mumble words to him she could not hear.

With a final, complicated look at Aldrua, he turned, and slunk away.

She let him go.

*　*　*

Herendak couldn't control his chest. It was heaving wildly; he couldn't get enough air. His throat burned. He knew Rilenheim had walked away, but he could barely see. He clutched at the numbness where he would normally expect his stomach to be, but felt only something slick and steaming into cold. His legs wouldn't move, but more worryingly he couldn't move the magic; it was leaving him, slowly flowing away into the ground.

He spluttered and moaned in his own private darkness.

But then, impossibly, someone was at his side, and a soft, warm hand cupped his cheek, stroked his stubble. He gasped urgently, his breathing slowed. He strained his useless eyes, reached out, and, after wiping whatever was on his hand onto his cloak, found an arm and followed it to reach the other's face.

"Meryn," he said. "You are alive! I'm so thankful you are still alive." His breathing almost stopped, and it was just about possible to imagine his broken face was smiling.

The hand tensed and pulled away.

"Don't," Herendak spluttered. "Don't leave me."

He was staring upwards, aware of the shadow over him, aware that someone was there, but unable to see. He felt detached from so much of his own body. He could still feel some magic, though, even if he couldn't will it. He felt it seeping further away around him, fading invisibly from its long-time home. Moving into another.

"Meryn? Please don't say anything."

The hand came back, and he held and kissed it. "I was wrong," he said simply, and lay still enough to be dead. But, after a time, he coughed violently back to life, and spoke quickly, "I know now I was wrong. I didn't mean to cause harm. I don't expect forgiveness, but please just understand... I was trying to put the world back together, but I couldn't without... Just please understand. The truth is. You are as I, in all the ways which count."

The words made him feel hollow, along with the magic, now almost all gone, now flowed almost entirely away. That was worse than the blindness.

The magic flowed into the silent woman by his side. He could feel her through it, and he knew it wasn't Meryn. He kept babbling all the same.

"I am sorry. Rilenheim... was right about some things. I... have much to say to you, Meryn-"

"Shh," soothed the woman, running her other hand over his heated brow. The hand of someone he had greatly wronged. Someone more worthy even than he, a Geomancer.

Herendak sighed, almost empty now, the last of the magic tingling somewhere in his chest. What use were words, in the end.

"Meryn," he said, finally, slowly, rolling the name, trying to hold on to it, but he felt emptier than ever, as if his life had been nothing but the lost power he had once wielded.

"Herendak," the cracked voice of Aldrua broke close to his blinded face. "Herendak. I promise this. Meryn understood. She understood this. All that you've said."

His face creased into a desperate smile, and for the longest time he felt full of something which made him want to laugh, and cry, and weep with loss all at the same time.

* * *

Aldrua held him long after he had gone. She rose unsteadily to her feet only when she was beginning to feel as cold as he felt.

"Damn you," she whispered. "Damn you Herendak."

She looked out over Ilris, and over Draldorn, spread out all around, more visible to her now than it had ever been before.

Thousands of people were watching her. Rayant too. He had sat up – he wasn't dead. He held his bloodied head in his hands.

They were all waiting to see what she'd do next.

END

Comments, suggestions or constructive abuse?

Email: theunending@outlook.com

Join the email list: http://eepurl.com/bdO4or